DOWN BY CONTACT

LA WOLVES BOOK THREE

CADENCE KEYS

Editors: Happily Editing Anns

Cover Design: Kate Farlow, Y'all. That Graphic

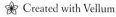 Created with Vellum

For my goofball husband for saying some of the most ridiculous things, which inevitably end up in my books.

Matt

I did not see this coming. If you had told me three months ago that I'd be standing here at a wedding reception desperately hoping a woman would look at me, I would've laughed in your face.

First of all, I'm *never* desperate.

Second, there's always another woman that'll warm my bed. Why would I be hung up on only one?

But here I stand, watching her body sway to the music, her blonde hair flowing in soft waves around her perfect, porcelain face, and her blue eyes shining bright.

And all I want—more than anything in the world—is for her to look at me.

For her to want me.

Who the hell am I right now?

But as fucked up as I feel right now, as confusing as all of these stupid feelings are, there's nothing I would change about ending up here in this moment, except for the fact that for the first time in my life I wish I was here with a date.

With that beautiful blonde bombshell to be exact.

But despite all the feelings between us, there's too much against us to ever make it work.

So here I stand, wishing for her to be mine, and knowing she never will be.

ONE

Nikki

3 months earlier

"Luther, you can't be serious." I stare at him in disbelief. "You want Matt Fischer to lead the new Wolves campaign?"

My eyes scan the marketing materials sitting before me, and I shake my head.

This has to be some kind of mistake.

Luther, my co-worker in the marketing and promotions department and one of my dearest friends, nods his head and confirms, "Definitely. The group testing verified he's the way to go for our campaign this year. He's on fire this season, and he's hotter than ever. He's a tight end with a *tight* end." Luther tosses me a wink that makes me want to roll my eyes. "Women want to be with him, and men want to *be* him. This is definitely his time to shine."

I shudder and look back down at the face of the one man on the team I can't stand. His pretty-boy features on his insanely strong, defined, athletic body really shouldn't be allowed. And don't even get me started on his piercing cerulean-blue eyes and the charming smile he tosses at every woman.

"He's practically a walking STD. The last thing the Wolves need is to tie our brand to one of our most notoriously slutty players. He's an unabashed womanizer." I force my gaze from the picture of Matt's ridiculously handsome face—ignoring the slight uptick in my heartbeat—and stare sternly at Luther. "No, we should definitely go with someone more wholesome. What about Jack Fuller?"

He shakes his head. "Jack has done several campaigns for us, but he's pulling back in preparation for his wedding to Paige. Plus, the group tests showed that while everyone loves him because he's the NFL's golden boy, they prefer Matt. I'm telling you, he was the choice by a landslide."

I wrack my brain for another alternative, *anyone* who might be a better draw than Matt "Manwhore" Fischer. But no names come to mind. It's a lot harder than one would think to find a wholesome player on our team. They're good guys, but they definitely get around.

My shoulders sag in defeat. You'd think on a team of fifty-three players, we'd be able to choose one who isn't the biggest ladies' man on the team.

I groan and fight the urge to bang my head on my clean and meticulously organized cherry wood desk. "Is he seriously our only decent option?"

Luther just smiles at me like he thinks I'm adorably naïve. "Sex sells, Nikki. Let's give the people what they want."

I throw my head back and take a centering breath, already dreading the next few months where I'll have to work closely with Matt. As a manager in the marketing and promotions department, I don't normally have to interact with the players—that's a task I can delegate to someone else—unless I'm directly in charge of their campaign. However, as the head coach's only daughter, I've met and talked with pretty much every player on the team.

Out of all the players my dad has ever coached, no one has ever rubbed me the wrong way like Matt Fischer does. From the very first time I met him, and he threw me his stupidly charming smirk, I knew he was trouble with a capital T.

I had walked into the locker room looking for my dad after a game, and my eyes locked on Matt's. Other players surrounded him, sweating and exuding the energy I've become used to from players after a victory—that explosion of excitement and adrenaline that's practically tangible in the air. I'll never forget his warm voice floating over me and the way my blood heated and tingled in ways it never has. Or the way my breath stuttered momentarily in my chest before his words finally registered. "Well, well, well, who do we have here? I call dibs. Move aside, guys, the lady needs a place to sit." Then he laid back on the bench and gestured to his face. "I've got the best seat in the house right here, honey." My cheeks flamed with embarrassment while the other players laughed uncomfortably at his antics toward the coach's daughter, a fact Matt was unaware of at the time since he was new to the team.

I may or may not have reported him to my dad, which resulted in what I heard were some torturous three-a-day practices.

Needless to say, I think he's a disgusting chauvinistic pig, and he thinks I'm a stuck-up princess. I already wish I could speed up time and get these next three months over with.

I enter my house and immediately line up my shoes in the shoe caddy by the front door. Rubbing the tight muscles in my neck, I attempt to work out the tension that's been growing since my conversation with Luther. I walk through the hallways of my house, barely noticing the pretentious artwork Anthony insisted we get when we were decorating our new house. It looks like a kindergartner threw paint on a canvas. I still can't believe the outrageous price Anthony paid for it, but he claims the artist is someone up and coming. Anthony loves to be ahead of the trends. Personally, I'd rather have gotten some landscapes or something calming, like a beach or forest scene.

But Anthony was adamant, and it didn't seem like it was worth arguing over. If there's anything I've learned in my life, it's that you have to pick your battles.

I walk into the kitchen, stalling slightly in wonder when I see Anthony standing near the stove, stirring a pot of something delicious smelling. Anthony never cooks for me.

"What's the special occasion?" I ask, walking toward him with a surprised smile on my face as I take in the aroma of whatever he's cooking.

He turns to me. "What do you mean?"

"You're cooking."

He shrugs indifferently and asks, "So? I cook."

My smile falters as he turns back to the pot. "Not usually for me. You usually order us takeout."

"Only when I know you're too tired to clean the kitchen. But I figured you'd be willing to clean up tonight since you have tomorrow off," he says, never once looking back at me.

I stare at his back, my smile now completely gone, half expecting him to tell me he's joking.

"It's not like I have the day off to lounge around the house, Anthony." I can't hide the tension in my voice. My breaths are already coming in short pants as I try to fight the emotion bubbling up in my chest.

He still doesn't turn to look at me. "True, but you won't be at the cemetery all day. Just for part of it. I'm sure even your folks don't want to spend their whole day there."

I can't respond to his comment, for fear I'll scream at him for his insensitivity to what tomorrow means to me. And screaming isn't something I do. I'm nothing if not composed and competent, always.

It's why Anthony loves me. At least it's one of the few reasons he's given me for why he wants to marry me.

The wine fridge under the counter to my right catches my eye, so instead of trying to come up with some semblance of a response, I grab a wine glass from the cabinet and open up a bottle of red wine—not paying any attention to the brand of the bottle in my hand. I pour a generous amount into my glass and then take a large, fortifying sip.

"You really should let that breathe to get the full robust flavors. That's too good a year to waste."

I can feel the cracks in my carefully composed foundation beginning to crumble. Ignoring Anthony's advice, I mumble a lame excuse about not being hungry and take my wine upstairs to our giant master bedroom. Frankly, I think this house is too big for just the two of us, but Anthony wanted something appropriate for our wealth, and, like I always do, I went with it.

I place my wine glass on my nightstand and slip out of my blouse and skirt, throwing them in the hamper because I know how much Anthony hates it when I leave my clothes on the floor, and I'm not in the mood to deal with his reproach tonight. I slide off my panty hose, grab my wine glass, taking a generous gulp when I do, and walk into our luxurious bathroom wearing my matching La Perla cream bra and underwear.

Standing in front of the mirror, I stare at the woman looking back at me. I set my wine glass on the counter and brace my hands against the white and gray marble sink hoping to relieve the weight of this burden I carry, if only for a moment. A tear slides down my pale cheek, and my gaze stares back at me, red rimmed and swirling with all the pain I normally keep buried so no one will know how I really feel.

A heavy breath leaves my chest as I exhale slowly, working to compose myself in case Anthony comes up here. I take one more for good measure before washing my face and making myself a bubble bath so I can ease some of the stress from today. But I know it's pointless because tomorrow will come with its own unique stress.

Tomorrow is the anniversary of my sister's death. The one day a year when my family and I go to her grave. I go on my own sometimes—although not often—as I'm sure my parents do, but the anniversary is always a day when we go and relive the pain of losing her together.

As I immerse myself in the hot lavender- and peppermint-scented bubbly water and take another generous sip of my wine, I ponder what my life could've been like if things had been different. If my sister hadn't died that day so many years ago. If my role in her death didn't eat me alive.

I quickly shut down the thought.

Things aren't different.

This is the bed I've made myself, and now I need to sleep in it.

Whether I like it or not.

TWO

Matt

"Oh, yes, yes, yessss! Matt. Ohmigod, right there. Don't stop. Harder, harder!"

I couldn't pound this woman any harder if I tried. I'm surprised I haven't pummeled a hole in her vagina at this rate. I mean, fuck, I know it's hot in porn, but this is real life. There isn't any harder than this. I'm only a man.

One hell of a man, and a sex god, if my past partners' cries of pleasure are any indication, but a man, nonetheless.

I pump furiously, feeling her tighten around me as her words turn into meaningless screams of pleasure. Veronica, or Vicky, or maybe it was Val...whatever. She comes. That's what matters.

Now, if only I could do the same.

But my dick and I haven't exactly been on the same page lately. Apparently, he's getting picky—stupid bastard. Pussy is pussy. He should be happy he gets it as much as he does. But *noooo*, now he's acting up.

I try to mentally encourage him to finally give me my release, but instead of feeling the familiar tingle in my spine, I feel myself starting to soften up. Fuck that.

I slide out of her and pull her up by her arms.

"Suck me, baby."

Baby, because now that I'm thinking about it, I'm not sure her name even starts with a V, and I know—unfortunately, from experience—that women don't like it when you don't remember their name while you're fucking them. I can't really blame them, but at the same time, we're only having sex. I always make my intentions clear beforehand not to expect anything more from me. I've never met a woman who made me consider changing my rules. This woman is no different.

Fortunately, the generic endearment doesn't seem to faze her. She eagerly gets on her knees and takes me into her mouth.

Fuck, yes. I tip my head back and close my eyes, relishing the sensation of her lips wrapped tightly around my cock as I hit the back of her throat. That feels so damn good.

This girl definitely knows how to suck dick.

It takes me longer than usual, but eventually the tingle I've been waiting for shoots down my spine, and I pull out of her mouth just in time to come hard all over her tits.

I drop to the bed, spent, but also unexpectedly restless. That was...not as satisfying as it should've been.

My fingers slide through my sandy-brown hair, while I try to figure out what the fuck is going on with me. This isn't the first hookup lately that's left me feeling unfulfilled.

I feel the bed dip next to me and look over to see her lie down beside me. I really wish I could remember her name, so I don't come off as a total dick when I ask her to leave.

I think it was Veronica. Sure, I'll go with that.

"Thanks, Veronica. I had a great time."

She shoots up from the bed, her eyes that were filled with pleasure and contentment seconds ago now flaming with anger, and my stomach drops.

"My name's Brenda!"

Fuck. I was way off.

I throw her a sheepish look and move to smooth things over, but before I can even get another word out, she throws her clothes on—screaming at me the entire time—and stomps out of the hotel room.

Okay, so that could've gone a little better.

I lie back against the bed, my eyes closing as I attempt to relax, but that niggling thought I've been trying to suppress by fucking jersey chasers comes back. The same thought that has my boners dying before I even get a chance to come in a woman.

It's not enough anymore.

I scrub my hands over my face and let out a groan of frustration. Fuck this. Meaningless sex has worked for years. Hell, since I lost my virginity at sixteen with Gabi Jimenez, a senior, at a pool party. I don't understand why it's suddenly not enough. I sit up and push off the bed, heading for the shower.

I turn the dial and step in. The hot water pelts my body, releasing the tension in my shoulders from my wayward thoughts and easing the other aches and pains from our away game yesterday. I think about my game-winning touchdown and how good everything feels when I'm out on the field. It used to feel that way when I was buried deep in a woman, too, but not so much anymore.

I wish I could pinpoint why.

I rinse the suds off my body and get out of the shower, grabbing a plush white towel off the towel rack and patting myself dry. I wrap the towel around my toned waist and walk toward my suitcase—no sense in unpacking when we're only here for two days—and then get dressed in a pair of jeans, a fitted black long-sleeved shirt, and a Wolves sweatshirt. I pack up the rest of my shit from around the room and then head out to catch our plane back to LA.

When I arrive at the airport, my teammates are spread out

on chairs at our gate, most distracted by their phones with their headphones on. Jack Fuller and Will Edmonson are huddled near each other, as usual. Jack and I aren't that close, but we're friendly. I'm closer to Will, but my best friend on the team is definitely Luke Carter. I look around and finally catch him drinking a coffee and staring at his phone.

I wander over and sit down. "Hey, man, what's up?"

He looks up from his phone. "Nothin' much, you?"

"Not much."

He looks me over and asks, "Did you hook up with someone last night?"

"You know it," I reply with a smirk. He doesn't need to know it was a less than stellar hookup. "And again this morning before she left."

He shakes his head, laughing. "Dude, you have a hickey on your neck."

Shit.

I didn't notice that when I got out of the shower. Then again, I didn't really spend much time looking in the mirror since I was in a hurry to get out of there.

I shrug it off, pretending it doesn't bug me. Truth is, I hate hickeys. I hate when women try to mark me as theirs. I don't belong to anyone but myself. No woman gets my heart, no matter how hard they try.

I've seen what falling in love does to people. It destroys them. Better to never bother. Meaningless sex is all I'm willing to give to a woman, and it works for me.

An unwelcome thought tickles my mind. *Does it?*

I try to push the thought aside, but it lingers during our entire flight back to LA.

When I pull up to my house, I see my agent sitting in his car waiting for me. He gets out as I pull into the garage.

"Hey, Steven, what's up?"

"I've got good news," he declares with a huge smile.

"Oh yeah?"

"Guess who's the new lead of this season's Wolves campaign?"

Hope and excitement flicker in my gut. "No way."

"Yes way. You did it, man. I got the call from Luther in the marketing department while you were on the plane back here. They want you to be the face of the Wolves this season."

My smile can't be contained as this news hits me full force. This is exactly what I needed to get out of my head. My face is going to be plastered all over the stadium and the entire city of Los Angeles. Frankly, I didn't think they'd choose someone with my reputation. I've tried to be discreet about my hookups, but when you fuck primarily jersey chasers, it tends to get out.

"Did they say why they were choosing me?"

"Who fucking cares *why*? The thing that matters is that they *did* choose you! Do you know how huge this is? This is going to open the door for so many sponsorship deals. I'm already getting calls from a couple of apparel lines and even some yogurt companies wanting to feature you."

"Which apparel lines?"

He smiles like the cat that ate the canary. "I'll give you one hint. It rhymes with Mikey."

My jaw drops. "Get the fuck out."

"Nope. I'm totally serious. You're doing it, Matt. This is going to be your year on top. I can feel it."

I huff out a laugh, giddiness coursing through my veins while my brain is still in shock.

"So, I'll call Nikki Denton and get the first meeting scheduled."

If this were a movie, you'd hear a DJ scratch a record right about now. "Woah, hold up. Nikki Denton is leading this campaign? As in, Coach Denton's daughter?" All my excitement disappears at the drop of a hat as dread sits heavy in my gut.

"The one and only." Steven looks at me closely, his smile slipping slightly. "Oh, for fuck's sake, Matt, please tell me you didn't fuck and run on her?"

I can't hide the immediate grimace from my face. "Fuck no. I wouldn't fuck Nikki if she was the last woman on earth. Please, give me a little more credit than that. I don't go for stuck-up princesses who only get where they are because Daddy paved the way for them. Yeah, that's a big fat no."

"Careful, Matt. Her *daddy* is also your boss and can bench you in a heartbeat. Plus, I didn't think you had any standards when it came to who you'd fuck." He smirks at me and offers a wink. He's one to talk. He loves the ladies as much as I do.

But then his entire comment registers. Her dad is my boss, and I'm sure he would love an excuse to bench me. I'm well aware I'm not his favorite because of my reputation, and if I wasn't as good as I am, he would've traded me ages ago.

"So, if you didn't fuck her, why do you sound like you'd rather get a root canal than work with her?"

"I just said why. She's a snooty little princess who thinks she's above everyone."

He frowns in confusion. "Are we talking about the same Nikki? I've never gotten that impression. I mean, sure, she's a little uptight and a bit of a control freak, but she's always been the consummate professional. Hell, there's talk she'll be the director of the entire marketing department in no time."

"Yeah, because her dad got her the job in the first place."

Steven rolls his eyes. "If you don't like nepotism, you should go hide under a rock. It's the way of the world."

"Whatever." I point at my chest. "I busted my ass for my spot on the team. It wasn't handed to me."

"My impression is that Nikki works plenty hard. Her dad may have helped her get her foot in the door, but he's definitely not why she's worked her way up to leadership. Maybe you should give her a chance."

I grab my suitcase out of my trunk and head into my house, ignoring his remark. I turn around right before Steven's about to get back in his car. "Let me know when the meeting is."

"I will. It'll probably be in the next few days. I know they're eager to get everything scheduled. Don't stress about working with Nikki, man. It'll be great."

Doubtful, but I want this campaign. It'll be huge for my career. I can work with Nikki if it means a boost to my profile.

Hell, it's only a few months. What's the worst that could happen?

THREE

Nikki

I glance at my mom, a smile on my face that won't reach my eyes, no matter how many times I attempt it. I haven't seen her since we all visited my sister's grave last week. A part of me wishes it had been longer because lately I'm having a tough time maintaining my usual cool composure, but we always have a weekly meal together as a family. So instead of ditching on tonight like I wanted to, I inhale deeply and listen to her and Anthony plan all the details of our wedding a year from now.

Both of Anthony's parents join in on the discussion, his mom just as eager as mine about our big day. I've barely managed to say a word about the wedding. Not that anyone would ask my opinion anyway. I tend to go along with what they want, just like I have since I was eight.

Their voices drone on as they continue to make choices about what's supposed to be one of the biggest days of my life. A little voice in the back of my mind screams at me to tell them what I want, but I ignore it, my hands squeezing under the table and my shoulders stiff as I fight an instinct that lately keeps trying to claw its way out.

My dad turns to me and asks, "What do you think, Nikki?"

I glance to my right, where he sits regally, with the air of authority he always carries. He asks my opinion like this all the time, but I know I can't really give it. "Sounds great."

He smiles wide, happy with my answer, and another piece of my heart cracks.

"Excuse me, I need to use the restroom," I say softly as I place my napkin on the table and slide out of my seat, making my way to the bathroom down the hall. As soon as the lock clicks, I lean against the door and take my first real breath since we arrived here an hour ago.

I've played the happy, devoted daughter and I've gone along with everything that was decided for me since I was eight years old.

Since the night everything changed.

The same night that altered my family in unimaginable ways.

It used to be easy to play this role. To be okay with whatever was decided for me. I don't know what changed, but lately, my skin feels tight and uncomfortable whenever people talk about my future or make decisions that affect my life without really wanting to know what I think.

Maybe it's because I'm about to marry a man who expects me to continue living this way. I always thought maybe I'd find someone who would make me feel free instead of locked away in this cage of my own making. But Anthony loves getting to decide everything for us. And my parents love Anthony. Hell, my mom is the one who set us up to begin with. They'd be crushed if I broke things off with him, and I just can't find it in my heart to do that to them. I've caused enough damage as it is.

I wash my hands to complete the pretense that I was actually using the bathroom and then go back out to dinner.

"What are we talking about?" I ask as I sit back at the table, catching the tail end of a conversation between my mom and Anthony's mom, Liz.

My mom turns to me, a smile bright on her face. "We were just talking about moving the wedding up six months."

"What?" I'm barely able to keep the shock off my face and my voice neutral and composed. I turn to Anthony to see what he thinks of this.

He grabs my hand as he fills me in on what I missed. "There was a cancellation at The Lexington Ballrooms, and they've offered it to us. You know how prestigious it is, and it would definitely be more fitting of our status than the place you wanted to book."

The Garland, the "place" he won't even name, was the only thing I requested of this wedding. When we first started touring venues, I made him check it out with me because it came highly recommended, and I instantly fell in love with the location and the décor. The lush greenery and beautiful flowers instantly put me at ease, and I knew that's where I wanted to get married. It was the only piece of our wedding I'd been vocal about, and now he was changing things. Was he even planning on talking with me about this?

"And you want this change? It would move things up quite significantly, which could be difficult for the wedding planner," I say, hoping he'll be on my side and not take away the *one* thing I wanted from this wedding.

He gets that smug look on his face he often gets when he's proud of himself. "I've already talked to Bridgitte. She's making the arrangements as we speak and said it wasn't a problem."

He already talked to our wedding planner, which means he already made these plans without asking me.

I look to both our moms who are practically bursting at the seams in excitement and choose to swallow down the words attempting to come out of my mouth.

So, we're getting married six months sooner. That's okay. That's fine.

I take a sip of my wine and follow the conversation just enough to show I'm paying attention, but without actively participating.

No one wants to hear my thoughts anyway.

"I heard you're going with Matt for this season's campaign."

I look up from the papers neatly lined up on my desk to see my best friend, Cassie Jones, standing in the doorway of my office. She works as the stadium experience coordinator, but we've known each other almost our whole lives. I'd be lost without her. She's one of the rare few people I actually feel I can be myself around.

"You heard right. According to Luther, he's our best bet." I fight against the urge to roll my eyes.

She tips her head from side to side. "I guess I can see where Luther is coming from. He's hot from both sides of the field, and his game was on fire last season. He's looking pretty good this season too." She throws me a wink I promptly ignore.

"He's a player," I state.

"Uh, you do realize we work for a football team, right?"

"I meant a womanizer player, not a football player."

"And your point?"

"I don't exactly feel good about having a guy like that as the head of our campaign."

She rolls her eyes at me, as she probably should because I feel like a broken record. I know my argument is weak, but I don't want to work with him. Every interaction I've had with Matt in the past couple of years has been...tense, for lack of a better word, and I always end up irritated and cranky. There's just something about him that makes me want to slap that charismatic smile off his handsome face.

Okay, yes, I'll admit, he's...attractive, if, you know, you're into that sort of thing. But I've always preferred business types who wear suits to work instead of sweats, regardless of their sex appeal. That's why Anthony is so perfect for me. He's put together and a very successful businessman. He's handsome in a politician's son kind of way. He's everything any woman would want in a partner. Driven, loyal, secure.

Cassie sits down in the chair in front of my desk. "So, how'd the dinner go with the in-laws last night?"

I let out a deep exhale, something I find myself doing a lot lately. "It was productive. I'm getting married in March instead of next September."

Her eyes widen. "Uh, what?! Way to give a warning to your maid of honor!"

"I would've given you a warning, but I just found out last night."

Her eyes darken and a frown mars her pretty face. "Anthony changed the date of your wedding without talking to you about it?" I don't miss the accusation and anger in her tone.

"It's no big deal," I state with a shrug. "A date opened up at the Lexington Ballrooms and he wanted to snatch it up before someone else did."

Frustration is apparent on her normally soft features. "I hate that you let them walk all over you. Did he even know why you originally wanted to get married at The Garland?"

Shaking my head, I respond, my voice smaller than I intend, "It doesn't matter. You should've seen the look on my parents' faces. They love Anthony, and my mom was so excited about the change."

"Are you ever going to tell them what *you* want? Or are you going to live the rest of your life doing whatever they tell you to do?"

My shoulders stiffen as I attempt to defend myself. "It's not that bad. It's not like they're telling me to walk in front of a bus or something. And it makes them happy. They deserve to be happy."

"So do you," she says emphatically.

"I am happy."

"Liar."

I play with the silver ring sitting on my right ring finger, the one that used to belong to my sister.

"I *am* happy. It makes me happy to make my parents and Anthony happy."

Cassie stares at me like she's pondering my response. "I think you actually believe that."

I avert my gaze back to the papers on my desk, unable to hide from her. She's always been able to see through the front I put up for everyone else. Probably because she's known me since before the accident.

"I'll let this go for now, but we're definitely coming back to this conversation later," she says.

I finally look up at her and nod my head.

"So, when is your first meeting with Matt?" she asks.

I look at the calendar I keep open on my computer. "In an hour. We're meeting with him and his agent to go over the specifics and the schedule. He'll have to be available for events that I'll need your help organizing."

"Sure thing. Well, I'll leave you to prepare. Don't kill him until after all the promos are done." She smirks at me before walking out.

I walk into the conference room and stop in my tracks, my breath trapped in my chest. My eyes scan the deliciously fitted suit of the man whose back is to me. I casually admire the way the pants hug his ass and the suit jacket tightens around his biceps and fit shoulders. When he turns around and my blue eyes meet his bright blues, my heart stops.

"Matt?" I stutter, my voice a near whisper of shock.

Matt's eyes are heated as he peruses me from head to toe and back again. My breath stalls in my chest, and my heartbeat kicks up a notch. His intense gaze has my skin prickling with a sensation I'm afraid to actually name. He opens his mouth to respond, but Luther speaks before he gets a chance.

"Matt and his agent, Steven, were able to get here a little early. I just got off the phone with your assistant to see if you could pop down ahead of schedule, but I should've known better. You're always early." Luther gives me a warm smile.

"It's rude to be late." I say the line automatically, since it's been ingrained in me to always be prompt, if not early, to any meeting.

The heat in Matt's gaze evaporates before my eyes, and I hate that it leaves me feeling cold. I need him to say something arrogant so I can remind myself why I hate him so much.

"Great, now that we've thoroughly discussed the importance of punctuality, can we get this meeting started?"

And there it is.

I nod, and everyone sits while I lay out our campaign agreement. "We'll need you available for several events and promo shoots. We'll try to schedule as many of the shoots bunched together or reuse some photos, but the events are spread out over the next three months and you are required to be in attendance for all of them per the contract. Once you sign it, we'll get everything scheduled. I believe you already had a chance to look it over?"

Matt and his agent both nod in agreement.

"Do you have any questions before you sign?"

He shakes his head, replying, "It seems pretty straightforward." He turns to his agent. "Can I borrow a pen?"

Steven digs around trying to find one. My impatience gets the best of me and I offer my pen to Matt. When he takes it, our fingers touch, and the sensation from when I first saw him earlier spreads through me, warming me like I've just been standing in the sun. His gaze snaps up to meet mine for the briefest of seconds, his eyes flaring, before he averts his gaze back to the contract in front of him.

My gaze drops to the table and I slide my hand back, bringing it up to brush against my smooth hair that's secured in my usual tight high chignon.

I glance back up to watch Matt sign the contract, completely unaffected.

Did I just imagine that moment with him?

What the hell is happening with me?

He signs the papers and places my pen in front of me on the table—careful not to touch me—before sitting back in his seat. I don't think he means it as a slight, but it feels like one.

And why do I even care?

I don't.

I compose myself and school my voice before speaking. "Excellent. Let's pull out our calendars and get this all scheduled."

FOUR

Matt

Nikki and Steven figure out my calendar for the next three months while I watch in fascination as her tongue slides over her plump, pink lips right before she speaks. I think about the moment she walked in and I turned to find her checking me out. Then when our fingers touched as she offered me her pen—she might as well have gripped my dick for the effect it had on me.

Why, for all that is good and right in the world, is *this* the woman who's making my dick take notice? She is the exact opposite kind of woman I should be interested in. Not to mention it's hard to miss the giant rock sitting on her left ring finger.

I don't fuck with taken women. It's a rule I have, and one I'll never break.

Attempting to pull my thoughts from the distracting blonde in front of me, I turn to Steven right as he asks me, "Do you have any questions?"

"Nope. Seems pretty standard to me."

"Great," Nikki says, a small smile on her face. It seems forced, and the idea that I bug her as much as she annoys me pleases me. I'm about to say something snarky to see if I can get her to make that squishy face she gets when she's really annoyed with me, but she cuts me off before I ever get the chance.

"I'll have copies of this forwarded to both of you before the end of the day." She turns to Luther and asks, "Can you finish up in here? I have another meeting I need to get to."

He looks at her curiously for a moment but then replies, "Sure thing."

I'd bet my left nut she doesn't have another meeting. She just can't stand to be in the same room as me any longer. That makes two of us.

Without another word, she turns and walks out of the room, her lithe little body practically floating gracefully out the door. I watch enthralled, despite my own dislike of her, at her peach of an ass in her form-fitting business skirt and her toned calves enhanced by her four-inch stilettos.

It's really too bad such a smoking hot body is wasted on such a frigid woman.

I use my key to open the door of my childhood home, and immediately notice the mess of dishes all over the living room.

"Fuck, Dad," I mumble to myself before I go in search of the man himself.

I find him still in bed, even though it's noon in the middle of a weekday, which isn't a good sign. I open the blinds, causing him to grumble loudly behind me. Turning around, I see him burying his head underneath his pillow.

"Come on, Dad. Time to get up. Didn't you have work today?"

He mumbles into his pillow.

"What was that?" I ask.

He lifts his head just enough I can actually hear him clearly this time. "Bastards let me go."

Of course they fucking did. I wish I could say I'm surprised, but this isn't the first job my dad has been fired from. Hell, it's not even the tenth job. He's lucky if he can hold down a job for longer than a couple of months before they let him go for a slew of different reasons, all revolving around my dad's inability to stop drinking his life away.

"Come on, Dad, let's get you in the shower and put some food in your stomach. When was the last time you ate?"

A garbled mess of words comes from his pillow. It doesn't matter. I know his routine, which means I can pretty much guarantee he hasn't eaten in at least a day, instead choosing to drink. I help him out of bed, ignoring his complaints and yells for me to leave him be. I get him into the shower and then go back to his room, stripping his sheets off the bed and throwing them into the wash. I open all the windows in an attempt to get the smell of body odor out of the room.

He wasn't always like this. I can still remember clearly when my dad was the stereotypical suburban dad with a good job that got him home every night for family dinners. He used to toss the football with me in the backyard and help me with my homework. He was a great dad.

Then my mom left us when I was eleven, and the man I knew and loved disappeared. In his place was a drunk who couldn't keep a job and would sob into his beer before passing out. The worst nights were when he got drunk at the bar, and I would have to find a way to get him home. By the time I was fifteen, he was well into a routine with his constant downward spiral. I was able to get a job that paid me under the table and kept our house running. When I got drafted by the NFL and received my first signing bonus, I paid off my dad's debt and the mortgage, so at least I knew he'd always have a roof over his head.

Watching my dad completely fall apart after my mom left convinced me love wasn't worth it. Why would I bother loving someone when the end result is turning into someone completely unrecognizable? Becoming someone who can't even function like a normal human being? Who can't even take care of his damn kid? Why would I put myself through that when ultimately, they'll leave you? Love is a disease.

One I'm luckily immune to.

I hear my dad get out of the shower, so I move to pick up the kitchen so he can get dressed in peace. I'm just starting the dishwasher when he comes around the corner looking more human than he did only half an hour ago.

He looks at me sheepishly, like he always does when I catch him like this. "Thanks for picking up, Matt. You didn't need to do that."

I dry my hands with a kitchen towel. "I could hire a cleaning lady for you."

He shakes his head. It's not the first time I've offered, and I'm sure it won't be the last.

I plant my hands on the counter behind me and try again, saying, "I could pay for rehab."

"No. I've got it under control."

My shoulders sag, the little boy in me wishing I could get my old dad back. "You keep saying that, but you can't hold a job for longer than two months, Dad. You can't keep living like this. I'm going to be crazy busy this season, so I won't be able to check on you as frequently as I usually do."

"I'll be fine."

He won't. He never is.

"Dad, please," I beg, wishing for once he'd try to get better.

"Don't you think this has gone on long enough? Mom's been gone for seventeen years."

He looks at me sadly. "You think I don't know that? I know she's gone. I know she's not coming back."

No, she's definitely not. He doesn't know this, but I found her once. It took me months of searching, but I finally found her, and when I did, she broke my heart all over again. She'd married someone else, some rich guy who made her his trophy wife. She was living large without a care in the world, while I had to grow up too fast in order to take care of my alcoholic dad and keep a roof over our heads. When I reached out to her in a moment of weakness, begging her to come home, or at least come see me, she responded that she just wasn't cut out to be a mother.

Yeah, no shit.

I haven't spoken to her since.

"Dad, I love you, but you can't keep living like this. Just think about it, okay? I'll pay for everything. You just have to go."

He shrugs and nods, but I know he won't consider it. I've been offering to pay for rehab since I got drafted six years ago right out of college, but he never takes my offer.

"I gotta head home. You gonna be okay?"

"I'll be fine," he assures me.

We stare at each other, knowing his words are a lie, but I pretend to believe them and walk out of his house.

Someday he'll hit rock bottom, and I'm both terrified of what that will look like when he does and eager for it to happen so I can finally get my dad back.

FIVE

Nikki

I readjust the takeout containers in my hand and dig around inside my bag for my keys. I'm home way earlier than I expected since my last meeting got cancelled, but I'm grateful. This has been a grueling week at work, and all I want to do is get into my comfy yoga pants and ratty college sweatshirt and curl up with my e-reader. It's been ages since I've been able to get home this early and relax.

I open the door and am about to shout out to Anthony but stop in my tracks as I hear the moans coming from upstairs. I smile and shake my head. I've never caught Anthony watching porn, but it makes him a little bit more human to me. I know he does it, but he's never admitted to it.

I mean, hell, I've done it when I just needed a little "me" time and a quick release, especially if Anthony wasn't home. I walk up the stairs, the sounds getting louder. I hesitate for a minute, thinking I should let him finish in peace before I disrupt his alone time, but then remember how horny I was earlier today—I mean, that's the only explanation for why I reacted to Matt the way I did—and decide maybe his solo session can turn into a couple's session.

I open the door and step into our bedroom. The smile on my face evaporates the moment my gaze lands on our bed. *Our fucking bed.* My breath stalls in my lungs, and my entire picture-perfect future shatters in an instant. Anthony isn't having a solo session, not if the naked brunette riding him like her life depends on it is any indication.

I stand there, my stomach rolling and clenching in disgust, while my brain tries to process the visual in front of me. My feet are frozen to the floor and my eyes are glued to the writhing bodies on the bed. It's like I'm watching a train wreck and can't turn away even though I know it's about to be a disaster.

I must make some kind of noise because Anthony turns his head mid-groan, his eyes widening when they land on me.

"Oh, fuck."

He quickly pushes the woman off him and she turns to face me for the first time.

"Bridgitte?" My voice is breathy and shallow.

He's fucking our wedding planner?

What. The. Actual. Fuck?

I turn around and walk out of the room, a weird calm encompassing me and carrying me down to the kitchen. I think about pouring myself a glass of wine but decide against it. I definitely need to be sober for the conversation that's coming.

What is even happening right now?

How, in the blink of an eye, did my life go from perfectly planned to crumbling right before my eyes?

I go to reach for a glass so I can drink some water and notice that my hands are shaking. I do a mental check and realize my whole body is vibrating with an emotion I can't quite place—shock, maybe?

I move to the living room and sit down on the couch, trying to take deep breaths to calm myself down. This is not how tonight was supposed to go.

"Nikki, I can explain."

I look up to see Anthony standing at the opening of the living room, panic clear on his features. It's possibly the first time I've ever seen him look anything but composed.

"You can explain?" I'd like to see him explain his way out of this one.

"It just happened. It was a one-time thing."

"It just happened?" That's really the direction he wants to go with this right now? "You just *accidentally* stuck your dick in our wedding planner? And then kept going since you were already there? How does something like that *just* happen, Anthony?"

"You've been so busy with work lately."

Oh, fuck no. He does not get to give me some cliché bullshit. I know I may sit back and take a lot of crap to make my family happy, but this is where I draw the line.

"Fuck you, Anthony." I seethe, finally channeling all my emotional shock into cold hard rage. How *dare* he blame this on me after all the concessions I've made for him.

His eyes widen in surprise, probably because I've never talked back to him before.

"The wedding is off, so you can continue to fuck Bridgitte all you want."

I grab my purse and walk past him, but he grabs my arm, stopping me in my tracks.

"Where are you going? We need to talk about this."

I look him straight in the eyes. "There's nothing left to talk about. Let me go."

His mouth gapes open but no words come out, thank God, because I'm already starting to shake again, and I am desperate to get out of here.

I pull my arm out of his grasp and head out to my car. The radio plays in the background, but I don't hear a sound. I don't even register where I'm going until I pull up to her house.

Cassie opens her door after the second knock. "Nikki? I would've expected you to be curled up enjoying your first actual night off in ages." She appraises my appearance and must notice the tremor of my body I still can't seem to get rid of because her brow furrows and her voice drips with concern. "What's wrong?"

"I caught Anthony fucking our wedding planner."

Saying the words makes the whole scene come back into full focus, and for the first time since I walked into our bedroom, the consequences of his actions hit me full force. The whole situation is so cliché. I've defended him on more than one occasion saying he was loyal, and now here I stand in front of my best friend because I walked in on my fiancé cheating on me.

Tears start falling down my cheeks, more over the loss of the life I worked so hard for and less about the man himself—which is telling. Regardless, I can't stop the flow of tears. Without another word, Cassie drags me into the house she shares with her boyfriend, Max Donnelly, and sits me on the couch.

Max walks into the room, slowing his stride when he sees me—the tears streaming down my face giving away that this is not a happy visit. He walks over to Cassie and places a tender kiss on her forehead before whispering, "I'll leave you girls alone. Holler if you need me, okay?"

Cassie nods at him, and the love shining in her eyes when she looks at him makes my insides shrivel up. I can't remember ever looking at Anthony like that. I don't think I've ever looked at *anyone* like that. Tears fall faster, and I'm no longer sure what I'm mourning—the loss of Anthony, the loss of my perfectly planned life, or the fact that all the events of tonight have made me realize I've never been in love and my life is an even bigger sham than I knew.

Feelings bombard me from all sides—some even from as far back as when I was a little girl—and tears continue to cascade in a steady waterfall down my face. Cassie holds me while I cry into her shoulder, letting out all the emotion I've been holding in.

I don't know how long we sit there, but eventually my tears subside. I sit up and look at Cassie.

"I don't know what to do now."

"I have an idea," she confides with a soft smile.

"What's that?"

"Why don't you actually live your life for yourself now?"

Well, isn't that an idea.

SIX

Matt

I push forward at the sound of the snap, weaving through defenders to propel my body toward the goal. After fifteen yards, I glance behind me, noticing the linebacker right on my heels about to reach out to grab me. I take a sharp left and shoot forward, putting my entire body into the movement and hoping to gain further momentum to push myself down the field. I reach the thirty-yard line and turn just in time to see the football spiraling in the air toward me.

Instinctively, my hands fly up in the air, grabbing the ball the moment it connects with my gloves and immediately bringing it down to my chest, tucking it close to my body. Unfortunately, the seconds it took to turn around and catch the ball slowed me down enough for the linebacker to catch up to me. I feel his body slam into mine, and I grip the ball tightly as I hit the ground with a thud. I hear the whistle signaling they've called the obvious—down by contact.

The linebacker rolls off me just as one of his teammates reaches out to help him up. I hand the ball off to the ref standing next to me, and then see Luke reach out his hand. I grip it and he pulls me up.

"Thanks, man."

He pats me on the back. "You good? That seemed like a hard hit."

I rotate my shoulder knowing it'll be sore later if I don't ice it after the game. "Nothing an ice bath won't fix."

We head back toward the huddle, eager to hear the next play from our captain and quarterback, Jack Fuller. We join the circle and gather around, the air thickening with adrenaline at how close we are to victory. When the huddle breaks, we get in position, ready and eager to make it happen. I get tackled another dozen times, but it feels worth it when we get one more touchdown and win the game.

After the game, I soak in an ice bath for ten minutes and then shower again before joining Luke at a local bar we like to frequent. I pat his back when I find him sitting at the bar flirting with a stacked blonde.

The moment I see her, my mind immediately thinks about Nikki's lighter blonde locks, and I shake the thought away as quickly as I can. The last person I need to be thinking about is Nikki fucking Denton.

"Hey, dude," I say.

He turns to me, "Hey! Glad you made it." He points to the blonde and a brunette I hadn't noticed standing next to her. "This is Jessica and her friend Natalie."

I nod, catching the brunette checking me out. I toss her a quick smirk right as the bartender walks over to us and asks, "What'll you have?"

"Can I get a beer?"

"Any specific one?" he asks.

"Whatever IPA you recommend," I say as I tap the bar top.

He pours my beer and asks before handing it off to me, "You wanna open a tab?" I shake my head and hand him twenty dollars.

I don't get wasted anymore. Not after I got shitfaced at a club event with the team and unintentionally assisted in Jack and his girlfriend-at-the-time, Paige's, breakup. Thankfully they were able to work through it all and are now soon to be married, but that was a huge wakeup call for me. My drinking had never really impacted anyone else before, but as soon as it ended up hurting someone, I couldn't do it anymore.

I know firsthand what it's like to be on the receiving end of someone who drinks too much, not caring about the consequences of their choices. I'm not about to do that to someone else. That night turned out to be exactly what I needed to show me that I was on a slippery slope to becoming my dad.

I take a sip of my beer and look over at the brunette who's currently eye-fucking me. She's hot—stacked like her friend and wearing a tight little black dress that leaves little to the imagination. I bet if she bent over right now, I could see her pussy on full display. Her towering heels barely bring her to my chin, which is something I'm used to given that I'm six feet four. Her brown eyes are nearly hidden underneath her overdone eye makeup, but she's still hot.

She'll do.

I really need to get laid, and I'm not one to be picky. I'm also a little desperate to get a certain blonde princess out of my fucking head, and nothing should do that quicker than fucking a woman who is her exact opposite.

I walk over and chat her up, ready to put on my most charismatic charm. I'm surprised when after only a minute or two of talking, she stops me with her hand to my chest. She leans close, her breasts rubbing against me.

She whispers in my ear seductively, "We both know where this is going, so why are we still standing here talking? Meet me in the bathroom in two minutes."

She pulls back and gives me a sexy smirk before she sashays

back toward the restrooms. I glance at the clock, count to sixty and then follow her, not caring that it hasn't been a full two minutes. The second I open the bathroom door, she pulls me in by my shirt before reaching up and pulling my mouth down to hers. My body leans against the door and I kiss her back, shoving my tongue against hers, but quickly notice that nothing is happening down south.

This is hot. This woman can't keep her hands off me and clearly wants to fuck my brains out, but I couldn't be less hard right now. I'm as flaccid as a windsock without even the slightest breeze.

Her hand slides down to grip me through my pants, then eagerly rubs up and down. I toss my head back against the door and close my eyes, sending a silent prayer to my missing boner that he'll show up.

"Looks like you need a little help," Nadia says—wait, no. Luke said her name was...*Fuck me*, why can't I remember this chick's name? I used to be better than this.

I look down at her as she unbuckles my belt and opens up my pants while she gets on her knees. I'm distracted thinking about how painful that position must be on these hard floors.

Not what I should be thinking about when a woman is about to blow me.

She pulls out my cock, which thank fuck is now at least a semi. She licks me like a lollipop and starts sucking on me slowly.

I close my eyes trying to focus on the movements of her tongue and mouth, but the second my eyes close, I see Nikki's heated look when she walked into our meeting the other day.

She hums happily and pulls her lips off with a pop. "There he is. God, your cock is so fucking big."

I look at her and then at my cock. I'm slightly mortified my dick went full alert at just the thought of Nikki Denton.

What the actual fuck?

I look back at the chick who's currently going to town on my dick like he's her last meal and try to get into the moment, but my thoughts are totally sidetracked by the fact I just got hard for Nikki. Nikki, who does that condescending tweak of her eyebrow when she thinks I'm being ridiculous and acts like she's above me.

Fuck, now I'm thinking of her being above me on a bed doing her eyebrow tweak while she rides me, her blue eyes dark with pleasure and her plump lips open in a scream.

Blinding pleasure overtakes me, and I rest all my weight against the door as I come down from my massive release. Belatedly, I realize Natalie—that was her name!—is licking me clean, and guilt overwhelms me.

I might be a massive player, some might even argue manwhore, but I've never fucked a woman while I thought about someone else. For the first time since I discovered sex, I excuse myself before pleasuring my partner. It's a douche move, but I can barely look at her right now, let alone think about making her come.

I find Luke still at the bar with the blonde and clap him on the back.

"I'm heading out."

"Already?" He looks behind me. "Where's Natalie?"

"She's in the bathroom."

He smirks at me knowingly but stops when he notices I don't return it.

"Did something happen?"

"I'm in a weird headspace." I shake my head at that understatement. "I don't know. I just gotta go. I'll catch ya later."

He nods slowly, his brow furrowed, but I don't acknowledge it and instead make my way toward the exit.

This is not what I had in mind when I started thinking I needed a change.

I watch Nikki walk around the space, talking to the photographer's assistant while I'm getting my hair worked on for the first photo shoot. I haven't been able to stop looking at her all day, curious as to why my brain went straight to her during my bathroom hookup a few days ago. I haven't thought about her since—thank fuck—but it's still left me feeling unsettled.

She definitely owns the room when she's in it, which I guess is objectively hot. Who doesn't like a woman who knows what she wants? But that's not what's captured my attention today. There's something different about her posture, and her eyes seem a little, I don't know, dimmer than they did before.

It's when she gets closer, holding her clipboard against her chest with her left hand, that I finally notice what's different.

Nikki's not wearing her obnoxiously large engagement ring today. I haven't seen her without that ring since she got engaged nearly a year ago.

She walks over to me. "Are you all set?"

I nod, my eyes locked on her face. "Yeah, I think so." I glance down at her hand white-knuckling her clipboard. "So, what, your man dumped you? Couldn't handle you having to be in control of everything?"

Yeah, I know, that was an asshole thing to say. I'm normally a lot smoother about my insults with her, but this weird chemistry that's been brewing between us, combined with my recent string of unsatisfying hookups, is throwing me off balance.

I shouldn't have even bothered to bring up her missing engagement ring.

Nikki's business is none of mine.

I bite my tongue to stop myself from saying anything else, but the damage is already done. Nikki's jaw is clenched, and her knuckles are nearly translucent from gripping her clipboard.

When she finally speaks, she practically spits her words at me, her voice lowered so as not to be heard by anyone around us. "You think you know me, but you don't know a damn thing."

My stomach rolls slightly at her words, mainly because I really don't know her, but also because I'm feeling guilty about being such a jackass when I can clearly see she's not in any mood for it.

During the shoot, she avoids me like the plague. Despite her efforts at avoidance, my body is constantly in tune with wherever she is in the room, and my eyes manage to find her whenever they stray from the camera.

For the first time, I notice how Nikki completely commands a room without being a dictator about it. She is focused and efficient, but gentle with her redirection when people aren't doing things the way they're supposed to.

I try to focus on the photographer. Today's shoot is fairly mild. Just me in my Wolves uniform in various poses. Next week's shoot will be a bit more interesting. I'll be posing with a couple of other models for an athletic brand that is sponsoring the Wolves this season. I try to think about the possibilities of hooking up with both models instead of obsessing about the blonde standing only twenty feet away and looking sexier than she should in a well-fitted pantsuit.

I do not think Nikki Denton is sexy.

My dick twitches.

Yeah, okay, keep telling yourself that, buddy.

Fuck me.

SEVEN

Nikki

Babysitting a manwhore like Matt is not generally my idea of a good time. As the light flickers on inside my office and I take a seat at my immaculate cherry wood desk, I have to admit our first photoshoot went off about as well as could be expected, except for his complete insensitivity toward me at the beginning. Then again, that's nothing new.

What was new was the way he constantly watched me for the remainder of the shoot.

My pulse quickens at the memory of the lingering weight of his eyes on me during the shoot, and how shivers raced down my spine the few times our gazes clashed. I shake my head, annoyed with myself. This has to be some strange side effect from the emotional upheaval I've recently gone through.

Honestly, I shouldn't be all that surprised this shoot went so well. Matt's great in front of the camera. It's the next one I'm concerned about. He'll be modeling with two other athleisure models, and Lord knows he'll probably try to get in their pants. I don't care what he does on his own time, but I'm not going to let his Casanova ways derail the shoot.

I'm just about to sit at my desk when I see Luther pop his head through my still open door.

"How'd it go?" he asks leisurely.

"As well as can be expected. The proofs looked great, so I feel confident it'll turn out even better after the edits."

"And Matt behaved?" For the first time, a hint of concern tinges his tone.

"Yes. For this one at least." He doesn't need to know about our one-on-one interaction.

Luther takes an obvious relieved exhale. "Excellent."

I squint at him. "I thought you weren't worried about him."

"I never said that. I said he was the best choice based on the group tests we ran. Doesn't mean I'm not scared shitless he's going to flirt with or fuck the wrong person and then we'll all be screwed, and not in a good way."

"There's a good way to be screwed?"

He tosses me a pitying look. "Oh, honey. You really need to get laid. I thought getting sex on the regular was supposed to be a perk of being in a committed relationship."

I look down at the papers on my desk, trying to find the composure I usually wear so well in the office.

"Yes, well, I'm not in a relationship anymore, so I definitely won't be having regular sex." Not that Anthony and I were having much sex lately to begin with.

Luther's eyes widen in shock. "What? What happened?"

"Turns out he wasn't as committed as we all thought."

His eyes soften with sympathy. "Honey, I'm so sorry." He reaches out and places his hand over mine on top of my desk.

"Thanks, but I'd really rather not talk about it."

He sits back in his chair, observing me. "You know, for someone whose fiancé just cheated on her, you seem to be handling it awfully well. If my man cheated on me, I'd be pulling a *Waiting to Exhale*."

"A what?"

"Please tell me you've seen the movie! It's a classic." When I shake my head, he throws his hands up. "In a stellar display of giving zero fucks about the consequences, she lights her cheating douchebag's car on fire with all his things in it and burns his shit to the ground. Oh, girl. We need to have a movie night with a giant tub of ice cream and pizza. Or, better yet, we'll take you clubbing and get you good and laid. Good riddance to bad dick!"

I can't help but laugh at Luther's comments. He's seriously the gay best friend of my dreams.

"I don't think I'm up for clubbing quite yet."

"Come on, girl. Time to hop back on the horse. I mean, fuck, when was the last time you were even at the rodeo?"

I twist my head to the side, my eyes going to the ceiling as I try to ponder when Anthony and I last had sex. My cheeks pink up when I realize I honestly can't remember. Maybe three months? I kept trying to initiate something, but he kept telling me he was too tired. A girl can only take so much rejection from her partner before she stops asking.

My blood heats when I think about the possibility he was turning me down because he was getting it elsewhere. He said that night was the first time, but clearly Anthony is a giant douchey liar, so who knows what the truth is anymore.

"Okay, you're taking way too long to answer, which means it's been too long. And if he couldn't please you, then you're definitely better off without him."

"Are we talking about Anthony?" Cassie's head pops around the corner of my door, her eyes bright with excitement. She was never the biggest fan of Anthony's—something she mostly tried to hide from me in the name of being a good friend, but fully admitted to when I ended up at her place after I left him.

Luther turns toward Cassie. "Girl, you knew and didn't tell me? Come on, you're supposed to always give me the tea first."

She rolls her eyes. "It happened barely a week ago. I haven't even seen you to be able to tell you."

"Helloooo," Luther exaggerates, clearly exasperated with her. "That's what phones are for."

Cassie places her hand on her chest. "You're right, how silly of me. I give you my humblest apologies for not alerting you first when I was trying to make sure my best friend was surviving the worst kind of betrayal."

Luther's lips pucker at her sarcasm, but then he nods when she finishes. "You're right. Your priorities were in the right place."

I swear, watching these two is like a tennis match but a million times more interesting. Their tiff apparently over, they both turn to me.

"So, how are you getting over the dirtbag?" Luther asks.

I shrug. "I figured I would just focus on work. I don't need to jump into anything serious right now."

"Honey, I'm not talking about jumping into serious. I'm talking about jumping into bed."

Cassie giggles and concurs, "He has a point, Nik. It might be good for you to have a meaningless fling with someone."

I look at her, my eyes wide and my mouth parted in surprise. "You agree with him?"

She nods, looking at me like she thinks his suggestion is exactly what I need.

I look between them and point out, "I'm sorry, but have either of you met me?" I nearly shriek, "I do *not* do flings. I've never even had a one-night stand!"

"Exactly!" He looks at me critically and then leans back. "Although, I'm not sure you could do a one-night stand."

Cassie nods and agrees, "Yeah, she'd hate that. What she

really needs is someone she can explore with and who will get her to try new things. Someone who will push all her sexual buttons."

"Absolutely."

While incredible sex doesn't sound too bad, this is so completely out of my comfort zone that the idea has my heart beating like a hummingbird's wings in my chest.

"You guys," I say, unable to hide the minor panic thrumming through my veins, "I appreciate where you both are coming from, but really, this is a terrible idea."

Cassie turns to me. "Nikki, I love you, but you're in a rut. You've lived your whole life for everyone else. It's time you lived for yourself. It's time you did something just for you. This is your chance. If not now, when? When are you going to explore your sexuality or let yourself really *live*?"

She eyes me earnestly, and my heart sinks and soars at the same time as I process her words. She's right. This might be my only chance to really be myself and try something new. But how do I let go of nearly twenty years of always doing what others expected of me?

How do I let myself be *myself*?

Do I even know who I really am anymore?

My shoulders sag in defeat. This feels impossible. Hell, my skin is already itching at the idea of disappointing my parents. What if they find out?

"Get out of your head, Nikki," Cassie says softly. "It's time to spread your wings, or you're going to regret it for the rest of your life that you never took this time for yourself."

She's right. I know she's right. But that doesn't change how impossible this all feels.

"I don't know how," I choke out. I fidget with my sister's ring, my constant reminder about why I make the choices I make. Usually, it reassures me that those choices have been for the best, no matter how miserable they sometimes made me.

Now, it offers me little comfort and almost feels like a burden sitting on my finger. This is my chance to do something just for me, and I'm frozen in fear, completely unsure about how to even begin.

Cassie can read the fear in my face. I see it in how her eyes soften to match her voice. "Nikki, you just have to decide to do it and then take the leap."

"Oh, that's it, huh?" I ask sarcastically. She makes it seem like it's no big deal. Like I'm just walking up a flight of stairs.

"Can you think of anyone you could ask for a friends with benefits arrangement?" Luther asks.

I toss him an *are you serious* look. "I've been engaged for the last year. All our friends were couples. The only friends I have outside of Anthony anymore are you and Cass."

Luther and Cassie look at each other. "Cass, do you know anyone who's a sex god and available?"

A sex god? My body warms and my core tingles at the thought of having a sexual partner who could make me feel things I've only read about or seen in movies.

But like hell I'll let them see they're actually getting me to consider this craziness. "You guys, I really don't think this is a good idea, or even necessary. Frankly, I think this whole thing is ridiculous and not something that's ever going to happen anyway, so let's just talk about something else."

Ignoring me, Cassie sits back against her chair, tapping her finger on her closed lips and humming while she thinks. Luther does the same, pacing back and forth and mumbling to himself, while I sit in my chair and process the idea of having meaning-less sex with someone. Could I actually do it? Would I even be able to find someone who can get me out of my head long enough to enjoy a sex-only fling? It would certainly be interesting to be with a man who knew how to find my clit.

Suddenly, Cassie shoots up, a radiant smile breaking out on her face and her eyes wide with delight. I hold my body stiff, bracing for whatever she's about to say.

"Oh my God, I can't believe I didn't think of it before. I know the *perfect* man for you, who is a sex god and all about no-strings sex."

"Who?" I ask nervously. She's way too excited about this, and I have a sneaking suspicion that it's not someone who *I* will think is perfect.

The second her mouth opens, I know I'm going to hate the name that pops from her lips.

"Matt Fischer."

EIGHT

Matt

The set for the photo shoot is already buzzing with activity, even though I arrive early. People are flitting around, trying to get everything ready. The second I get fully through the doors, a woman with a clipboard comes up to me.

"Mr. Fischer. Thank God you're early." She lets out a sigh of relief and looks down at her clipboard. "Okay, I'm going to have you get started in hair and makeup with Eileen. She's the redhead over there. I'll come get you when we're ready for you in wardrobe."

"Sure thing." I walk over to the redhead she pointed to. "Are you Eileen?"

She turns to me, and I glance at the laugh lines around her eyes and mouth. She looks to be in her forties and appears to be sans plastic surgery, a rarity for people in her line of work in this city.

She smiles at me. "I am. You must be Matt."

"That's me." I grin and reply back, trying to place the hint of accent I heard when she spoke.

I sit in the chair she points to. "Are you from around here?" I ask.

"No. I grew up in Dublin. Accent's a bit watered down since I moved to the states twenty years ago."

I start to ask her if she misses it. I've always wanted to travel to Dublin, but never seem to find the time between making sure my dad doesn't drink himself to death and all my football responsibilities. But before I can speak, I hear a woman throwing a diva-level hissy fit behind me. I turn around to see some buxom blonde ripping Nikki a new one.

Nikki's face is flushed in anger she's barely containing, her fists clenched at her sides and her eyes sparking with frustration and annoyance.

She looks fucking hot when she's pissed off. I've been on the receiving end of her annoyance more than once, but I've never made her this mad before. Clearly, I need to try harder because she is a sight to behold.

Discreetly adjusting myself in my suddenly uncomfortably tight pants, I watch as her jaw clenches, her lips purse, and her chest starts to rise and fall in a false attempt to control her temper and her breathing.

Fuck me. I've never seen her have so much fire, and it's seriously doing something to me. I hear the blonde call Nikki a bitch and that pulls me temporarily out of my lust haze.

I should *not* be lusting after Nikki.

But I also don't like the way this blonde is tearing her down, and while I may not like Nikki, I doubt she deserves this treatment. I get up from my chair, asking Eileen to give me a minute, and walk over just as Nikki is about to open her mouth in response to the blonde towering over her.

My movement must register, because her eyes swing to meet mine, and my heart rate quickens having all that heat and fire directed at me. God, why is that so sexy?

"Everything okay over here, ladies?" I ask, trying to compose my voice so as not to expose the lust coursing through my veins, while at the same time attempting to diffuse the situation.

The blonde turns to me, and I immediately recognize her as one of the models I'm supposed to be working with today, Nadine Monroe.

"No, things are not okay. I was supposed to have Aqua Deco water, and instead they put this generic bullshit." She points to Nikki and continues, "*This* woman has one fucking job, and she can't even do it right."

As Nadine talks, I recall hearing she was a diva to work with, but now that I know she's caused this huge scene over a brand of water? Yeah, she's next level crazy in my book. And not sex-will-be-off-the-charts crazy, but roll-your-eyes-at-the-diva and don't-let-her-come-near-you-with-a-sharp-object crazy.

I look around the room and see nearly everyone has stopped what they're doing and is staring at the scene in front of them. I start to feel the pressure of needing to de-escalate this quickly, but I have no idea how. Just as I'm about to open my mouth—to say what, I have no idea—the photographer's assistant comes hustling over, her eyes set and determined.

"Ms. Monroe. The photographer already made it clear this behavior would not be tolerated, and Ms. Denton was not in charge of handling your rider, so your anger is misplaced. I'm only going to ask once that you go back to your dressing room and calm down."

I wince. Damn, she was on a roll, but even I know you don't tell an irate woman to calm down.

Nadine's eyes turn to slits, and her icy voice whispers softly, "Calm down? You want me to calm down? Who the hell do you think you are?"

Out of the corner of my eye, I see the photographer, Jimmy, walk up with security. I've never been at a shoot where they had to call security. This is insane.

"Nadine, you're fired. Get your shit and get out. I'm done with this. You've not earned the right to be this big of a heinous bitch," Jimmy says with no hint of remorse at losing a model.

Nadine's mouth opens and shuts like a fish out of water sucking desperately for air. Security escorts her out, and Jimmy tells everyone to get back to it. I turn back to Nikki about to remark on how crazy that was when I see her face is still flushed, her expression enraged, and her fists clenched tightly at her side.

She looks insanely sexy all fired up, but there's also something in her expression that makes me think Nadine said something before I walked up that hit a nerve.

I look around and see an unoccupied room tucked off to the side. I gently grab her upper arm and pull her into the room before closing the door. It's a totally unconscious move when I push the lock.

I swear.

When I turn around to look at her, her chest is heaving and her eyes are sparking with rage. When she bites her lip and lets out a guttural groan of frustration and anger, my dick gets impossibly hard.

"I..." she starts to say as she begins pacing, clearly unable to articulate all her anger or what has really triggered her. Her nostrils flare while her hands clench and unclench at her sides. I find this side of her completely fascinating, and while I've never been a masochist, the idea of letting her take out all that anger on me stirs my body further.

She starts muttering to herself, and her hands fly up to harshly slide through her hair, pulling strands from her normally tight and perfect bun. Her cheeks tinge a dark pink as she lets out another growl, and I can't take it anymore. She's doing things to me, and I'm not a guy who sits around, especially not when my body is demanding I act.

On her next trip past me, I grab her upper arm and twist her to face me, sliding my other hand up to wrap around her neck. Our eyes lock—hers full of fire, mine full of lust—then I cover her mouth with mine in a searing kiss that lights my whole body aflame. Her teeth gnash against my lips, and she lets out the smallest groan of protest before her body melts into mine. Her mouth ravages me in a way I've never experienced before.

Holy fuck, this woman can kiss.

My mind is spinning out of control at the revelation, when I feel her hand slide over my dick. I let out a groan, and the noise must register with her because she pulls back slightly, her chest heaving, her breaths uncontrolled and the flush on her cheeks darker than when she was spitting mad. Her lips are red and swollen, and I want nothing more than to claim them again.

God, I want to fuck her so bad.

"Don't stop," I say, with the tiniest hint of begging in my tone. I'm pretty certain if she stops right now, I will die of blue balls. Literally. My dick hasn't been this hard in months, and all it took was a thirty-second kiss from her.

She looks at me, and I see a million thoughts spinning in that head of hers, but I won't be the one to initiate a kiss again. I've already taken more than I should. If we do this, it needs to be her decision.

"I hate you," she whispers.

"Right back at ya, Princess."

Her eyes spark. I know she hates that nickname, and it sends a thrill through me.

"Fuck you, Matt." Her voice is stronger now.

"That was the idea."

The next thing I know, her lips are mashing against mine and she's grinding her body against me and I swear to God I've never been this turned on in my life.

I grip her ass and lift her up, her legs wrapping tight around my hips as she finds the perfect spot to grind against my steel erection. I groan into her mouth, loving the pressure and hating it at the same time because I'm desperate to be buried inside her.

I also fucking hate that she's wearing pants.

Fuck pants.

I spin so her back is against the wall next to the door and drop her down, just long enough to undo the button on her slacks and watch as they fall to her feet. She must be in as much of a daze as I am because she quickly steps out of them, while simultaneously working on unbuttoning my pants. Every time her small hands graze my dick, I want to weep at how fucking good it feels. It's the perfect tease of things to come.

I rub her through her panties and watch in fascination as her head drops back and she lets out a soft moan, grinding against my hand. Her panties are soaked and now all I can think about is tasting her, but I know we don't have time. Everyone is right outside, and I'm sure they'll come looking for us soon.

I refuse to leave this room without feeling her come on my cock.

I pull her panties off, shoving them in my back pocket and grabbing a condom before pushing my pants down to my knees. I put it on in record time. When I lift her up, her legs automatically wrap around me again, sliding her wet heat over my hard dick. I slide inside her with no resistance and let out a groan in relief and awe at how goddamn good she feels.

Nikki is *nothing* like I imagined.

She's so insanely tight, and hot, and wet. Fuck, I'm in heaven.

Her pussy clenches around me, and I let out another groan. I'm not going to last long at this rate, which is a shame because Nikki's pussy is perfection and I really want to spend forever in it right now. Her hips thrust in rhythm with mine, and her clit grinds against me as I pound into her. Her legs start to shake around me, and she lets out a soft moan at the same time I feel her squeezing my dick with her pussy. My eyes roll back in my head at the bliss shooting through my body and the feeling of her coming around me. She lets out the faintest whimper and I lock my lips on hers, desperate to taste her in any way I can while I fuck all her anger and frustration away.

I'm normally known for my stamina, but when she comes again within seconds of her last orgasm, I can't fight it anymore. Her tight little pussy milks my cock for all it's worth and I come hard.

My head rests on her shoulder, as I come down from my release. Her arms are lax around my neck, but still holding onto me as we both attempt to catch our breath and process what just happened.

What the fuck *did* just happen?

I feel her body stiffen as we both realize what we just did, and I gently pull out of her. She winces, which doesn't surprise me given my size and how tight she was. I'm guessing she's going to be a bit sore.

The idea sends another little thrill through me, knowing she's going to feel me for the rest of the day.

She bends down and quickly puts her pants back on—sans panties. She won't look me in the eye as she straightens out her shirt and attempts to fix her hair.

"Nikki?"

"That never should've happened," she whispers, all her fire from before completely vanished.

Maybe it shouldn't have happened, but it *did* happen. And I, for one, don't regret it. Maybe I should, but I don't.

Clearly, I'm alone in that sentiment because without another word, she opens the door and sneaks out, never looking back at me.

I stand there trying to process everything, but I barely even start when there's a knock on the door, and I hear Eileen on the other side telling me they really need me to get my hair and makeup done for the shoot so they can get started.

I pull up my pants and discard the condom in a nearby trashcan before I open the door and follow Eileen to her station. I can't stop myself from looking around for Nikki, but I don't see her anywhere.

Thirty minutes later, I finally break and ask the photographer's assistant if she's seen her.

"Yeah, she said there was a work emergency and she had to go."

Right.

A work emergency.

My princess is a big, fat liar.

"I thought she had to be here for these things."

The PA shrugs and offers, "We prefer if we have a representative here, but technically we can run the shoot without her. It's just not something we do regularly, since they have the final say on things."

I nod and let her walk away while I try to pull my thoughts together. It takes me the entire shoot before I come to any sort of conclusion.

I'm not done with Nikki Denton.

Not by a long shot.

NINE

Nikki

My entire drive back to the Wolves business office is spent internally yelling at myself for the colossal mistake I just made. I mean, I know Cassie joked about me having a fling with Matt, but I had argued it was the most ridiculous idea she'd ever suggested.

An argument that was sound.

It made sense.

Having sex would be a disaster.

Now I'm desperately trying to forget the feel of him sliding inside me and making me come so hard I swore I saw stars. Twice! I've never come twice. Hell, I can count on one hand the number of times Anthony actually made me come from penetration at all in the last year.

I know that's horrible, and feminists everywhere are probably outraged that I ever considered marrying him when the man couldn't even give me a proper orgasm, but my parents loved him. So, I stuck it out and came to terms with the fact I would have mediocre sex for the rest of my life, which at the time didn't seem like a big deal since sex had never really been that mind-blowing.

But I get it now.

Oh boy, do I get it.

Sex with Matt was...there aren't even words for what it was.

Oh wait...yes, there are.

Mistake. Disaster. Mistake—it's worth repeating, that's how big of a mistake it was.

Oh God, but what a delicious mistake.

Wait, no. It was just a disaster. A very bad decision.

A mistake.

Did I say that already?

My head is a mess, and my body is still humming from the pleasure overload as I walk in a daze to Cassie's office area. Her head pops up when I walk in, and fortunately, there's no one else in her office.

"Nikki? I thought you had the shoot with Matt today?"

I look at her, convinced guilt is marring my features. "I did something bad."

She puts down the paper she's holding and gives me her undivided attention. "What happened?" Concern is evident in her tone.

She should be concerned.

"I made a horrible mistake. I..." Oh, God. I have to say it out loud. "I had sex with Matt." I drop my head into my hands, unable to look at what I'm sure is her horrified expression.

When she doesn't say anything after a minute, I look up and am dismayed to see her face in a huge grin, her eyes alight with excitement.

"Are you serious? Or are you fucking with me?" She looks like a kid at Christmas.

Did she not hear me?

"I wish I was fucking with you," I say cautiously.

She claps giddily before jumping out of her seat and running around her desk to me. She pulls me up into a big hug, squealing in my ear and forcing my stiff body to hop up and down with hers.

What the hell?

"I'm so proud of you!" she squeals.

"What?!"

She pulls back, and when she notes my serious demeanor and lack of smile, her own falls from her face.

"Was he not good?" she asks fearfully.

"What?" I shake my head. *That's* what she's worried about?!

"You think I'm upset because the sex was bad?" I ask in disbelief. I shouldn't even have had the sex!

"Why else would you be upset?"

"Because I had sex with Matt! Matt Fischer," I enunciate, in case she didn't catch it the first time. "Walking STD Matt Fischer. Manwhore of the Wolves Matt Fischer," I say, nearly hysterical now.

"So, the sex wasn't bad?" she asks hesitantly.

I shake my head. "Why does that even matter?"

She tilts her head and sighs heavily like she's trying to explain something to a small child. "You really want me to answer that?"

I don't say anything.

"Okay, but really, I need to know. Was it good?"

I give up.

I throw my arms out and my head back. "Yes!" I shout, looking back at her. "It was mind-blowing." I start pacing around her office. "It was the best sex I've ever had, okay? Are you happy now?"

I turn back to her to find her eyes wide and her mouth twitching while she fights back a shit-eating grin. She looks at me like she doesn't know what to do with me.

Well, joke's on her, because I don't know what to do with me either.

God, I'm a mess.

"Okay, so if it was the best you've ever had, why are you having a toddler-level meltdown right now?"

Leave it to Cassie to call me out.

I sag into the chair across from her desk, physically, mentally, and emotionally exhausted.

"Because I...I don't even know what happened, Cass. One minute, I'm getting bitched at by some diva model and the next Matt has me against the wall in the most passionate kiss I've ever experienced."

"You guys had wall sex?!" she practically squeals. I throw her a look, and she composes her face to a more serious expression. "I mean, so, you had wall sex."

She's trying to contain her joy and excitement, I'll give her that—failing miserably, but trying, nonetheless.

I slide my hand through my hair, my finger catching on a knot, and I realize I never truly fixed it and I've been walking around with sex hair since I left Matt. Good God, what is happening to me?

I close my eyes, take a fortifying breath, and then walk Cassie through the events that happened at the shoot. I tell her all about Nadine and her meltdown. I even tell her the nasty comment she made about how she'd fucked my fiancé. At first, I thought she was making it up—I didn't realize Anthony even knew models—but then she mentioned how they'd laughed at how clueless I was when he still went to Tahoe on a trip we'd planned. I had gotten sick the day before we were supposed to go, and he claimed he couldn't get a refund, so he decided to go and let me get better at home.

Apparently, he didn't go alone. There's no way she could know about that weekend unless she was there. It triggered something in me, some emotion buried deep. I sacrificed so much of myself for him, for my parents, and he'd made me a fool. I thought it had just been our wedding planner, but apparently not. Fury burned through me when I realized the depth of his betrayal. And to cheat on me with a bitch like Nadine was a new low.

I had a moment where I could relate to Midge on *The Marvelous Miss Maisel*. She was the perfect housewife, but it still wasn't enough for her cheating husband. Although, I guess in the end, that spoke more about his failings instead of hers.

When Nadine exposed Anthony's continued betrayal, I could barely hold myself back from lashing out at her. My body was shaking with rage by the time Matt intervened and guided me into that side room.

All I could think about when he touched me was that I hadn't had sex in months, and I'd been with a lying, cheating, asshole for the last year. When he kissed me, I heard Cassie's voice in my head talking about how perfect Matt would be for a fling because of how good he must be at sex and I just snapped. I kissed him and then got completely carried away.

And my God, the man is good at sex. Like, should be illegal level good.

But when it was over, I couldn't even look at him while shame coursed through me like a tsunami.

What had I done?

He's a player! In more ways than one.

Not only is he a player with women, he's a player on my dad's team.

I tell Cassie everything, ignoring her claps of excitement when I tell her how quickly he made me come. When I finally finish, we sit there in silence for what feels like hours but is probably only a minute or two.

"So, what now?" she asks.

"What do you mean?" I ask, my body sagging from exhaustion in the chair next to her desk.

"Are you guys going to hook up again?"

My eyes wide in shock, I spit out, "Um, NO!"

"Why the hell not?" she asks, clearly frustrated with me.

Has she not listened to a word I've said? Not only now, but when I told her from the beginning that this harebrained plan of hers had bad idea written all over it?

"Uh, for a million reasons, first and foremost being it's completely unprofessional."

"So? Please, like these types of things don't happen all the time."

"I can't, Cassie. What if my dad found out? His number one rule has always been I can't date any of his players. Can you imagine his reaction if he found out that not only was I sleeping with one of his players, but that I was sleeping with the most notoriously slutty player on his team?"

Cassie shakes her head and sighs. "Forget your dad, Nik. What do *you* want? This is about you, not anyone else. Do you want to have sex with Matt again?"

Do I?

Short answer is yes.

Long answer is I don't see how I can. Our situation is so complicated, not to mention I doubt Matt would be open to it. It's pretty common knowledge that he doesn't fuck the same girl twice.

But I don't want to lie to Cass. This is the first thing I've done for myself in as long as I can remember. The fact my body is still humming from our encounter only solidifies my answer, despite all the excuses I've been using for why this is such a terrible idea.

"Yes," I whisper.

She gently wraps her hand around mine. "Then I say you go for it."

"He doesn't do repeats."

"I have heard that." She sits back in her chair and bites her lip while she thinks. After a minute of us both sitting in silence, she leans forward. "Okay, here's what I think you should do. If the situation presents itself where you get the opportunity to establish a friends with benefits thing with him, take it. Don't wuss out. Don't worry about what your dad will think, or your mom for that matter. Don't think about anyone else but you. What *you* want. Okay?"

"Okay," I promise. It's an easy one to make because I know it'll never happen.

There's nothing to worry about.

TEN

Matt

My palms are sweaty as I brace myself for what's coming. I take a deep breath before knocking on the door and peeking in. "You wanted to see me, Coach?"

Coach Denton looks up from his desk, a TV with game tape playing on the wall beside him and the bookshelf behind him covered with Wolves memorabilia. I catch sight of a picture of him and Nikki sitting in a prominent position on his desk, and my dick twitches at the sight of her smile.

Was it really just yesterday she was coming on my cock?

I can't get the look on her face out of my mind. I mean, yes, Nikki has always been hot.

Uptight, stuck-up, and definitely spoiled. But still hot.

But seeing her come and feeling her vise-like pussy clench around my dick has made her next level hot. Like, can't get her out of my mind hot.

And that doesn't happen to me.

I'm a one and done kind of guy. A fuck and run type. I'm not ashamed. I'd rather be that than a sorry sap who falls in love.

Yeah, no thanks.

I don't know if it's my restlessness about how unfulfilling my latest hookups have been or if I'm coming down with a cold, but for the first time in my life, I'm actually seriously debating a repeat.

"Matt, are you listening to me right now?"

I pull my gaze from the picture of Nikki and turn back to Coach. He glances at the picture before returning his gaze to me. He squints, obviously suspicious.

"I recommend you keep your gaze averted if you know what's good for you."

I hear the threat in his words, loud and clear. And I know I should listen, heed his warning, probably even feel a little guilty about what I've already done. I should definitely let my little tryst with Nikki be a one and done.

But see, here's the thing. I can't. I don't know why, so don't ask me, but I just *can't.*

Pretending I hear him and will stay far away from his one and only daughter, I offer him a two-finger salute.

"Got it. So, what'd you call me in here for, Coach, if not to check out your daughter?"

Yeah, I know, I'm a dick and playing with fire, but I just can't help myself sometimes.

"Careful, son. You're already on thin ice in my book."

Coach has been up my ass this season. I'm playing better than ever, but suddenly nothing's good enough for him. I don't know what crawled up his ass, but it's really starting to piss me off.

"I called you in here to see how the campaign is going."

"It's going. Just finished another shoot yesterday. We're doing one here at the stadium next week."

He nods before folding his hands and leaning his forearms on his desk. "I also want to warn you to stay away from my daughter."

"Uh, that's a little hard to do seeing as how she's running the show. I kind of have to work with her."

"I understand that, I do. And I expect you to be the utmost professional and not give her any trouble. She's having...well, things have been difficult for her lately." His normally gruff appearance softens slightly when his gaze dips down to the picture on his desk.

My ears perk up, wondering if this has to do with her sudden lack of a fiancé. Not that I'm complaining, or else I wouldn't have been able to fuck her yesterday.

"Oh yeah?" I want him to tell me more, and I'm disappointed when he doesn't.

"I want you to leave her alone outside of your obligations to the campaign. I know about your reputation, Matt. As a man with a daughter, I've never liked the way you treat women, but as a coach with multiple players who do things I'm not a fan of, I've kept my mouth shut. But now that you're working with my daughter, I want to make sure we're clear that I will trade you faster than you can blink if you mess with her. You are not to interact with her outside of a professional capacity. Am I making myself clear?"

My eyes lock on his, registering his serious expression. I've never had a girlfriend, so I've managed to avoid the whole "meet a girl's dad" situation, but I imagine it would've been close to this.

"Got it." I understand where he's coming from. Really, I do. But at the same time, Nikki has stirred something in me, something new and exciting. I'm intrigued by her.

Plus, I really want to fuck her again.

I want to taste her on my tongue and feel her thighs squeeze my head while she explodes from my oral expertise.

The idea alone is making me hard, which is awkward since her dad is staring at me like he knows exactly what I'm thinking and wants to murder me.

I clear my throat, attempting to banish the visual of Nikki in my head. "Is that all?"

He nods, a little reluctantly it seems, and then dismisses me.

I walk out of his office and immediately adjust myself once I'm out of his line of sight.

"What was that about?" I turn to see Luke standing there.

"He was warning me to stay away from Nikki."

Luke tilts his head to the side. "Why would you ever go for Nikki? Not only is she completely out of your league, but she's also the exact opposite of your type."

"She is not out of my league."

"Dude, she's the little darling of our coach, who is practically football royalty." He pats me on the back as he continues, "Trust me, she's out of your league. But it's not like it matters, because you'd never go for someone like her."

"What do you mean?" I ask as we get to our cubbies.

"You know, you usually go for jersey chasers."

"I don't *only* go for jersey chasers."

He shrugs. "I guess that's true, but I can't remember the last time you went for a girl who wasn't one, a girl who had any substance to her whatsoever. Nikki doesn't seem like a one-night stand kind of woman, and those are the only ones you hook up with."

I can't argue with him there. It's true I typically do one-night stands, and Nikki is definitely not a one-night stand kind of girl.

So why can't I get the idea of fucking her again out of my head?

I grab my towel and head to the showers, hoping the steady beat of the water will wash away these thoughts. I need to get my head straight and figure my shit out. This isn't like me. I don't sit around thinking about women.

After my shower, I make a decision.

I need to talk to Nikki.

I'm just about to knock on her closed office door when it opens abruptly.

"Oh!" Nikki's eyes connect with mine and she freezes, her lips holding a perfect O position, and I immediately imagine what they'd look like wrapped around my cock.

Nope. I need to focus.

Which would be a lot easier if I couldn't still remember what Nikki feels like wrapped around me and what her face looks like when she comes. I can't help but look at the gorgeous woman in front of me and wonder why *this* is the woman I can't seem to get out of my mind. Of all the women in the world—hell, in Los Angeles alone—why is it the one woman who drives me up a fucking wall most of the time?

"Hi," I say, while still trying to get my head to focus on why I'm here. I came here to end this. I didn't take Coach's warning seriously until I was lying in bed last night thinking about all I'd be risking by pursuing her for more sex. I can't lose this team. No woman is worth that.

"Hi," she says softly. She peeks behind me and then steps back, opening the door farther and gesturing for me to come on in. "Did you need something? I didn't expect to see you until the stadium shoot next week."

"Actually, I thought maybe we should talk," I say as I sit down in one of the chairs in front of her desk.

She audibly swallows, before readjusting her blouse—that didn't need any adjusting to begin with—and making her way to her desk chair.

"Um, sure. What did you need to talk about? If this is about

Nadine, I can assure you we won't have you working with any other diva models."

I look her straight in the eye and say, "It's not about Nadine."

I watch her body slouch slightly like she's dreading where this conversation is going.

"I thought we should talk about—"

"Oh, I'm sorry. I didn't know you were in a meeting."

I turn around to see Cassie Jones standing at the door. I look back at Nikki just in time to catch her sending bug eyes to Cassie. I glance back and forth between the women, noticing Cassie's growing smile each time I turn back to her.

"We can get lunch tomorrow. Have fun." Cassie emphasizes fun with a pointed look at Nikki. When I turn back to Nikki, she's still staring at the door like her ship is sinking and she just watched the last lifeboat float away without her.

I gesture with my thumb to the door. "Did you need to go with her? I didn't mean to ruin your plans."

Nikki finally looks at me, and there's the slightest hint of fear in her eyes that concerns me.

"Is everything okay?" I ask seriously.

"Y-yes." She clears her throat and starts again. "Yes. Everything's fine. We had lunch plans, but it's no big deal. We get lunch together most days." She looks at me for a moment longer before she gazes down at her desk. She quickly shuffles around a couple of papers before looking back at me.

It's amusing to watch her freak out. I don't know what's happening in that beautiful head of hers, but she's clearly having some kind of internal struggle. I'd laugh, but she'd probably kick me out and I really want to see how this plays out.

She must come to some sort of decision because she takes a deep breath and then speaks. "I'm glad you came in."

My eyebrows arch in surprise.

"I...I actually wanted to talk to you too. About...the shoot. Well, what happened at the shoot....You know...between us...in that room...after, the, you know..."

It's adorable watching her stumble over her words. I don't think I've ever seen Nikki so...flustered. She's always organized, put together, and in control. This is a side of her I'm definitely enjoying. I lean back against the chair, relaxing my body as I watch her continue to try and find her footing, already feeling the resolve I walked in here with softening.

"Um," she says as she slides her hand over her forehead and then mumbles something that sounds suspiciously like she said *fuck it*. "I enjoyed our...moment together the other day."

"Our *moment*? Is that what we're calling hot wall sex now?"

Her face flushes and a thrill shoots through my body.

"I didn't want to be so crude."

"It's okay, Princess," I say with a smirk. "I don't mind hearing you have a dirty mouth. So, you liked having sex with me?" I lean forward and whisper, "I kinda already figured that out since you came twice."

Her eyes widen slightly, and I watch in fascination as her chest starts heaving.

"Uh, I did." She closes her eyes, taking a deep breath through her nose I'm sure she wouldn't do if she knew how spectacular her tits look when she sticks them out during her inhale. Her body is tense, something I can tell even from across the desk.

I bet I could fuck that tension right out of her. That thought should remind me why I came here—to do the opposite of fuck her—but instead, my original plans fly out the window as I continue to watch her have some kind of internal debate. I hate that what I want most right now is to kiss her again.

Suddenly her eyes pop open, and I see determination clear

as day in her expression, which is even hotter than seeing her flustered.

"I think we should do it again."

My eyes widen in surprise, and a smile breaks out on my face. Without even thinking twice about it, I answer, "I agree."

Her determination morphs to shock. "You do?"

I nod slowly, already imagining how many different ways I could take her in this office.

"But...you don't have sex with the same woman twice," her words come out breathy and uneven, like this isn't what she was expecting at all, which makes two of us. Somehow it only turns me on more.

I like pushing Nikki out of her comfort zone.

I nonchalantly shrug. "Not usually. I'd be willing to break the rules for you." I shoot her a wink because I can't help myself.

She bites her lip, and I'd pay a million dollars to know what she's thinking.

"What if it's more than one more time?"

Now I'm even more intrigued.

"What do you mean?" I ask.

"I'd like to propose a...well, I guess, a friends with benefits situation."

"We aren't friends."

She takes a deep breath before nodding. "No, I suppose we aren't, but that doesn't change the idea."

"You want to be fuck buddies?"

She nods again, suddenly looking more vulnerable than I've ever seen her.

I know why I'm motivated to agree to this arrangement—the one-and-dones aren't doing it for me anymore, and Nikki felt sinfully good—but why is she?

"Why?"

"I'm sorry?" she asks.

"Why do you want to be fuck buddies with me?"

She hesitates for only a second, then whispers, "Because I've never had sex like that before."

She not only looks vulnerable now, but something else. Something sad, and part of me wonders if the sadness has to do with the ex.

"What happened with your fiancé?"

"What?" She sits back in her chair, clearly surprised by the question.

"What happened? Why'd the wedding get called off?"

"How'd you know?"

I throw her a look. "You haven't been wearing your engagement ring. That thing was a little hard to miss. Also, you really think I would've fucked you when you were engaged to someone else? Good to know you think so little of me."

It actually burns and pisses me off that she thinks I would do that. I get I'm not exactly the most noble guy when it comes to women, but not fucking taken women is my number one rule I *never* break.

"I'm sorry. I didn't mean it like that. I just haven't made a formal announcement, and I didn't think anyone would notice my engagement ring missing."

I shrug like it doesn't bother me.

"Does it really matter what happened with my fiancé? All you need to know is it's over."

She's right. I don't *need* to know, but I want to. Which bothers me a little—okay, maybe a lot. If this is just sex, then she's right, it shouldn't matter.

"Fine. You don't need to tell me. So, you want to be fuck buddies?"

She nods slowly.

"I'm in."

ELEVEN

Nikki

My ears must be ringing. Did he just say he was in?

He's not supposed to say yes!

He's supposed to let me down easy!

What. Is. Happening?

"You're in?" I can barely get the words out.

He gives me a slow smile and nods his head.

He's in.

Oh my God, what have I just done?

I blame Cassie. I wasn't even going to say anything, even though I knew he was here to talk about what happened last time we saw each other. I was going to sidestep the whole conversation and get us back on professional footing. Then Cassie walked in and saw him sitting there. I could see in her eyes that she vividly remembered our conversation and my promise to pursue this absurd, ridiculous idea.

Oh my God.

I'm going to have sex with Matt.

Again!

The shiver flowing through me is not repulsion at the idea like I *should* feel. No, it's a thrill knowing what he could do to my body again. The things he could make me feel. My breathing accelerates and my heart beats rapidly in stupid anticipation.

He sits up from his relaxed position and claps his hands together. "So, should we start now?"

My eyes go wide, and if I thought my heart was beating rapidly before, I was wrong, because it's practically pounding out of my chest now. "Now?" I look around. "We're in my office! There are people outside the door," I whisper-yell, pointing to said door.

He smiles at me like he thinks I'm adorable. But then his eyes change, looking heated as they start to slide down the parts of my body he can see from his position on the other side of my desk.

My skin responds like he's actually touching me, and goosebumps break out along my arms.

His gaze slides back up and locks on mine. "I bet your panties are soaked right now, aren't they?"

"No!" I shout.

They are. Oh, God, they *so* are.

He gives me that Cheshire cat grin again and then stands and leans over my desk, his palms resting flat against the surface, his presence dominating the room with just that one movement.

"It's okay. I'm already hard for you."

My mouth falls open in shock, letting out a quiet gasp as my gaze drops to his pants. The stiff bulge is impossible to miss. My cheeks burn as I realize he really is into this idea.

I look back at him. Have his eyes always been this bright blue? This piercing? Like he can see every thought in my head.

"You really want to do this?" I ask, still in disbelief he wants this, with me of all people.

"I really do."

I swallow down all my trepidation and remind myself this might be my one and only chance to do something just for me.

And I want this, dammit.

"Okay," I whisper, a tremble in my voice as my gaze locks on his. "Okay," I repeat, firmer this time.

He stands up, readjusting himself in the process. "Great. I'll see you next week then." And then he turns and starts heading to the door.

I stand, completely baffled by the change in him, and stammer, "Wait, what?" He looks back at me and I look around my office. "I thought you wanted to...you know...here, right now?"

He smiles. "Oh, Princess, I do."

My blood stirs, and not in passion, at his use of the nickname he knows I hate.

"But I also want you to beg me for it."

He tosses me a wink and heads toward the door while I clench my fists, annoyed with his arrogance and the fact he's actually going to leave me hanging like this after he got me worked up. He pauses at the threshold, turns back to me with a smirk on his lips and says, "On second thought..."

In three strides he's at my desk, his hand in my hair, while his other wraps around my waist. His takes my mouth with his in a kiss that leaves me breathless and dazed. The second I grip his light sandy-brown strands he breaks the kiss and steps away. "Just wanted something to tide me over." His voice is soft and ragged, but at least he can speak, which is more than I can do right now. He turns around and this time walks out the door, closing it softly behind him.

Dropping to my chair like a stone in water, I try to process what just happened.

A startled laugh hits my ears, and I realize it's me.

He actually said yes. And he kissed me!

I'm about to get fucked, possibly in more ways than one, and

I can't even be mad about it because I can still remember what he feels like inside me, and my lips are still tingling from his mouth on mine.

A smile breaks across my face, and I spend the rest of my lunch break soaking in the excitement of what's to come.

I'm not at all surprised when Cassie comes back from lunch and comes straight to my office.

"Well?" she asks excitedly.

I roll my eyes, but I'm secretly—okay, maybe not so secretly—thrilled. "He said yes."

"Ahhh," she squeals, jumping up and down like she just got free tickets to a Rapturous Intent concert.

"Would you calm down? This is still an office, you know. It's not that big a deal."

"Not that big a deal? Nikki, honey, I love you, you know this, but this is a huge deal, and you're delusional if you think it's not. You're finally doing it, babe. You're finally asking for what you want, and I'm just so effing proud of you."

I don't acknowledge her praise because I can only handle one major life change at a time, and I'm not convinced this will lead to a major character change.

It's just sex.

"I can't believe he actually said yes." I keep hoping if I say it enough, it'll fully sink in.

She smiles at me. "I can. Girl, you're hot. He'd have to be blind not to notice. Of course, he wants to bang it out as much as he can."

"It's not weird?"

"Only if you make it weird." She gives me a stern look. "Do *not* make it weird, Nikki. You need this. Hell, *I* need this. I need you to do this."

"You're right."

"Of course I'm right. So, when are you guys hooking up?

Wait..." she looks at my desk before leaning in and whispering, "Did you guys have a quickie during lunch?"

"What? No! He left after we agreed to the arrangement." Although, I'm still aching and wet and wishing we actually did have a quickie. Then I remember his parting words and suddenly my enthusiasm dampens, and my blood starts to simmer. "Actually, do you know what that arrogant jock said to me when he left?"

"What?"

"He told me he wanted me to beg for it!"

"God, that's hot." She fans herself.

"Cassie!"

"What? It is! Sue me."

I roll my eyes. "Can you be serious for five minutes?"

Her eyes widen. "I *am* being serious. Have you ever tried it? Begging can be very sexy."

I stare at her in disbelief.

"You've really never begged? You've never had a man withhold your orgasm until you thought you were going to die if you didn't get release?"

I open my mouth to respond, but she stops me by holding her hand up. "You know what? Pretend I never asked because I know all the men you've dated, and it no longer surprises me you've never had a man drive you crazy or demand you beg him to fuck you. All your exes were wet blankets."

"I can't argue with you there."

"So, when are you going to do it?"

"I don't know."

"Well, when do you see him again?"

"Next week. We have a shoot at the stadium."

Her eyes light up, and I don't have to be a mind reader to know what she's thinking. The thing that surprises me most is I'm thinking it too.

TWELVE

Matt

The buzz going through my body should concern me, right? I don't get excited about seeing a woman. That's not who I am. But I *especially* should not be this excited to see a woman I was explicitly told to keep my hands off of.

And yet, I can't deny I'm excited to see Nikki today. She might be a stuck-up ice princess, but I'm dying to hear her beg for me. The idea I could get her so worked up she's begging for me to bury myself inside her stirs my blood in a way it never has before.

All thoughts of Nikki evaporate when I walk on to the field where we're doing the shoot. There's something about the smell of the turf—it's not real grass, but it has a unique smell of its own that always sends me back in time to when I first fell in love with football. It was the one place I got to be a kid. I was taken care of instead of having to do the taking care. I got to relax and just *be*. It was my favorite place and the respite I needed from my daily life. And I was good. I'm better now, but even as an awkward teen, I was better than most. Enough that my coach made sure to hone my skills so I could get a scholarship and play in college.

I feel the ground beneath my feet and look up at the empty stadium seats. Even empty, being in this stadium—on this field—is almost a religious experience for me. It feels like the home I always craved and wished for. I love playing for the Wolves, not just because it keeps me close to my dad so I can look out for him, but also because I love everything this team stands for. I love the community, the staff that work for the Wolves organization, my teammates. Everything about this team makes me feel alive and damn near invincible. It's a heady feeling sometimes, but one I'm grateful for every day.

Not even being inside a woman has offered me the same feeling I get from being on this team. The thought makes me pause. Aren't I risking all this by being with Nikki? Her dad made it abundantly clear he wouldn't hesitate to trade me if I messed around with her.

Why does the thought not scare me away from her like it should?

The photographer's assistant runs up to me, pulling me from my thoughts before I have any more time to evaluate what I'm doing with Nikki Denton, or about to do with her. "Matt, we actually want you in your full uniform for this shoot. We've got hair and makeup waiting in the locker room for you."

"Oh, sorry. I thought we were starting out here."

"That's totally okay. We got some things mixed up, so you got the wrong info. It's not a big deal. Just head to the locker room and then come back out when you're ready. We still have quite a bit to set up." She leans closer to me and says, "Sam is upset with the current lighting, so you'd be doing us a huge favor if you take a little longer than normal, but you didn't hear that from me."

"Got it."

I turn and head back to the tunnel, knowing my way around this stadium like it's the back of my hand. I'm just about to reach the edge of the tunnel when I spot Nikki walking my way, her head down, her eyes glued to the papers in her hand. I stop in my tracks and quickly scan her body. Her long blonde hair is up in her signature bun, and I wonder what she'd look like with all her hair down around her face.

Fuck, I bet she'd look stunning.

Her pouty pink lips are slightly pursed, and her brows are furrowed, leading me to believe she's not happy with what she's reading. I move to my left and stand still, knowing if she doesn't look up soon, she'll walk right into me, which will probably piss her off.

The idea sends a zing of excitement through me.

Sure enough, not a minute later, she does.

"Oh my gosh, excuse me, I'm so..." She looks up, her quick apology dying instantly. "Matt?" She looks around me at the setup happening out on the field. "Are we not meeting out there?"

"Apparently they want me in my full uniform, so I gotta go change."

"Oh, right. That makes sense." Her eyes slide down my body before coming back to mine. Her cheeks flush slightly when our eyes meet, probably because she just realized I caught her checking me out. I don't mind.

"Like what you see, Princess?"

Her eyes squint as she spits out, "I hate that nickname."

"I know," I say, a smile wide on my face. That's why I use it. It's one of the only times I see her perfected control break, or at the very least stumble.

"I should get out there to see what they need," she says, never looking away from me.

"You should." I nod but don't move. Neither does she.

I lean in, catching her scent. She smells like an orange

creamsicle, citrusy and sweet but not overpowering. I let my lips graze her ear as I whisper, "I'm waiting."

Her body shivers, and I don't miss the goosebumps covering the side of her neck. I gently slide my pointer finger from that spot right behind her ear down to her clavicle.

"Matt," her voice breaks, her eyes pleading with mine. But I want her words.

"Yes?"

Her aqua-blue eyes are bright and reflect the need I feel humming through my own body. She visibly swallows. "You have to go get ready," she whispers.

I'm disappointed and a little annoyed. Even when she's obviously turned on, work comes first. I'm determined to get under her skin enough that she chooses a quickie with me over the job one of these days—our first time doesn't count. If I'm willing to risk my job, I'd like to see her willing to do the same. Plus, I'd love nothing more than to see her all mussed up instead of the buttoned-up, always put together and in control woman she presents to the world.

I wonder if she ever just lets her hair down and has fun. Probably not. Hmm, something to work on then.

I pull away from her, taking in her dilated eyes, flushed cheeks, and parted lips. Oh yeah, she's hot for me. I toss her a wink and then walk away, heading farther into the tunnel and toward the locker room. I don't look back for two reasons. First, because I want her to think I don't care, and second, because I'm about ninety-eight percent certain if I looked back, I'd fuck her right here.

I wish I could understand what it is about her that just really fucking revs my engine.

I get into the locker room and quickly change into my uniform—full pads and everything. A woman named Sally fixes my hair how they want it for the shoot, and thankfully goes minimal on the makeup.

I still remember the first time I had to do a photoshoot when I made it into the NFL. When the woman started to put makeup on me, I asked her what the hell she thought she was doing. I'm a man. I don't wear makeup. I'm not a rock star who uses eyeliner, or guy liner, or whatever they call it these days. I'm an athlete. A man's man. I fuck women who wear makeup. I don't wear it unless I've just kissed it off a woman's lips.

She explained to me how the camera lights work and assured me no one would even notice. Sure enough, she was right. I looked at the finished photos and couldn't tell at all.

It's still crazy to me, though.

In what feels like no time at all, I'm walking back out onto the field. My gaze catches on Nikki talking to the PA who ran up to me earlier. I'm far enough away I can let my gaze scan up and down her body without anyone noticing. My gaze slides over her tailored pantsuit and perfectly composed expression. She has this tough as nails persona when she's all business. Always in control.

But I've seen her when she lets go. Seen her face when she's completely lost in ecstasy. Maybe that's the reason I can't stop this arrangement—or don't want to stop it, even when she drives me crazy or it risks my job—because she's shown me this glimpse of her that is undeniably alluring.

She glances my way and her eyes fix on mine. For the briefest moment, my breath catches in my chest, but I quickly shake it off.

What the hell is that about anyway?

Fuck, I'm turning into a pussy.

I walk over to her and the PA, my attention focused on the PA. It's time to put my game face on now that we're around other people.

"Hey, you guys ready for me?"

"Yes, we are. You have perfect timing. We just got everything all set up. Right this way."

She leads me over to the shoot area. I glance over my shoulder to see Nikki following us, her eyes glued to the PA's hand at my elbow guiding me toward our photographer, her brows pinched in a slight frown.

My lips quirk up in a small smile, but I school my expression before she can catch my enjoyment at her hint of jealousy.

"Alright Matt, here's what I want you to do." I listen attentively to Sam, the photographer, as he tells me where he wants me to stand and how he wants me to position myself. I've done many different kinds of photoshoots in my career so I understand how all this works by now. I get in position and move my body the way he directs.

I swear I try to pay attention solely to him.

Really, I do.

But I can't help it when my gaze keeps sliding over to Nikki as I get in the different poses. More than once I catch her biting her lip while checking me out.

I flex my biceps, really making my muscles pop, and glance over at her. Her bottom lip is grasped firmly between her teeth, her cheeks have a sexy rosy glow I'm coming to crave, and her eyes look heated and wanting.

My ice princess is horny. It's written all over her face.

However, the longer the shoot goes on—and I'm out on this field, the only place I've ever felt I truly belong—everything I'm risking settles deep in my bones. By the time the shoot ends, I'm second-guessing everything and whether she's really worth it.

The photographer wraps the shoot up and dismisses me to go change. I walk past Nikki on the way to the locker room, our eyes briefly meeting before I look away. My uncertainty swirls in my gut, while at the same time this undeniable connection to her draws me in.

The sound of steps following behind me pulls me from my thoughts, and I glance back to see Nikki, her eyes watching me with an intensity that's a mix of determination and concern.

God, why does she have to be so fucking sexy?

"Matt."

My dick pulses hearing her voice, and all the reasons why this is a bad idea start to vanish behind my desire to feel her again.

Just one last time.

I turn around when I get inside the tunnel, just out of the line of sight from where the crew is still set up, with Nikki right on my heels. "Yes, Princess?"

She frowns. "Stop calling me that."

I lean down to be eye level with her. "Make me," I taunt.

Her eyes flare, her lips part slightly, and then the next thing I know our mouths are joined in a greedy kiss. I couldn't tell you who kissed whom first, all I know is I don't want to stop. Her lips taste divine, and her tongue dances with mine like they were made for each other.

I pull her body tighter to me and deepen the kiss, showing her with my mouth all the things I want to do to her body. She sags against me and hums in the back of her throat.

A groan rumbles from my chest. Fuck, I want this woman.

But I don't want her more than I want this team.

I break the kiss and take an unsteady step back. Her eyes open slowly, her lips swollen and red, and it takes everything in me to keep from pulling her back into my arms.

The truth is, I'm not sure she's worth the risk.

THIRTEEN

Nikki

Something's changed.

I can tell by the way the energy around us shifts from charged and needy to something else. Something that makes me brace for what I'm afraid is coming.

He looks down at his jersey before his gaze comes back up to mine. Emotion swirls in his eyes and his jaw clenches.

"I need to get changed."

I stand taller, trying to show I'm not affected by him stopping what was one of the most passionate kisses I've ever experienced. "Sure. I'm going to head back to see if they need help wrapping everything up."

"Good idea. See ya around, Nikki."

He walks away from me, and I let the frown I've been holding back take over my face. *See ya around?* Why does that sound like he's ending things?

Nothing's even really started yet.

I go back out on the field and oversee cleanup and make sure everyone gets out of the stadium. I'm waiting for Matt to show up when I see one of our security guys lock up the locker room.

"Hey, Reggie, I think Matt's still in there."

He turns to me, shaking his head as he replies, "No, I saw Matt leave about twenty minutes ago."

"Oh." He already left? "Okay, thanks, Reg."

"No problem, Nikki. Have a good day."

I nod, a more polite goodbye trapped in my throat while I try to figure out what it means that Matt left without saying goodbye.

Is this supposed to be some kind of payback for how I left after the first time we had sex?

Is this a test to see if I'll beg?

I leave the stadium with more questions than answers.

My phone rings in my purse right as Cassie's front door shuts soundly behind me. I drop my keys on the side table and quickly dig in my bag trying to find my phone before the call goes to voicemail. *Why do I have so much crap in here?*

I catch it right as the ringing stops and see Anthony's name as the missed call. Tipping my head back, I close my eyes and take a deep breath, letting my shoulders drop on the exhale, heavy from the weight of all the tension I'm now carrying at just the sight of his name.

I don't want to talk to him. I know I need to. I still need to get all my stuff out of our house. Hell, I need to start looking for my own apartment. Cassie has been nice enough to let me stay with her and Max in their guest room while I'm figuring everything out, but I can't stay here forever.

I look back down at my phone. God, I really don't want to call him back. I can't stand the idea of listening to his condescending tone over the phone. Honestly, I can't believe I was going to marry him.

Cassie was right when she said I was more upset about how this threw my life plan off course and less about losing the actual guy. The more days that pass, the more I realize I never loved Anthony. My parents loved Anthony.

Once again, I put their wants and needs before my own. I don't really know how *not* to anymore. This little arrangement with Matt is the closest I've ever gotten to doing something *I* wanted to do since I was eight years old.

My phone rings in my palm and I look at it, expecting to see Anthony calling me again, but instead Cassie's name shows on the screen. I quickly accept the call.

"Hey, Cass."

"Hey, I'm on my way home and today has been stressful, to say the least. How do you feel about a giant pizza?"

"Sounds perfect."

"Great, I'll pick one up and then be home soon."

"Okay, see you soon."

We hang up and I grab my sweats out of the suitcase I brought to Cassie's. By the time I've washed my face, changed my clothes, and let down my hair from the tight bun I usually keep it in, I'm starting to feel more relaxed.

I sit down on the plush brown couch in the living room and turn on the TV, pulling up the latest offerings on Netflix. I've just pulled up *The Great British Baking Show*—because I'm a sucker for cooking competition shows—when Cassie walks through the door. The cheesy aroma of pizza quickly fills her living room.

"God, that smells heavenly."

She smiles. "I know. You're lucky I didn't eat the whole damn thing on the drive home."

"That bad of a day?"

Cassie places the pizza on the coffee table and then plops down on the couch next to me. I cross my legs like a pretzel and turn toward her. Her head is resting against the back of the couch and she's staring at the ceiling, but she doesn't say a word.

"Cass?"

Without lifting her head, she turns to me. "I think Max might be planning to break up with me," she whispers.

"What?" There's no way. I've never met two people more in love with each other.

She nods sadly, her eyes filling with tears.

Cassie did this flirty dance with Max, Jack Fuller's personal assistant and best friend, for years before they got together almost a year ago. They've been inseparable since, and as far as I know, rarely even argue.

"What makes you think that?"

She blows out a breath. "He came in today asking for some swag and tickets for a kids' charity that Jack and Paige want to donate to. Max is apparently helping Jack come up with a bunch of different bid items, and Max figured I could help."

"Okay," I say, my tone encouraging her to go on.

"But then he got kinda dodgy when I asked him what time he'd be home tonight. And there have been other things, like he looks at me differently. I don't know." She shakes her head and runs her hands over her face, wiping away the tears escaping her eyes.

"And that makes you think he's going to break up with you?"

She says sadly, "It just feels like maybe he's keeping something from me. He's being distant all of a sudden."

"Do you think he could be doing it because I'm here? Maybe he's trying to give us space so we can have girl time," I suggest.

She turns to me with her whole body, her eyes misty and her voice hoarse from the emotion she's trying to hold back. "No, because it started right before you moved in. He's never done this before. Not in the entire time we've been together. He wasn't even this distant during the two years I was dying for him to make a move!" Her voice lowers as she expresses what's clearly her deepest fear, "What if he's met someone else?"

I immediately place my hand over hers and squeeze. "There's no way, Cass. That man is completely lost without you. There's no one else."

"How do you know? You didn't even realize Anthony was cheating on you." Her eyes go wide as the sting of her words penetrates my bones.

I'm not proud of being duped. Not by a long shot. But it didn't hurt the way it should, most likely because I never loved him. My tears were never for him.

"I'm so sorry, Nikki," Cassie whispers, horrified. "I didn't mean it like that."

I reassure her, because I know she didn't, and then try to calm her down. "Have you talked to him?"

"And say what?"

I shrug. "Maybe ask him if everything is okay. Talk to him instead of worrying over something that might be nothing."

"But what if it is something?" Her breath catches in her throat in a small hiccup as worst-case scenarios clearly play out in her head.

"Cass," I whisper softly, wishing I could comfort her the way she needs, but what she really needs is Max.

Pain laces her words. "I love him so much. He's more than I ever dreamed of having. I don't want to lose him."

I wrap my arm around her shoulder and pull her close. "Talk to him, Cassie. That's the only advice I can offer."

She nods solemnly before picking up the remote and turning up the volume on the TV. We eat pizza silently, Cassie's eyes focused on the screen while my gaze floats back and forth between the show and her.

When the episode ends, she turns to me. "How're things going with Matt?"

Sighing heavily, I respond, "I have no idea."

"What do you mean?"

"I thought everything was going fine. We kissed after the shoot today, but when he pulled away, he had this weird look on his face, almost like he was disappointed, or maybe second-guessing this. I don't know. But then he left the stadium before I had another chance to talk to him. So, I have no idea what's going on with us."

"Hmm, maybe he just had other plans and didn't have a chance to say goodbye."

I toss her a *really?* look.

"Okay, yes, it's a weak reason, but you never know. I'm sure you guys will figure it out."

Three days later, I'm still no closer to figuring out if we're doing this fuck buddies thing or not. It's been radio silence from Matt, and my body is aching for what he gave me against the wall when we had sex nearly two weeks ago.

A part of me wonders if this is all a ploy to get me to beg him for it.

If it is, it's working.

I can't remember another time in my life where I've been so sexually frustrated. I reach over to my nightstand and grab my vibrator. I'm desperate for a release, even one by my own hand.

I slide off my silk sleep shorts slowly, letting them graze across my sensitive nerve endings, already heightened from my arousal. With the press of a button, my vibrator pulses and I glide it over my peaked nipples, down my stomach, until it reaches the apex of my thighs and the bundle of nerves begging for release.

My mind immediately goes to that tiny room at our photo-shoot, and I can practically feel the hardness of the wall on my back while Matt's firm body pressed against my front. It doesn't take long for the memory—paired with the steady pulsing against my clit—to ignite an orgasm that starts deep in my core and thrums steadily throughout my entire body.

When the pleasure becomes too much, I turn off my vibrator, letting the little aftershocks of my orgasm settle before finally taking a full breath.

My eyes open and the empty room taunts me. I remember nights like this when I was still with Anthony, except the difference then was I often felt relief and satisfaction after my release. Now, I'm left feeling bereft because I know how much better it can be.

My vibrator is a poor substitute for what I really want.

What I'm craving.

Fuck, I think I'm ready to beg.

By the time my next meeting with Matt comes two days later, I'm practically a junkie in need of a fix. My vibrator officially got fired last night because no matter what lie I've been trying to tell myself, nothing compares to what Matt can do to me.

I need to feel him again.

I need to let go the way only he's been able to get me to.

He shows up for our meeting straight from morning prac-tice, his hair still damp from his shower, his upper body covered in a Wolves T-shirt, and jeans covering his toned ass that reminds me of Chris Evans as Captain America.

He looks edible, and my craving for him only increases.

Once the meeting starts, I go into work mode, only glancing at him when absolutely necessary for fear that my need will be written all over my face if I look at him too long. When we finalize the details of the next photoshoots and events we'll need Matt to attend, I turn to him, taking advantage of Luther starting a conversation with Matt's agent, Steven.

"Meet me in my office in five minutes," I say quietly before standing up from my chair, grabbing my folder of documents, and making a quick exit.

I practically count the seconds. When five minutes turn into ten, I start to worry he got held up talking to Steven and Luther. When ten minutes turn into twenty, my worry morphs into hurt as I realize he's not coming.

I slump in my chair, trying to figure out how I've messed this up before it even really got started when I hear a gentle knock on my door.

Hope blooms in my chest as the door swings open but is quickly dashed when Luther pops his head in. "Hey, are you going to lunch with Cass today?" At my nod, he says, "Mind if I join you? I need girl time."

I give him a soft smile, trying to hide my disappointment that he wasn't who I was hoping was at the door. "Sure. We'd love that."

"Great. See you in an hour."

Resigned to focusing on work, I shake my mouse and wake my computer screen. Another tap on my door has my gaze sliding up and clashing with the brilliant cerulean blues I was expecting over twenty minutes ago.

I stand from my desk, my nerves firing in excitement and my need sparking back to life just from his presence. "I didn't think you were coming."

He takes a noticeable breath and clenches his jaw before scrubbing his stubble with his hand. "I wasn't going to."

I bite my lip, fighting a frown. "Did I do something?"

He shakes his head before looking at the ceiling. "Nikki..."

He looks so torn, so conflicted, and I hate it. I need him to do this. He gives me the confidence to actually go through with this friends with benefits thing. There's no one else I could do this with.

I need this.

"Matt," my voice breaks, but I push my shoulders back and try to channel my inner vixen.

You can do this, Nikki. He's already had sex with you once. Clearly, he finds you attractive. Give him what he wants.

I walk toward him, my strides conveying a false confidence until I see his eyes flash with lust. He clenches his jaw again, and it somehow only makes him look sexier and his jaw more defined. My hands glide up his chest until they wrap around his neck.

He lets out a soft groan before his hoarse voice pleads, "Nikki."

I don't let him finish, afraid he's going to end this arrangement before it's even had a chance to start. Instead, I grip the back of his neck and give him what he asked for.

I beg.

"God, Matt. I need you to fuck me. Please. *Please* fuck me. Right now."

He closes his eyes and grimaces as if in pain. "Nikki, you don't know what you're asking of me."

I kiss his neck, sliding my hands down his chest and feeling how toned and fit he is. "Matt, please. I need you."

He groans again. "Fuck!"

And then his mouth is on mine.

Heat ignites instantly in my belly, and my whole body feels like it's on fire.

Yes! This is what I've been craving.

He slides his hands down my sides and then cups my ass and lifts me up, carrying me to my desk like I weigh nothing.

"God, I want you," he growls. "I've tried so hard not to, but I can't say no to you. You have no idea what you're doing to me."

"Probably the same thing you're doing to me," I say, kissing his jaw and down to his neck.

He groans as he places me on the edge of my desk and then strips me of my pants and underwear, smirking at the soaked fabric.

He undoes his pants and slides them down in record time. With deft movements, he slides a condom over his thick length and then impales me with his cock. I shout out at the delicious invasion, and he quickly covers my mouth with his own to muffle my sounds.

His body rocks into me with furious thrusts, and faster than I'm prepared for, an orgasm slams into me.

"Fuck, Nikki, you feel so insanely good when you come." He grunts and captures my gaze with his as he pumps two more times and then comes, triggering another orgasm to rock through me.

I lay back on my mostly bare desk, suddenly grateful I'm such a neat freak at work.

"Wow." That's all I can say. I finally feel the deep satisfaction I'd been craving all week that my vibrator had failed to give me.

Matt slides out of me and I sit up and point to a box of Kleenex sitting on the shelf behind my desk. "You can use those to clean up."

"Thanks."

We both clean up and get dressed, an awkward silence settling around us. Now that I'm not distracted by my lust for him, I can better read his mood.

"You were going to pull out of our arrangement, weren't you?"

He looks at me, not saying a word, but he doesn't need to. His expression says it all.

He was.

I cross my arms, closing off my body to him in some semblance of protection. "So, that was it then?"

He stares at me, his expression shuttered, hiding what he's thinking. I don't break eye contact with him and find myself nibbling the inside of my lip because I don't know what to say and I'm in uncharted waters here.

He drops his gaze to the floor before sliding his hands through his hair and sighing heavily. He looks back at me. "Despite what I know I should do, I can't stay away from you."

"What does that mean?"

He steps closer. "It means we can do this, but we definitely need to keep it quiet."

"I'm fine with that. I don't exactly want a lot of people to know about this."

"Good. Then if you still want to do this, I'm still in."

"No more pulling away or radio silence."

He shakes his head, his eyes alight with a smile. "No more. Nothing but lots of mind-blowing sex."

I smile back at him. "It's about damn time."

FOURTEEN

Matt

My phone feels heavy in my hand as I pull up Nikki's number. I made sure I had it before I left her office a few days ago. I'd been so good about staying away from her—even when she found her way into nearly every thought I had the week I avoided her. But when she begged me, when she said she needed me, I couldn't deny it anymore.

I know it's reckless and massively risky, but if we keep this thing a secret, we can just let it run its course, and when we're done, no one will know we were ever fuck buddies.

"Hello?"

"Nikki?"

"Yes?" she asks hesitantly.

"Hey, it's Matt. Matt Fischer." I wince. *Smooth, dude.* To be fair, I've never really done the whole call a woman thing. I'm not usually trying to see them again.

"Hi, Matt. Why are you calling me?"

I roll my eyes. God, this woman sounds uptight even through the phone, which both annoys me and makes me want to dig underneath her hard exterior to where she's soft and pleasant like she is right after she comes. "Why do you think, Princess?"

"I'd really appreciate if you'd stop calling me that, especially if we're going to continue to...you know."

My eyebrows rise. Can she really not say it? Oh, we'll definitely need to work on that. I bet there's a very dirty girl buried under her buttoned-up exterior.

"If we're going to continue what, Princess?"

I can practically hear her eye roll.

"You know what, Matt."

I smile wide, my heart beating a little faster hearing her irritation with me. "You know, I don't think I do. I think you're going to need to spell it out for me." God, this is fun.

"Fine!" she huffs. "Sex. If we're going to continue to have SEX."

My dick stirs at the angry frustration in her tone. I don't know why pissing her off turns me on so much. That's never been my thing before, but with Nikki it's like an instant aphrodisiac.

"Ohhhh, sex. Right, well, speaking of, I thought we should talk more about what this little arrangement of ours will look like."

"Okay," she says, not sounding sure in the slightest.

"First of all, I think we should have some rules."

"Actually, I think that's a great idea." Ah, there's the confident tone I'm so used to hearing from her. I shake my head and take a breath, already feeling my blood pressure rise. While I definitely think we need to have some ground rules, it's going to be really annoying if she tries to micromanage me, which by her tone is the exact direction she's heading.

So instead, I take the lead. "Great. First rule is we don't go to each other's places."

"Wait, so you want to just keep hooking up in random side

rooms at photoshoots or my office?" She sounds like she just stepped in shit.

"I was thinking a hotel. I'll get us a room and we can meet up whenever either of us wants to fuck." Thinking about her last remark, I add, "And it won't be some slimy pay-by-the-hour dive, if that's what you're concerned about. It'll be nice."

She doesn't say anything for a beat before finally responding. "A hotel is a good idea, especially since I'm still staying with Max and Cassie at the moment. A hotel is less personal."

"Exactly." I want to ask about her living situation, but I don't.

"Okay. I'm on board. What else were you thinking?"

Well, that was easier than I expected. I really thought she'd put up a fight and demand to be in charge of everything. "Second rule is no sleepovers. We fuck and then we go home."

"That works for me."

"Great. That's really all I've got. Do you have any rules?"

"Actually, I do." She sounds nervous and I sit up a little taller, curious what she'll ask for. "I'd like us to be exclusive while we're doing this. I know this isn't a relationship—that's the last thing I'm looking for right now—but I also want assurances that I don't have to worry about you giving me some STD from one of your jersey girls."

"They're called jersey chasers."

"Whatever."

I love that I can hear the indignation and eye roll in her voice. "I'll agree to exclusivity, as long as we're both clear this is just sex."

"That's all it will ever be."

"Good," I respond. So, why am I slightly disappointed at how easily she acquiesced to nothing more than sex?

"So," she sounds nervous again, further reinforcing how out

of her comfort zone she is with all of this. "When...I mean... should we...I guess what I'm asking..."

I finally rescue her from herself with, "What are you doing tonight?"

She exhales heavily and relief floods her voice. "Nothing."

"Not anymore. Meet me at The Ritz-Carlton at seven. I'll have a key waiting for you at the front desk."

"The Ritz? Well, that certainly isn't a pay-by-the hour place."

"I can afford the luxury, so why not?"

"I guess you're right."

"I am."

"Okay, I'll see you at seven."

"See you then."

I hang up the phone, dropping it to my side as I take a deep breath. The weight sitting on my chest when I first called her is now completely gone. In its place, desire and excitement thrum through me, headier than even my victories on the field.

Nikki Denton is about to get the best sex of her life.

FIFTEEN

Nikki

"Enjoy your stay," the hotel concierge says with a bright smile on her face.

"I will. Thanks." I wish I could be as friendly as her, but my nerves are a mess. My hands are clammy, my pulse is beating frantically, and my breaths are shallow. I've tried breathing exercises in an attempt to calm myself, but to no avail. Wringing my fingers, the weight of the key card sitting heavy in my pocket, I make my way to the elevator.

I absently press the button to the floor indicated by the front desk clerk when she gave me my key and then go back to worrying my fingers. The sterling silver ring that never leaves my right hand acts as a talisman—a reminder of why I'm doing this. Why I'm putting myself so far out of my comfort zone.

Who am I kidding? I left my comfort zone behind the moment I let Matt fuck me against a wall at a photoshoot.

The memory of his hard body thrusting into mine makes my body heat up in a different way—my core throbbing with a level of desire that is still new to me. Both times Matt's fucked me, he's taken me to a place I didn't even think existed.

I never knew sex could feel this way. This...freeing.

And terrifying.

There's a ding as the elevator stops and the doors slide open. I walk out, readjusting my oversized purse with a change of clothes and fresh underwear on my shoulder.

I walk toward the innocuous door that looks like all the rest on this floor and pull the key card out of my pocket. My feet halt at the door, my breath caught in my throat. There's no going back if I slide the key in the door.

Maybe I'm already too far gone.

I mean, this isn't even the first time we're having sex, or the second. The line's already been crossed.

With one more deep inhale—attempting composure I know will be gone the second I see Matt—I slide the key card in the door, and at the beep and glow of green, I press down on the handle and push the door open.

Immediately, I'm overwhelmed by the sight before me—the room, which I belatedly realize is a gorgeous suite, the last thing on my mind.

Matt stands in front of the windows overlooking Los Angeles covered only by a tight white towel around his hips.

If I thought I was having trouble breathing before, I was mistaken.

He turns around, his beautifully sculpted body on nearly full display for me. I ogle his toned arms from hours at the gym and the tattoos covering his shoulder, part of his other arm, and one sliding around his waist. His washboard abs are lickable, and I have to actively prevent myself from moving forward and doing just that.

But all of that is eclipsed by his gorgeous face and the intensity in his cerulean-blue eyes which feel like they're piercing through all my armor.

I attempt to shore it up, but it's a useless effort. It's mesmerizing and addicting feeling seen.

Truly seen.

He doesn't look at me like a trophy.

He looks at me like a gift.

Emotion clogs my throat—no one has ever looked at me like this before.

It wasn't supposed to be like *this*. It's supposed to be just sex.

But this doesn't feel like just sex. The air in the room feels heavy, the tension fraught between us.

He tips his head down slightly, staring deeper into me, but doesn't move. Why isn't he moving? Can't he see I'm frozen? I made the first step by coming here. I can't take another. I need him to tell me what to do now.

I need him to lead this because I've never felt so lost, and yet his eyes are telling me for the first time, I'm found.

Our gazes are locked on each other, our breaths beginning to match and the desire between us almost like a tangible thing in the room.

"Matt," my voice cracks and panic fills me.

Before I even have a chance to let the panic take over, Matt's hands are in my hair and his lips are owning mine.

I didn't even see him move, but all I can think about now is how incredible his lips feel against mine. Our mouths mold like they were made for each other, seducing each other the way our bodies will soon.

He slides the purse strap off my shoulder without breaking the connection of our lips. His arms wrap around my body, pulling me against him so I can clearly feel the effect I have on his body. His erection presses hard and thick between us and I moan, aching to feel him inside me again.

I want to feel the euphoria only he seems to be able to give me.

He growls deep in his throat, the vibration flowing to me

through our kiss, and my blood heats. My hands reach up, pulling on his hair and holding his mouth tight to mine. He uses his strength to guide my body deeper into the room while we continue kissing like we're starved and our mouths are the last meal we've been craving.

The back of my legs hit something soft, and I break away from him to look down and see I'm leaning against the arm of the couch. I turn back to Matt, his gaze watching my face, the desire in his eyes unmistakable.

"Shouldn't we go to the bedroom?"

"I can't wait." His voice is gruff, and he's still watching my face like he's trying to memorize every minute detail. "I think I'll taste you right here."

"What?" Panic is clear in my voice, but he remains calm.

"You heard me, Princess."

My eyes turn to slits at the name he *knows* I hate, but all it does is make him laugh.

"You wouldn't look at me like that, *Princess,* if you knew what it does to me." He looks down and I follow his gaze to see his hard—and large—erection tenting the towel he's wearing.

"I like pushing your buttons, just the same way you like pushing mine," he says as he leans forward and nibbles on my lip.

I don't confirm or deny it.

There's no point.

"It's time to let go and feel. Feel everything I want to give you," he says softly.

My chest heaves at his words and, unable to find my voice, I nod my head.

He presses on my sternum until my upper body falls back on the couch, my lower body lifted by the arm I had been leaning against. My legs spread of their own accord and I'm suddenly thankful I thought to wear a dress tonight.

Easy access.

He slides his hands up my legs from my ankle to my inner thigh, my breath catching in my chest and heat rising to the surface of my skin at his touch. He gives me a wolfish grin before dropping to his knees and ripping my panties off my body.

Literally ripping them off.

My head pops up at the sound of the lace tearing, and if he had any doubts what he does to me, I can guarantee they're gone now with the flood of moisture I just felt.

His head dips, his eyes locked on my core. "Fuck, Nikki, you're so wet." He looks up at me, that snarky grin I know too well back on his face. "Looks like your pussy likes me, even if you don't."

I'm about to spit out a snarky reply of my own, but before the words even reach my lips, he licks my clit and my brain goes blank.

Matt uses his mouth on my pussy the same way he used it on my mouth, thoroughly owning me with his indecent kiss.

My thighs start to shake when he slides two fingers inside me while continuing to suck and lick my clit. He pumps rhythmically and sucks hard causing my head to spin. I gasp loudly, reaching out and gripping his hair as my orgasm hits me and tremors wrack my body. It's not a slow build like I'm used to, but an abrupt shock rocking me to my core. His fingers slow, but he continues to kiss and lick me through my release until I'm a pile of mush on the couch, my body completely slack.

He kisses my thigh and then stands up, his erection prominently tenting the white towel he wears.

He watches my heaving chest—or maybe he's just checking out my breasts that are still confined by my dress—and smiles at me.

"Proud of yourself, aren't you?" I ask, wishing it came out more controlled and less breathy.

"Are you saying I shouldn't be?"

I shake my head, giving in, because if we're really going to do this then he deserves honesty. "You should be."

He grabs my hand and pulls me up off the couch. "Come on, Princess. There's plenty more where that came from."

As soon as my butt hits my chair, Cassie demands details about Matt.

I glance around the mostly empty restaurant where we're having lunch today. "Do we have to talk about this here?"

She looks around. "There's hardly anybody here, so yes. Now spill."

I take a resigned breath and try to organize my thoughts. "It's weird having sex with someone I hated," I admit to her.

She perks up. "*Hated*? Does that mean you don't hate him anymore? Wait! Did you guys hook up again?"

When I just stare at her, she grabs my arms and squeals, "Oh my God, you did, didn't you?! When? Where? I need details ASAP!"

I laugh but shake my head at how ridiculously excited she is about this. You'd think she's the one getting earth-shattering sex.

"I don't even know where to start."

"With the sex, duh! Was it hot? What am I asking? Of course, it was fucking hot, it's Matt fucking Fischer!"

"Okay, calm down, crazy. It was just sex."

She gives me a look that says *you're full of shit*. She's not wrong.

I don't know what it is about him that just lights up my

entire body, but I've never been so excited to find out. Even if I can't stand the actual man the body belongs to.

"Okay, fine. It was...God, Cassie, he...it...I..."

She gives me a knowing smile. "That good, huh?"

"There are no words. It was unlike anything I've ever experienced before. I mean, it was just as hot as our first couple of times, but it was also really different."

"Different how?"

I think back to our rendezvous at the hotel the other night. "He was...almost gentle with me. It wasn't frantic like before, and I'm sure part of that was because we had more time and no risk of someone catching us. I don't know—it also felt deeper than that.

"The first time we had sex, I was so angry that it didn't even fully register with me what we were doing until I was coming. Which is insane! I've never been out of my head like that, and certainly not during sex. But this time...it's like he knew exactly what I needed. It started as soon as I walked in the door. Right as I was about to panic, he kissed me, and I got so swept up in it that all my panic and nervousness just evaporated. Then, when we finally had sex, it was slower than the other times we've hooked up, and he was so attentive."

"It almost sounds romantic."

"No, it wasn't. That's the thing. Matt has this weird way of being reassuring and sweet, and yet domineering and passionate at the same time. I don't even know if that makes sense."

"Do you like him, Nikki?"

I turn to her, shocked she'd even suggest it. "Absolutely not! It's just sex. Isn't that the whole point of a friends with benefits situation?"

She nods.

"That's why I think you were right in encouraging me to do

this. I'm at no risk for actually falling for him because he's the exact opposite of the type of guys I've dated."

She smiles and agrees, "Exactly."

I look at her, a little concerned that we're thinking two different things about my fuck buddies arrangement with Matt.

It's just no-strings-attached sex. Nothing else.

I'm definitely not at risk of falling for Matt Fischer. He is the last man on earth I would *ever* fall in love with.

SIXTEEN

Matt

The water runs in the bathroom, the sound making anticipation spike in my veins as I lie back on the bed waiting for Nikki. This is our second meet-up in this suite at the Ritz-Carlton. It's been nearly a week since I've been inside her, and I'm practically busting the seams of my pants at the idea of finally pushing into her tight wet heat again.

I prop my hands behind my head and think back over this week. I thought it would be hard to not fuck other women while I was away from Nikki, but it was easy.

Too easy.

Even when the team went out to celebrate our victory, no woman even came close to catching my eye. I never gave much thought to exclusivity before this little arrangement of ours. Now I can't help but wonder, why am I so invested in this thing with Nikki? Why doesn't it freak me out when I think about our time together going on for another month or longer?

The idea should definitely unsettle me more than it does.

Instead, anticipation pulses through me at just the thought.

The bathroom door opens wide, pulling me from my

thoughts, and my breath locks up in my chest as soon as I see the vision before me.

Fuck me.

I sit up in absolute awe, the words I should say trapped in my throat and desire pounding through my body. I'm frozen in place, my gaze tracing every exposed inch of Nikki's fucking gloriously sexy body wrapped only in the sexiest red lacy lingerie set I've ever seen. Her perky breasts look plump and ready for my hands and mouth, while the scrap of lace at the apex of her thighs already shows signs of her excitement.

Red is definitely Nikki's color. Why she's always wearing muted colors at work is beyond me.

She stares at me, nervously fidgeting with that silver ring of hers while I stare dumbfounded and realize belatedly she probably needs reassurance. I've noticed in the little time we've spent together that Nikki always seems to struggle most when it's something new. By her fidgeting and nervous expression, I can tell sexy lingerie is definitely new. Possessiveness overwhelms me at the idea that she's not done this for anyone else.

This is mine.

She's mine.

Except she's not.

Because that's not what we are.

I dial back my inner caveman and find my voice. "You look... hot." *Stunning.*

She releases a noticeable breath. "It's not too slutty?"

"You know I like slutty."

I internally wince at the reminder of my playboy ways. Why the fuck did I say that? The last thing I need is to remind her of what a manwhore I've been, even if that's the only reason she chose me for her fuck buddy.

She frowns at me, causing my heart to drop a little. "I get

this isn't a big deal for you because I'm sure you've seen women in more scandalous attire than this, but this is a big step for me."

I quickly get out of the bed and walk purposefully over to her. "I didn't mean it that way, and I never said this wasn't a big deal for me. You know I've never done anything like this either."

Her pinched brows ease as she stares at me, searching for something in my eyes. I'd give it to her if I knew what she was looking for.

Which should scare me.

So, why doesn't it?

What is it about this uptight, infuriating, control-freak woman that makes me want to soothe her, calm her, pleasure her?

"I've got another rule to add to this little arrangement of ours," I say softly, leaning in close enough to catch a whiff of her usual citrusy scent.

She squints at me and wraps her arms self-consciously around her exposed stomach. "What is it?"

I gently pull her arms away, allowing me to see her in all her splendid glory. "You let me push you out of your comfort zone."

"You already do that," she says softly, her doe eyes looking up at me with both annoyance and innocence.

Smirking, I reply, "Good. Then let's start with this insanely sexy outfit you wore for me."

"I didn't wear it for you." Her response—or should I say lie—is immediate.

"Oh, really? Then who did you wear it for?"

She throws her shoulders back and looks me straight in the eye. "I wore it for me. I wanted to feel sexy, and I've never splurged on sexy lingerie like this before."

I knew it!

She continues, her voice taking on that air of haughtiness that used to annoy the shit out of me but now just makes me hard. "It just so happens I wore it today, not knowing we would end up seeing each other, but it most certainly was not for you."

I think she might even believe that.

I run my hands up and down her arms, causing goosebumps to follow the trail of my fingers. "This whole strong woman routine is hot and all, but I'd rather get to the fucking already."

She huffs. "This is not a routine! I am—"

My mouth cuts off her protest, my tongue sliding along the seam of her lips looking for entry which she grants almost immediately.

She lets out the softest sigh, and then her body melts against mine as I plunder her mouth.

Fuck, she's delicious.

If I've learned anything in the short time we've been fucking, it's that Nikki does best when I take the lead. She's too clinical in how she looks at our arrangement, trying to organize and orchestrate the moves.

Until I kiss her.

Then she turns into someone else entirely. Someone who follows instinct and desires and wants. She becomes needy and greedy, strong and sure. Only occasionally will moments of insecurity pop up, but I can easily push them away with the stroke of my cock, flick of my tongue, or owning her mouth like it actually belongs to me.

Sometimes I'm even convinced it does.

No woman has ever made me feel this way, and instead of running away like I know I should, I push her and taunt her to get the reactions from her I'm so used to.

To get her spite and her annoyance.

To rile her up the way I know only I can.

We eat dinner in between rounds, something I insisted on because I wasn't finished with her yet. And when she eventually walks out the door, I ignore the little voice in the back of my mind telling me I'll never be finished with her.

Luke and Will take seats at the table while I look around the room. The Edison lights hanging throughout the space give this restaurant massive hipster vibes, but it's one of our favorite places to eat when we're in Atlanta.

I'm excited to finally play a home game next week. I'm even more excited to see Nikki again, but I'm trying not to think about why. A thrill shoots through me whenever I think about her. Her bright blue eyes, lush pink mouth, and God, her laugh. I had her laughing so hard last time we were together, she could hardly catch a breath. It's crazy to think we've been fuck buddies for almost two months now.

"What are you smiling about?" Luke asks curiously.

Shit. Am I smiling?

My smile drops as soon as I take in his arched brows and soft smirk. I slide a hand through my hair and shake my head, hoping he'll drop it.

Thankfully he does.

"Hey, check it out. Your plans for tonight just arrived." Luke nods his head toward the door, a salacious grin on his face. I turn around and instantly see what he's talking about. A group of women wearing heels, short skirts, and low-cut tops stand at the entrance of the bar, huddled together and looking around like they have a specific target in mind. The second they spot us, their faces light up and their postures change as they walk over to us, swaying their hips and pushing their breasts out.

I turn back to him. "I'm good."

He stares at me like I just told him I was dying of cancer.

"Are you feeling okay?" He places the back of his hand against my forehead. "Are you sick?"

I brush his hand away and laugh. "Get off me, fucker." Before I have a chance to say any more, a delicate hand slides over my bicep.

"Hey there, sexy," a woman purrs in my ear.

I turn around to see a redhead leading the pack of women who had their sights set on us. But instead of turning on the charm like I used to, I gently remove her hand from my arm.

"I'm not interested, ladies. Have a nice night."

I turn back around in my seat and catch Luke's eyebrows drawing together in concern. I hear a huff behind me before the clacking of heels fades into the background.

"What?" I ask Luke.

He shakes his head. "I can't believe you just turned down easy pussy."

"She wasn't doing it for me. I just want to relax with my guys," I say, gesturing to the two of them.

Luke turns to Will, who's been stoically taking in our exchange. "See, this is what I was telling you. Something's seriously wrong with Matt."

"Dude, I'm right fucking here."

Luke turns back to me. "Yeah, but you're not acting like yourself. You haven't for a while now. For real, though, what's going on with you? You rarely hit on women anymore. I can't even remember the last time I saw you leave with a woman when we've been out. I'm genuinely worried about you."

I open my mouth to speak, but then close it again when I remember I can't tell him about Nikki. I decide to tell him a partial truth.

"Fucking jersey chasers has gotten old."

He grips my shoulder and leans forward. "Are you trying to

tell me that you aren't getting laid at all? The man who had a new woman nearly every damn night? No fucking way."

I grip the back of my neck and glance over at Will, silently begging him to rescue me.

Like the good man he is, he comes through. "Leave him alone, Luke."

I shrug off Luke's hand and ignore his pinched expression. Maybe someday I'll tell him about Nikki. About how I've been fucking her every spare chance I have. How I've discovered the thrill of having sex with the same woman and learning all her likes and dislikes so that sex is tailored to her specific needs and wants. How much better sex has been because I've gotten to know her so well.

How much I love that she's letting me get to know other parts of her too. I think about all the hours we've spent talking and laughing, getting to know each other in the moments in between mind-blowing sex.

"Fine. I'll let it go for now," Luke says and then proceeds to tell Will and me a story about the antics he and his best friend from back home, Drew, got up to in college.

As he talks, my mind drifts to Nikki. I wonder what she's doing right now. I glance down at my cell and calculate the time difference. She's probably at her weekly dinner with her folks. I wonder what she's wearing. Has she bought any more sexy lingerie?

Will's booming laugh pulls me from my thoughts.

What the fuck am I even doing? Daydreaming about my fuck buddy?

Is she really just *a fuck buddy?*

My chest feels tight and my breathing uneasy. I can't think about her. I *shouldn't* be thinking about her.

So why can't I fucking stop thinking about her?

Why does her face pop into my head whenever I'm not on the football field?

Why does my heart instantly accelerate whenever I see a blonde even though I know it couldn't possibly be Nikki because she's back in Los Angeles?

My callused fingers scrub across my face and I wish they could wipe all these thoughts from my brain.

It's just supposed to be sex.

And yet, every night, I've found myself lying in my hotel bed staring at the only picture I have of her on my phone. In a moment of blind insanity the last time we were together, I took a picture of her when she had her eyes closed, resting after one of our marathon sex sessions.

She looked so relaxed and peaceful.

That might've been the moment calling her Princess took on a completely different meaning for me. She still gets annoyed whenever I use it, but that's fine.

She doesn't need to know I don't use it to piss her off anymore, but as the only term of endearment I'll allow myself to use with her.

It doesn't give me away if she still thinks it's an insult.

Not that there's anything to give away.

There's not.

It's just sex.

Maybe if I keep telling myself that I can go back to believing it.

SEVENTEEN

Nikki

Leaning back against the wall, I try to take a breath and a moment to myself. My shoulders are stiff from the stress of the day, and my usual breathing exercises aren't doing a damn thing to help relieve the tension I'm carrying in my body. Frankly, I feel like a chicken with its head cut off.

Today has been a shitshow since the moment I woke up. I forgot to set my alarm, so I didn't wake up until Cassie popped in asking if I was okay. For once, I was grateful that it's been such a pain in the ass to find a place of my own, or who knows how late I would've overslept.

When I made it to work, Luther reminded me that today was the day of the last-minute campaign shoot which got scheduled at the end of last week. One of our sponsors changed their mind and decided they did in fact want to be involved in the campaign with Matt.

We'd thrown this shoot together by a miracle, and I should've been focused on making sure all my ducks were in a row for it, and I was.

Kind of.

Mainly, I was just excited to finally see Matt again. We

haven't been able to get together since he got back from Atlanta the other night and I was dying to see him.

Not that I'll ever admit that to him.

But then the photographer got the location wrong, and our sponsors were breathing down my neck. I'd hardly had a minute to myself all day. Let alone actually getting a moment with Matt.

Now I'm leaning here against a wall and I feel frazzled, which is not a feeling I like.

"Here." My eyes pop open as I turn to the familiar deep voice that never fails to send tingles through my body. I look at Matt standing next to me wearing a Wolves hoodie and gray sweatpants.

God, men in gray sweatpants really shouldn't be allowed in public.

He gestures with his hand, and for the first time I notice he's handing me a water bottle. Just the sight of it causes me to focus on how parched I am. I can't remember the last time I had water today, which speaks to how busy I've been.

I take the bottle from his outstretched hand and quickly drink half of it, the cool, crisp water helping wash away some of the tension.

I pull the bottle from my lips and focus my gaze on Matt's. His blue eyes are smoldering, and once again this man commands my body with just a look. On a breath, the rest of my tension releases for the first time all day. It should alarm me that I feel more relaxed *with* him than away from him, but I decide not to think about it. A habit I seem to be falling into with Matt.

"Drink it all so you don't get dehydrated. You haven't had any water the whole time we've been here." His demand should rankle me, but instead I'm distracted by his last statement.

"How do you know?"

He looks sheepish before schooling his features and shrugging his shoulders. My heart beats a little faster, my eyes transfixed by his. Has he been watching me all day? He says so much with just that look, but I'm afraid to trust it.

He's a playboy.

I'm an ice princess, according to him.

I must be projecting my own feelings into his look.

Wait, no.

I don't have feelings for him.

I *can't* have feelings for him.

My chest rises and falls at a rapid pace while I internally freak out. I need to pull myself together and get back out to the shoot before something else falls apart.

I duck my head and brush past him, the feel of his body setting all my nerve endings aflame. "Thanks for the water," I say softly.

"Sure thing, Princess."

His voice sounds like a caress, but the word at the end rankles me and reminds me he's just in this for the sex. Which is obviously the reminder I need because clearly I'm losing my mind.

I cannot, under any circumstances, start having feelings for Matt Fischer.

Or at the very least, I can never let him see that I might be having feelings.

My body shakes with the power of my release as I come apart on top of Matt. He bucks up into me, increasing his pace as he chases his own climax, and lets out a hoarse groan that always makes my pulse pound a little harder. I go to collapse next to him, but his arms wrap tight around my body, pulling my chest down to his. I rest my head against his shoulder, both of us catching our breath.

I wish I could say this has been a transformative experience for me, but it hasn't.

Well, not completely.

I've tried every sexual position imaginable and come in a myriad of ways, but I still feel tension in my shoulders before I arrive and the moment I walk out the door after.

Tension that carries the weight of all the expectations others have of me.

Matt's come to expect it because he practically pounces on me the second I walk in the room, kissing me senseless until I'm a heap of needy woman craving him in ways I never knew were possible.

But his powers only last so long.

I would give anything to be the woman I am with him when I'm outside the safety of this hotel room. He makes me feel strong, and sexy, and confident.

I don't second-guess myself as much anymore when we're together, but he sees it when we've had to work together. I've caught him looking at me more than once with his brows pinched like he's trying to figure out what it'll take to get me to truly loosen up. It's the same look he gave me when we first started this arrangement. The same look he never has to give me anymore when we're together in quiet moments like this.

But if I knew what it would take to loosen me up, I would've done it by now. I've been trying to figure it out for years.

Matt's fingers slide through my hair, sending pleasure through my body at the gentle caress. His chest is sturdy and strong under mine, and the calm rise and fall of it relaxes me further. I can't pinpoint when we started cuddling, but somehow it happened once and now it happens more often than not.

I run my index finger up and down his toned chest, enjoying the thrill when his breath stutters at my soft touch. The comfort of his arms around me and the satisfaction of my release has me looser than I've been in days.

"You're nothing like I thought you were," my honest words come out as a whisper.

His fingers halt briefly before he says with a gruff voice, "Right back at ya, Princess."

I lean up, placing my hand firmly on his chest. "Aren't we beyond that name now? Why do you still use it?"

He stares at me, his gaze gentle and tender. "I don't use it because I think you're spoiled—well, at least not anymore," he says with a wink. I roll my eyes, but before I can comment, he continues, his fingers still running soothingly through my long blonde locks. "Now I use it as a reminder of how you should be treated—like the royalty you are."

My breath catches in my throat, and my eyes have the vaguest hint of tears. His gaze is vulnerable now, appraising my reaction. But I don't have any words for him.

How can I tell him he's made me feel something I thought was lost? He's shown me glimpses of the woman I suspected lived deep inside me all this time—even if she doesn't stick around once I leave him. How can I articulate how he's changed me so completely in one area of my life, while my life outside these doors feels exactly the same?

How can I tell him this doesn't feel like just sex anymore?

I can't.

So, instead, I kiss him with everything I'm feeling. I speak with my body, which seems to be the best way we communicate anyway.

When we finish, exhausted and finally sated, I ignore the voice in my head telling me to get my ass out of bed, instead choosing to curl up next to him. As my eyelids get heavy with sleep, I ignore the fact that we made it a rule never to spend the night.

I ignore everything I'm *supposed* to do and instead fall into a peaceful sleep, wrapped in the arms of a man who is so much more than I ever gave him credit for.

I walk into Cassie and Max's house, attempting to be quiet. This is not a walk of shame.

It's not.

I just don't need her to know I didn't come home last night.

"And where have you been, young lady?"

Busted.

I look to the right to see Cassie sitting on her couch with a cup of coffee and the biggest shit-eating grin I've ever seen on her face.

She totally knows where I've been, but I also notice her eyes don't seem weighted down like they have lately. In fact, she seems happier than I've seen her since she confessed she was worried Max might break up with her.

As soon as she lifts her cup of coffee to take a sip, I see why.

"You got engaged?!" I can barely keep the excitement out of my voice.

She jumps up, laughing and nodding her head. "We got engaged!"

I run over to her, tossing my purse on the coffee table in the process, and wrap her up in a big hug before pulling away and grabbing her hand to stare at the gorgeous—and huge—rock on her hand.

"Oh my God, Cassie, it's beautiful."

"Isn't it?" She's practically gushing. I don't know that I've ever seen her this happy.

"Did this happen last night?"

"Yeah. I had no idea. He took me out and he was so serious the whole time. I was convinced he was finally going to break up with me like I've been dreading after he was acting weird a couple of months ago, but then he got down on one knee and proposed. Apparently, he got distant when he bought the ring because he was afraid he'd spill the beans, and he's been planning this for a while."

I give her another big hug. "I'm so happy for you both."

"Me too. He's...Nikki, he's the most amazing man I've ever known. I can't believe I get to be his wife." She has tears in her eyes, and immediately mine start to water.

"He's lucky to have you."

"We're lucky to have each other," she says, her eyes getting all dreamy and her face glowing with incandescent happiness.

"So, it was a good thing I didn't come home last night, then?"

She smiles knowingly. "Yes, it definitely worked out that you weren't here. Also, I wouldn't eat at the table yet. I need to clean it."

Gross. I won't be eating at that table ever again now.

She rolls her eyes like she can read my thoughts, but then shifts the focus to me. "So, you stayed the night. I thought that was against your rules."

I shrug. "It was, but we were both too tired after, so we just fell asleep. It seemed silly to waste such a great hotel suite anyway."

"Uh huh."

"What? What's with the 'uh huh'?"

"Nothing. I should be used to you living in delusion-land." She says it so casually.

"I'm sorry, what?" I say, indignation clear in my tone.

"You like him."

"I do not! It's still just sex."

"Like I said, delusion-land."

"I am not being delusional."

"Why won't you just admit you like him?"

Because I can't. Because that's not what we're supposed to be. But instead of saying any of that, I just stare at her.

The worst part is she's right.

I do like him.

But I'm still not ready to admit it out loud because once I do, there will be no going back. And because I'm afraid he doesn't feel the same, which means our arrangement will end.

I'm not ready for it to end.

EIGHTEEN

Matt

"What are you doing today?" I ask, eager to put my plan into action.

"I'm having dinner with my parents tonight."

"That's tonight. I asked what you were doing *today*. You know, like when the sun is up."

"Nothing, why?" she asks, her tone curious and skeptical at the same time.

"Because I want to fuck, and since you're my fuck buddy, I called you first." That's not really why I called, but I'm afraid if I tell her the real reason, she'll never agree, and I want to see her. I'm trying not to focus on how excited I am at the prospect of seeing her outside our hotel suite.

"Do you have to be so vulgar about it?"

"Oh, Princess, I can get way more vulgar if you'd like."

"Hard pass." God, I love when she's not amused with my antics.

"I'll give you something hard."

"Oh my God, stop! You're about to get your pussy privileges revoked." I'm relieved by the laugh I hear in her voice, because I was worried I might've crossed a line there for a second.

"Okay, I'm done. But seriously, do you want to see me today?"

The phone is silent, so silent I actually pull it away from my ear and look at the screen to make sure the call didn't drop.

Putting it back to my ear, I prod, "Nikki?"

"Uh, sure. Yes."

I ignore the hesitation I hear in her tone, knowing it's probably due to me going completely off-script on our usual plans of meeting at the suite. She tells me where to pick her up, and thirty minutes later, I pull up to a nice house in Pacific Palisades.

She walks out the door before I have the chance to even get out of my car, and my mouth drops at the sight of her. I've never seen her outside of her business attire—well, unless she's naked—but holy shit. She's wearing skin-tight skinny jeans that hug every perfect curve on her fit little body and make her ass look fucking delicious. Her top is a flowy, floral short-sleeved thing that doesn't quite reach the edge of her pants, so when she moves certain ways, I get glimpses of her toned stomach. It goes all the way up to her neck, so I don't see any cleavage, which almost makes it sexier. Very rarely do I meet women who dress so modestly, and there's something so sexy about a woman who lets your imagination run wild instead of showing all the goods.

What really kicks me in the nuts, though, is the fact her blonde hair is down, flowing in soft waves around her face. Fuck, I love how sexy she looks with her hair down. It always makes me feel a little breathless. She just looks so relaxed and at peace when her hair is down. Softer, almost.

She gets in the car and buckles her seat belt before turning to me. I'm still staring at her like an idiot, but I can't stop.

She just looks so *fucking good*.

She pats her hair and fidgets with her shirt. "Is something wrong?"

The vulnerability in her voice guts me. "No," I choke out as I shake my head. "No, you just look... Fuck, Nikki, I'm trying to behave myself, but you look fucking sinful."

She smiles shyly, and my heart does this weird clench in my chest.

Maybe I should get that checked out by the team doctor since it keeps happening.

"Thank you," she says softly. "You don't look too bad yourself."

"Thanks."

Okay, I need to pull my shit together and get this back on track.

I clear my throat. "So, don't take this the wrong way—"

"Why do I feel like you're about to insult me?"

I throw her my usual charming smile. "It's not an insult if it's true."

She shakes her head. "That's not at all true, but go ahead. Say whatever you're going to say."

"You're uptight. Like stick-permanently-resides-in-your-ass level uptight, at least outside of the bedroom," I say. "I think we should work on that."

"I thought this was a sex only arrangement."

"It was, but I think if you learn to loosen up a bit it'll make the sex even better, so it's kinda self-serving and still focused on sex ultimately."

That's how I'm justifying it to myself at least.

She purses her lips and looks out the front window. Before I have a chance to tell her it was a stupid idea, she opens her mouth. "You're right."

"I am?" I'm honestly surprised we didn't just get in an argument about this.

She nods. "Yeah. I do need to loosen up. I know I can be kind of..."

"Controlling, overbearing, borderline authoritarian?" I say teasingly.

"I was going to say difficult," she enunciates and shakes her head, a soft smile on her face. "But sure, all those things too. Anyway, I know this about myself and...well, I'd like to loosen up. I wasn't always like this." She whispers that last bit while looking out the side passenger window.

Now I'm curious what she means. I've known Nikki for five years and in that time, she's only ever been uptight and controlling.

I've never thought about *why* she was the way she was, but I am now.

Which I definitely shouldn't be.

Time to course correct—again.

"Well, I had an idea of something fun we could do."

She turns to me. "What's that?"

"It's a surprise," I say with a grin.

She looks at me skeptically but doesn't question it further. I take the short drive to one of my favorite spots. It's been a long time since I've been here, but I used to come here all the time.

We pull up to the red brick building and park in the otherwise empty parking lot.

"Uh, I think we have to find somewhere else to go," Nikki says, pointing to the closed sign on the door.

"Do you trust me?"

She looks at me for only a second before replying, "Strangely enough, I do."

Warmth spreads through me. "Then let's go."

We meet at the front of my car and walk together toward the door. I have the strangest urge to hold her hand, which isn't something we do—even though lately it feels like we've been blurring the lines that we established at the beginning of our relationship. I ignore the impulse and knock on the door.

A familiar short, bald, and portly man comes and opens it up for us.

"Matt! It's so good to see you, son." Scotty leans in and gives me a quick hug and pat on the back. "How long's it been?"

"Too long." I peek behind him. "You've gotten new games since I was last here."

He smiles wide. "Well, your donation allowed us to make quite a few improvements. I can't thank you enough for all your help."

I shake my head quickly, not wanting him to go too deep into detail around Nikki. I have a reputation to maintain, and philanthropic sap doesn't fit into it.

Scotty glances at Nikki and then looks back at me. "Right. Well, come on in, you two. The place is all yours for as long as you need it."

I gesture for Nikki to go ahead of me. She looks at me curiously as she passes, and I catch her citrusy scent in my nose. It reminds me of summers on the beach and is quickly becoming my favorite smell.

"Oh wow," she whispers when she gets fully inside. I come up behind her and try to see the space from her point of view. Classic arcade games, pinball machines, redemption games, and the like cover nearly every inch.

Scotty's Arcade was my childhood safe haven. Whenever I needed a break from my dad or my life, I would walk here and play for hours. It was the only time I got to be a kid after my mom left.

Nikki turns to me and the wide smile on her face makes this day so worth it. Even if I know we're playing with the line of our arrangement.

Or well beyond it at this point.

Watching her practically bubbling with excitement and joy sends one thought through my brain.

Fuck the rules.

NINETEEN

Nikki

I look around the room, unable to wipe the smile from my face. I remember coming to an arcade similar to this for a friend's birthday when I was eight. It was one of the best days I'd ever had. I planned to have my ninth birthday at one, but then the accident happened and what I wanted didn't matter anymore.

I turn to Matt and catch him watching me already. There's something in his gaze, a heat simmering under the surface, but something else too. Something I've been seeing more of during our time together, but I'm afraid to name. His lips tip up in a smile and he grabs my hand.

"Come on, let's play. Time to pull that stick out of your ass."

I laugh. "Gee, thanks."

He turns back and smiles at me, and my breath catches in my lungs. I've seen Matt smile a million different times, but never like this. This smile actually seems carefree. It's authentic instead of charming or for show like he normally does—his camera smile as I've come to think of it.

This smile is so much better than any other smile I've ever seen from him.

"So, what game do you want to start with?" he asks.

I look around. "I have no idea. I've only ever been to an arcade once when I was little."

His eyes bug out. "Wait, you've only been once? *In your whole life?*"

I nod, attempting to hold back my laugh at how put out he seems by the idea.

"Oh, no, we definitely have to fix this." He looks around. "Okay, we're going to start with Skee-Ball because it's a classic." He pulls me toward the machines and gets everything ready, showing me how to throw the balls underhanded.

"Cup it like you're cupping a man's balls."

I give him a look, which causes him to laugh. "Alright, I'll stop. For now."

I smile at him, enjoying this side of him. He's different here.

"Okay, give it a try." He hands me one of the balls, and I follow his instructions and throw it underhanded.

Turns out, I suck at Skee-Ball.

The ball doesn't even make it to the outside ring. On my second attempt, I throw it too hard and it bounces around the rings before falling in the outside one, giving me the fewest number of points. After several rounds of my failure and Matt's uncontrollable fit of giggles, I decide it's time to try something else.

We rotate through the games, Matt showing me how to do them and then us competing against each other. I beat him at the Cyclone game, but he kicks my ass on almost everything else. We lose track of time while we laugh, play, and tease each other relentlessly, always keeping the conversation light.

"I want a Skee-Ball rematch. I think I could do better this time."

He looks at me skeptically.

I slap his arm. "I'm serious."

He shrugs and smiles. "Fine by me. After you, Princess."

My heart swells at the nickname, especially since his confession the last time we were together.

We make our way back to the Skee-Ball machine and start competing with each other again.

"How'd you find this place, anyway?" I ask.

"I used to come here as a kid."

I turn to him, but his focus is still on the game. "You did? I didn't know you lived around here."

He stands up from his slouched position having just released a ball and turns to me. "Yeah, just a couple of blocks away." He hesitates before saying, almost reluctantly, "My dad still lives there actually."

"He does?" This is definitely news. He's never talked about his family before.

He nods.

"Did he come here and play too?"

Matt shakes his head and then grips the back of his neck, his shoulders getting visibly tense. I take in the change in his demeanor and am curious about why he's gotten so awkward.

"It was just me. Scotty became a good friend back then." He puts on his camera smile and my heart sinks a little. "He had more hair back then too."

I give him a small smile and then turn back to the game. I've spent enough time with him to know the camera smile means he's putting on his playboy persona. I'm beginning to believe it's really just that—a persona. He's much deeper than I ever gave him credit for.

I glance over at him and see him rolling the ball in his hand. He seems lost in thought when he suddenly looks up and catches me looking. Instead of turning away and focusing back on the game like I'm itching to do, I meet his gaze.

"I didn't have a great childhood," he says softly, almost like he's confessing to me.

I don't speak, afraid if I do, he'll stop sharing. We've talked a lot in the two months we've been together, but nothing heavy. Nothing truly important.

"My dad was kind of a mess. It's a long, depressing story, but this was my happy place, I guess." He shrugs his shoulder like he doesn't know what else to say.

"Thank you for sharing it with me."

He nods, and something passes between us while we look at each other.

His phone rings in his pocket, breaking us from our moment, and I turn my gaze back to the game in front of me. I glance to the side to watch him stare at his phone before he silences it and refocuses on his game. We only toss another ball or two before his phone starts ringing again.

When Matt looks at the screen this time, his eyes close and the quickest flicker of pain crosses his face. I watch him carefully, curiosity getting the better of me, as he brings the phone to his ear and answers.

"Yeah..." His eyes close again and he starts pacing in short lines back and forth in front of me. "Uh huh...Is there no one there who could take him home? No, I understand," he says, resigned. He looks at me, apologetic, maybe a little remorseful, but the emotion I see most clearly is fear. Fear of what, I'm not entirely sure.

He hangs up the phone, his voice tight. "We need to go. I have to make a stop before I take you home, and we need to go now if I'm gonna get you back in time for your dinner with your folks."

"Is everything okay?"

He lets out a deep exhale. "Not really, but fuck if I want to explain it right now. Let's go."

He heads for the door and I follow quickly. He gives Scotty

a brief hug and a thanks before he opens the door for me and we leave the arcade.

The car ride to wherever we're going is quiet, not even the radio playing. Matt is completely lost in his thoughts and honestly, so am I. I've seen so many different sides to him today. It's becoming increasingly clear he's not the shallow playboy he pretends to be. There's a lot more to him, and I can't help but wonder why he acts the way he does in front of everyone else.

We pull up to a small dive bar a few blocks away from the arcade, and Matt gets out of the car without a word.

Am I supposed to stay here?

Screw that. I want to know what's going on.

I jump out of the car and quickly follow after him. He's already gone through the door by the time I get there, so I pull it open and see him standing next to a man at the bar who looks like he can barely hold himself up. I look around at the dingy interior. The Formica table tops are cracked, and the chairs grimy like they haven't been cleaned in a long time. The air has that tinge of smoke that seems to be coming from the walls, probably from the old days when people could still smoke in bars. There are only a handful of people here, and all of them seem equally miserable, their heads bent down to their drinks and their postures slumped. I refocus on Matt, trying to figure out why we're here.

He grabs the man's arm and coaxes him to get up. "Come on, Dad. You've had enough. Sterling is cutting you off. It's time to go."

I stare at the man Matt's talking to, his clothes noticeably dirty and wrinkled. That's his dad?

When the man stumbles up from Matt's firm grasp, I get my first good look at his face. I can definitely see the similarities, but this man has not aged well, presumably due to the alcohol. His body seems worn and frail. His sandy-blond hair is disheveled, and his blue eyes are vacant and watery, whereas Matt's are a bright, vibrant blue.

"Thanks for coming to get him, Matt. I can't have him passing out on the bar again." The bartender—I'm guessing this is Sterling—looks at me before talking again to Matt. "I didn't mean to interrupt."

Matt turns around, noticing for the first time that I followed him in. He visibly swallows, and his eyes take on a haunted look. I recognize the pain and regret in his eyes instantly, since it's a look I'm all too familiar with, and I ache to wipe the look away, to ease his suffering.

Who would've thought Matt Fischer and I had anything in common?

"Nikki..."

I shake my head and tell him quietly, "It's okay, Matt. Take care of your dad." I move closer to him. "Do you want my help?"

He shakes his head, reaching out and squeezing my hand.

There's something so innocent about the gesture, and yet with that one move, I know we are no longer friends with benefits—or fuck buddies as he always put it.

We're something more.

TWENTY

Matt

Nikki's soft hand in mine soothes some of my worry over her seeing this part of my life. I give it a gentle squeeze and then turn back to my dad. My heart sinks at his condition. How his liver is even still functioning at this point is a goddamn miracle. He mumbles something—no doubt about my mom—and then lurches forward. I grab him around the waist and lift him, supporting him so we can shuffle out to my car.

Nikki opens the door in front of us and I give her a look I hope expresses my gratitude. As mortified as I was when I realized she followed me in here, I'm grateful for her help.

It's the first time I've had someone with me when I've had to come get my dad, and it's nice knowing there's someone here for *me*. I've been taking care of my dad for so long, I have forgotten what it feels like to be taken care of. Even though she's not really doing anything, just her presence here, and her support, makes it feel like she's taking care of me.

I can't help but think we're swimming in dangerous waters right now. Our whole fuck buddies arrangement was supposed to be sex only and yet we've basically spent the day on an hours-long date. Now she's seeing my dad at his worst and surprisingly hasn't run away screaming.

Nikki is a lot stronger than I've given her credit for because this is definitely above and beyond the call of duty for what our arrangement is supposed to be.

But I don't hate it.

The exact opposite in fact. I think I might like that she knows this about me.

It's the real me. The me no one else sees.

I push my wayward thoughts aside and focus on the issue at hand—my dad.

He stumbles to the car, and I gently help him get in the back seat. I get him strapped in and then close the door, taking a deep breath of the cool air and closing my eyes. I wish I could say this is new for him, but we've done this so many times now, it's almost a habit.

I turn to Nikki, who's standing outside the passenger door, staring intently at her phone.

"I'm really sorry about this. Do we have time to drop him off before I take you back to your place? His house is just around the corner."

"I cancelled my dinner plans." She waves her phone at me, and I can see her text messages open.

My eyes go wide. "You did?"

She nods, looking at me intently.

"Why?" The word comes out shallower than I intended, but I don't understand why she'd do that. I'm nothing special to her.

"I didn't want you to feel rushed, and I don't mind helping out." She bites her lip nervously like she's afraid I might push her away.

I'm speechless.

I don't have a charming comeback, and all the walls I keep

up against women are slowly crumbling in the face of her kindness and support.

I offer her a nod and then walk to the driver side, trying to get my scrambled thoughts together. What's happening between us?

The car is silent—apart from my dad's low mumbles—during the duration of the drive to his house. When we get there, Nikki helps me by taking my keys and running ahead of us to open the door. Inside the house, I turn on some lights and then turn to tell Nikki, "Make yourself comfortable. I'm going to get him into bed."

She nods shyly.

I take my dad to his room, help him get his shoes off and then into bed. He'll wake up at some point in the night and take off his pants and shirt, but for now I leave him be. He needs to sleep some of this off. At the threshold of his room, I turn back and watch his chest rise and fall with heavy breaths.

Gently closing the door, I walk back out to the living room to find Nikki tucked on the couch. I sit down next to her and let my head fall back with my eyes closed.

"We can leave soon. I just need a minute," I say without opening my eyes.

"Has he always been this way?"

"No."

Silence sits heavy in the room.

"Is he why you used to go to the arcade all the time?" she asks softly.

I open my eyes and turn my head, seeing her already looking at me with her gentle gaze.

I nod and try to identify this intense pressure that's suddenly present in my chest. It's like all the words are trying to burst out to spill my life story to her. The longer Nikki and I stare at each other, the more I want to tell her.

I turn my head, unable to look at her while I bare my soul, and stare blindly at the wall in front of me. "My mom left us when I was eleven." I hear her sharp inhale, but she doesn't say anything, so I continue. "She wasn't happy, I guess. She never wanted to be a mom. One day, I came home from school and my dad was sitting on the couch with his head in his hands crying. I knew something bad had happened, but I didn't know what. We had a pretty good life up until that point. I'd never had anyone die on me or anything tragic, so I was completely unprepared when he said Mom left.

"I remember asking when she was coming back, and when he looked up at me, he was so...broken. His eyes were filled with so much pain. I'd never seen my dad like that before. Hell, I'd never even seen him cry before that day."

I can see the moment so clearly in my head, even all these years later.

"Is that when he started drinking?"

I shake my head. "No. The drinking started when she sent him divorce papers."

"Did she ever give a reason why?"

"Not really. She just left a note saying she couldn't do it anymore. This wasn't the life she wanted."

I look at her, her eyes showing so much concern for me. I don't think I've ever had anyone look at me the way she does.

"I found her once," I say softly.

Her eyes go wide. "Did you talk to her?"

I nod, and my voice comes out in a whisper. "She said she never wanted me. She thought she loved my dad, but she didn't. She wanted to be free to party and do whatever she wanted."

Nikki's beautiful blue eyes fill with tears. "Matt," her voice comes out whisper soft, but there's so much care in the way she says my name that my heart nearly breaks.

She leans forward, placing her lips gently on mine. The kiss is soft, tender, and over far too soon. I blink my eyes open and watch her carefully.

Her gaze locks with mine, and the look there makes me feel like she truly understands this pain I've held on to for so long. She stands up from the couch and holds her hand out to me. "Come on. I want to show you something."

I give her a small smile. "I've already seen the goods, Nikki."

She rolls her eyes—fuck, I love when she's annoyed with me. "Come on, smart-ass."

I grab her hand and let her pull me from my childhood home.

Somehow, I think I'd let her drag me anywhere at this point.

TWENTY-ONE

Nikki

When we get to Griffith Park, Matt shoots me a look. Fortunately, there aren't too many people around. When we get out of the car, I take the lead, knowing the route to my spot like the back of my hand since I used to come here all the time. There's a bench that overlooks the whole city, and sitting there has always helped give me perspective. Although, sometimes it's hard to get a moment to myself when I'm here because it's been featured in so many movies and TV shows that tourists constantly want to come and get their selfies overlooking LA.

But to me, it'll always be the spot where I'm able to let down my walls and finally take a deep, guilt-free breath.

When I see that no one is sitting there already, I release a breath I didn't realize I'd been holding. I take a seat on the bench and Matt sits next to me, neither of us saying a word but just admiring the view.

I glance over at him and see the sag of his shoulders and the despondence in his expression. I look back out at the view, unable to look at him while I confess my greatest pain and biggest secret.

"Did you know I had a sister?" I see Matt's head whip to me from my periphery, but I still don't look at him.

"She was two years older than me." Deep breath. "She died when she was ten."

"Nikki..." The pain in his voice breaks my heart, and a tear slips unbidden down my cheek.

"It was my fault," I choke out. I finally look at him now, my eyes blurring with tears. His gaze is kind and sympathetic, yet still curious, waiting for me to explain.

I chew the inside of my lip and try to get my emotions under control. "I was so excited about an art show I was in at school. Nora had ballet which overlapped, but I begged her to leave early so she and my dad could be there. It was the biggest thing that had ever happened to me and I demanded they come, the way only an eight-year-old girl who's never had anything bad happen to her can." I roll my eyes at how dumb I was. How naïve. "I told her I wouldn't speak to her again if she didn't come."

I have to stop, my chest feeling tight and tears trickling down my cheeks as I remember that conversation. How badly I wish I could go back in time and change it. How bratty and entitled I was. If I'd known what would happen, I would've done so much differently.

I take another shallow breath and attempt to push through, but the words get trapped in my throat as a sob breaks loose. The warmth of Matt's hand covers the top of mine and I turn to him, seeing only kindness and encouragement in his eyes. The one time I attempted to tell Anthony about that night, he just looked at me like I was pathetic, so I never told him the whole thing. I couldn't take his derision.

Matt's gentle support is exactly what I need to finally get it all out. "My dad and sister were in a car accident on the way to my art show. A driver who was high ran a red light and T-boned them. He slammed into Nora's side of the car."

I let out another sob, reliving the moment the officer told my mom and me what had happened. "There was too much damage, and despite hours in surgery attempting to fix it, the doctors couldn't save her."

Matt's arm wraps around me and he pulls me into his body. Burying my face in my hands, I let it all out. I stop fighting my emotions and sob in the warmth and comfort of his embrace. He holds me tight, rubbing my back and whispering in my hair.

"Let it out, Nikki. I've got you." They're the words I need, and I wish I could explain to him what they mean to me.

I don't know how long we sit there, him holding me close and me soaking his shirt with my tears. Slowly, my tears subside, but I don't move from his hold just yet. He smells like bergamot and patchouli, and I close my eyes, letting his scent comfort me. Never in a million years would I have imagined a moment like this with Matt.

I reluctantly sit up. Matt seems equally reluctant to let me go and leaves his arm wrapped around my shoulders. He wipes my tears with his thumb and cups my face, looking deeply into my eyes.

"It wasn't your fault, Princess."

Tears start to fill my eyes again. "It was," I choke out.

He shakes his head. "No. It was the guy who decided to get high and then drive."

"But—" I start, but he cuts me off.

"No 'buts,' Nikki. It wasn't your fault. There was no way you could've known what would happen."

"If I hadn't been so selfish and demanding, she'd still be here."

He shakes his head. "You were eight. You acted like a little kid who wanted her family to support her."

I look at my hands, unable to see the compassion in his eyes anymore, because he's almost got me believing him. But his words will never truly assuage the guilt I feel over my sister's death.

"I miss her so much," I whisper. "It's been twenty years and I still miss her." My gaze slides up and over the view of LA. The city seems so small from up here in this serene spot, but so vast at the same time.

"My parents changed when she died. I changed. They were so sad, and I just wanted to make them happy. I felt so guilty, I couldn't bear to do anything that would bring them more pain." My hands are clammy and hot, despite the chill in the air. "I started doing whatever they asked, even when I didn't want to. Then I'd overhear them talking about things they wished for me, dreams they had, so I did those things too. I went into marketing because my mom thought I'd be great at it, even though my dream had always been graphic design. I dated Anthony because my parents set us up and thought he was a great guy, which he was on paper. But the reality was he was a cheating pig who constantly found ways to make me feel small."

Matt's arm tenses behind me, and I chance a glance at him, only to see his eyes have gone hard and his mouth is set in a firm line. "He cheated on you? That's why you broke up?"

I nod and huff out a laugh. "With our wedding planner of all people." I remember Nadine's cutting remarks about how she slept with Anthony. "Actually, turns out he cheated with multiple people, at least according to Nadine Monroe."

Matt's eyes go wide. "Nadine? The model from that shoot where…"

"Where you took me against the wall? Yeah, that's the one."

Matt looks out at the city. "Wow." He turns back to me. "Is that why you got so angry with her?"

I shrug and look back down at my hands. "She said some

things. Things I wasn't expecting, and it just made me feel so stupid that I never noticed or figured it out. That I never questioned his behavior. So, here I am at work and I find out not only did my fiancé constantly make me feel small, but he'd made me out to be a fool too. I just...snapped when she brought him up. It wasn't the most professional thing to do."

"Maybe not, but it was hot," he says with a small smile.

I slap his chest. He catches my hand in his and holds it there, our gazes locking on each other.

"Why'd you tell me all this?" he whispers.

"I guess I just thought we could have a secret for a secret. You shared the truth about your dad with me, so I wanted to even the playing field, I guess."

"You told me your darkest secret so I wouldn't feel bad about my dad?"

I nod.

He shakes his head, fighting a soft smile. "Nikki Denton, you are something else, you know that?"

"Is that a good thing or a bad thing?" I ask quietly.

He cups my cheek, his eyes searching mine. "Definitely a good thing," he whispers. He leans forward and softly places his lips on mine.

This kiss is unlike anything else I've experienced with him. It's tender, caring, and so sweet. It shakes my foundation in ways I can't even begin to explain, but it's clear things are shifting between us.

Which scares the shit out of me, but hell if I know how to stop it.

TWENTY-TWO

Matt

I knock on Nikki's open office door, alerting her to my presence. She looks up quickly, her mouth open with the slightest "O" and her eyes squinting at the door. She looks fucking adorable.

"Hey," I say, walking toward her desk. I hold up the plastic bag filled with white and red takeout cartons. "I brought you lunch."

She looks at me in surprise. "Lunch?"

"Yeah. When I called your secretary earlier to see if you were available, she said you'd been slammed in meetings and were planning to work through lunch."

"I was, I mean, I am," she stumbles over her words before closing her eyes and visibly composing herself. My lips tilt up in a small smile as I watch her organize her thoughts.

"We've been going through the proofs from your last shoot and organizing a bunch of other marketing campaigns for the rest of the season. Plus, one of our directors quit, so we've had to take over his tasks. It's been...stressful, to say the least."

"It sounds like you need a break." I hold up the bags again.

She looks at the clock on the wall next to the door. "I suppose I could take a small break."

"Great." I place the bag on her desk and carefully take out the cartons with different Chinese food. "I wasn't sure what you like, so I got a little bit of everything."

She looks ravenously at the boxes before lifting up the carton with orange chicken and inhaling deeply. "Oh my God, this smells amazing." She looks back up at me sheepishly and admits, "I didn't realize I was so hungry."

"Well, then I had perfect timing. Dig in."

She doesn't need any further prompting, and I watch in fascination as she devours every last bite of the orange chicken and half the carton of rice. She looks at me, her mouth full of food, and realizes I'm not eating.

She swallows and gestures to the food. "Aren't you going to eat?" I shake my head, letting my body relax into the chair, my ankle crossed on the opposite knee.

"Nope. This is all for you."

The room is silent, her stare weighted with questions, but she doesn't ask. We continue to stare at each other, each of us waiting until the other breaks and speaks first.

I decide to give her a break—just this once. "I wanted to see you, to see if things were still okay with us."

She stares at me for another few seconds before fully absorbing my words and nodding slowly. "You mean because of what happened the last time we hung out."

I nod.

"We're fine."

Somehow, I don't believe her. I haven't seen her in a week—since our day at the arcade and subsequent interaction with my dad and conversation at Griffith Park—despite the fact I had a meeting to further discuss some additional details of the campaign. She sent Luther to the meeting in her place, and I'm dying to know why.

Really, I'm just dying to know if she's done with me.

Because I'm nowhere near done with her.

"Are we?"

She nods but looks down at the papers on her desk.

"Why didn't you come to the campaign meeting yesterday?"

She looks at me, her brows slightly furrowed in a frown. "Didn't you hear me when I told you one of the directors in the department quit? The VP shifted all his assignments between the two of us that remain, and seeing as how Bill pulls the good ol' boys club card ninety-five percent of the time, I've had to do most of the work on top of my own. I've barely left my office in days." Her eyes search mine, and I see it instantly when it clicks.

"I wasn't avoiding you, Matt. I promise."

I take the first real breath I've taken all day—hell, all week— the stress of not knowing what I'd be walking into here causing me to worry.

She gets up and walks around her desk over to her office door. I watch her every movement, memorizing the lines of her body and lusting after her delicious curves in her uptight business suit. If she thinks those suits hide what she's got underneath, she's sorely mistaken. If anything, knowing what she's got under there makes those suits even more attractive to me.

She closes her door, the click of the lock thundering in the room and sending all the blood in my body straight to my dick.

She walks slowly back to me until I'm looking up into her bright blue eyes. Her makeup is light and natural, but her blush makes it look like her cheeks are flushed, and it sends my head thinking back to all the times we've hooked up in the past couple of months. I reach out and grab her hand, pulling it to my mouth and kissing the inside of her wrist.

"If you want to be done with me, you're sending the wrong message," I tell her quietly.

"I don't want to be done with you," she whispers.

My gaze slides up her body until I reach her eyes again. My

voice is gruff when I speak, "Good, because I'm not ready to be done either."

She smiles and then takes me completely by surprise when she straddles me, her hands gripping my hair. She pulls my mouth to hers in a kiss that nearly breaks down every last wall I have. I don't know how she does it, but she fucking consumes me. I wrap my arms around her, holding her as close to my body as I possibly can.

Our kiss is heated and hungry, our want and need for each other made clear with this one physical connection. I reach my arm out to her desk and slide the remaining Chinese containers to the side, then lift her up and place her butt on the edge. Without breaking my lips from hers, I start to fiddle with the button on her pants.

She moans deeply into my mouth when I pull the zipper down and then slide them over her hips, taking her panties as well.

She barely breaks our kiss, while her hands instantly go to my jeans. "I need you inside me."

I smile against her mouth, my heart soaring that she's as affected by this as I am. That she wants me as much as I want her.

As soon as she gets my pants undone, I grab a condom from my pocket and then push them and my boxer briefs down to my knees.

When I see her hand reach out to grip my dick, I quickly grab her wrist to stop her. "If you touch me now, I'll come like a fucking sixteen-year-old virgin."

She giggles but pulls her hand back. Thank God, because I wasn't joking. I'm so hot for her, I think I might nut the second I get inside her. I pull the condom on, then slide my fingers over her to make sure she's ready for me. She lets out a needy moan, and I pull my fingers away from her slick center.

I lick her off my fingers, wishing I could really taste her the way I want to, but I'm way too needy to take my time with her right now.

"Damn, that's hot," she whispers, her eyes glued to my fingers.

I smirk at her, then line up my cock with her warm, wet heat and slide home. I'm sure I could come up with a football metaphor—a touchdown, I reach her endzone, all that crap— but in this moment, sliding home feels most appropriate because she's quickly becoming a constant in my life. She makes me feel grounded and whole in a way I never have before.

It scares the shit out of me, but I won't let that stop me from taking everything she'll give me. I hate not talking to her, not fucking her, not seeing that adorable blush she gets when she's shy or embarrassed or turned on. I want to soak in every moment with her.

We both come quickly, our desire for each other driving us faster toward our release than either of us were fully prepared for. After we clean up and put her desk back to rights, I bring up the other reason I stopped by today.

"Are you going to Jack and Paige's wedding this weekend?" She nods. "You?"

"Yeah. The whole team was invited."

"I figured." She clears her throat and looks down at her desk nervously before looking back at me. "My dad will be there."

It hits me then that even though she's confessed her darkest secret to me, nothing's really changed.

We aren't anything real. At least, not to her.

"Right," I nod. "Okay, so I'll stay on the opposite side of the room from you then."

"Matt," she says with a mix of scolding and begging for my understanding.

I wish I did understand what was going on—both in her head and mine.

"It doesn't have to be like that. I mean, we work together on the campaign, so it's not like we'd completely avoid each other," she says.

"I just can't dance with you or touch you."

She looks at me, her eyes filled with regret, and then shakes her head, confirming that what her family thinks and wants still rules her life and probably always will.

She'd never choose me over them.

I mean, who am I except an easy fuck, a simple rebound after her broken engagement.

The thought leaves me feeling more gutted than I'm prepared to show her, so instead I just make my way to the door.

"Matt," she calls out.

My hand rests on the handle, but my body turns toward her.

When our eyes connect, she whispers, "I'm sorry."

My heart cracks, and I wish she would've let me go before delivering her final blow. I offer a simple nod and walk out, unwilling to turn back toward the only woman I've ever wanted, who clearly doesn't want me.

TWENTY-THREE

Nikki

The stunning display of twinkling lights, cream and pale pink flowers, and gold filigree on the arch at the end of the aisle screams elegance. I watch the various football players mingling before finding their seats. I recognize each and every one of them, but none of them are the one I'm actually desperate to see.

I hate how Matt left my office the other day. He tried to hide it, but I could see the disappointment, and maybe even hurt, in his gaze before he walked out.

I'd give anything to take it away, but I don't know how to change something that's been so ingrained in me for the past twenty years.

I don't want to be this person. But at the same time, I still don't want to disappoint my parents.

More than ever, I can't stop thinking about what my life could look like if I pursued the things that interested me instead of just going along with my parents' wishes.

But thinking about that is a lot easier than *doing* it.

"How do those seats look, honey?" I hear my mom's sweet,

melodic voice right behind me and turn to see her and my dad looking at three seats on the left.

Jack and Paige put a sign out letting people know there was no bride or groom side for the seating, but that we're all family here, so to sit wherever we want.

"They look great, Mom." I offer her a small smile that doesn't reach my eyes and let her and my dad pass in front of me. I discreetly look around again, hoping I'll catch a glance of the man who's consumed all my thoughts. My gaze passes over a group of women, but then I quickly do a double take when I realize what they're gawking at, or I should say whom.

Matt stands in the middle of the group looking delicious in a fitted navy blue suit, his light sandy-brown hair perfectly styled to look slightly disheveled. My heart aches at the sight of his charismatic smile—the one he displays when he's in player mode.

A flighty blonde—okay, maybe she's not flighty, but in my head she is—places her hand on his arm seductively and pushes her chest out in a way that accentuates her lush cleavage. My cheeks heat, and jealousy spreads through me like a wildfire.

What's worse, he doesn't move her arm away. In fact, he leans down and says something in her ear causing her smile to grow. A sharp pain shoots through my chest, nearly stealing the breath from my lungs.

Except, what right do I have to be jealous?

We aren't anything.

Not really.

Right?

Emotion clogs my throat because I wish desperately that I could walk over to the horde of women and claim him.

"Nikki?" I turn to see my dad who's already taken his seat next to my mom. "You gonna join us?"

I nod and then briefly glance back to Matt and his harem.

His eyes lock with mine, and I watch his carefully composed smile falter slightly before he looks away and continues flirting.

When I sit down next to my parents, my stomach is in knots.

A part of me understands what he's doing—this is the persona he's known for and he's keeping up appearances—but a bigger part of me wishes he weren't doing it at all. That he could be here with me.

I look over at my parents who are talking about how beautiful the venue is and remind myself why I'm putting myself through this misery—I need to make them happy.

I manage to fight the urge to look for Matt throughout the beautiful ceremony. When Paige and Jack say their vows, I finally let the tears I've been holding back slide down my cheeks under the pretense of how beautiful their vows to each other are. Which they are, but I'm really crying because while I'm sitting here watching them promise each other forever, I keep wishing I could have something real with Matt.

I want him to be mine—not just for fun or for sex, but for real.

I chew my lip and look back at my parents who are smiling at the couple at the altar. I face forward again, wishing harder than I ever have that things were different.

TWENTY-FOUR

Matt

I stare at the back of Nikki's head, wishing she'd look at me. It gutted me to see the pain in her eyes when I caught her watching me flirt with a group of women before the wedding. I was already feeling a little sick at the act, but that moment made me feel like the lowest scum of the earth.

The fact she hasn't looked at me since isn't lost on me.

Was she as affected by that moment as I was?

"You're going to burn a hole in her head if you keep staring," Luke whispers next to me. He drops his voice a little lower, "Not to mention what Denton will do to you if he sees you eyeing his daughter."

Yeah, I'm well aware that Coach is a major roadblock in me getting what I want right now. Just not the way Luke thinks.

"Why don't you worry about your own issues," I whisper back and look pointedly at the redhead sitting next to him. He says she's just his new roommate, that he's doing a favor for his best friend from back home, but I call bullshit. I know sexual tension when I see it, and you could practically cut the sexual tension between these two with a knife.

He frowns at me and turns back to the wedding ceremony

happening in front of us, his shoulders stiff and his body tense. I would feel bad, but if he's going to call me out, I'm going to return the favor.

I watch as the ceremony goes on. Jack and Paige are what any sane person would call couple goals, but I'm so tied in knots over Nikki I can't focus on the whole reason we're all here. I continue to stare at her from the corner of my eye, silently willing her to look at me.

She doesn't.

Her head dips, and I watch her dig around in her purse before she pulls out a tissue and delicately blots it under her eyes. My chest tightens. Why is she crying?

I subtly look around and notice quite a few people are crying and smiling, and I realize I just missed the vows. Except, even from my seat behind her and on the opposite side of the aisle, I can see enough of her profile to know she's not smiling.

I don't think those were happy tears.

I ache to go over to her and ask her what's wrong, to hold her hand in mine and offer her whatever comfort I can, but then I see her look over at her parents and I'm reminded all over again about why we're in this current predicament.

Because she can't stop being the perfect daughter.

I get why she does it—in fact, I understand her now in a way I never did before, and it all makes perfect sense—but that doesn't change how much I hate it. How much I wish she'd ask for what she wants.

How much I wish she'd want me.

The ceremony ends when Jack gives Paige a kiss bordering on indecent. They both pull back, smiling at each other like it's the best day of their life.

I look at Nikki and wonder what that feels like.

I swore I'd never fall in love with anyone, not after all the shit my mom put my dad and me through. And yet, here I am, wishing I was here with one woman, feeling sick to my stomach when I flirt with other women, and wondering what it would be like to kiss Nikki in front of our family and friends.

I shake the thought immediately from my mind, a little freaked out it even went there.

I stand, offering a small smile when Jack and Paige make their way down the aisle, bright wide smiles lighting up their faces, followed by Max Donnelly and Gina Rodrigo who were the best man and maid of honor, respectively. As they pass, I look back over at Nikki and catch her gaze. Our gazes lock onto each other, and I fight the urge to make my way to her.

I wish I could wipe away the hurt I see in her eyes. She looks beside her, her dad bending down and talking in her ear. She nods and ducks her head, joining the rest of the guests as they usher themselves out of the venue toward the reception area. When she passes by me, she gives me the briefest look, but that one look is all I need to know she's as tied up in knots over this as I am.

At least I'm not alone.

TWENTY-FIVE

Nikki

The reception is just as elegant as the wedding ceremony was, except everything feels more laid-back. I see Wolves' players dancing with their dates or taking shots at the bar in celebration.

Jack and Paige make the rounds, both glowing and happy and in love. Envy flashes through me, different than the spike of jealousy I felt when I watched those women fawn all over Matt before the wedding ceremony.

No, this envy is buried in the fact that I want what they have. They're so incandescently in love with each other. When they look at each other, there's an openness and trust that's obvious to everyone around them.

I've never had that with anyone. Well...I hadn't until Matt. Tears sting my eyes, but I fight them back and look over at my parents as they take their seats at our assigned table. My skin prickles with awareness, and when I glance up my gaze catches on Matt's like two magnets instantly drawn to each other. My heart beats steadily in my chest, warming at the idea of being wrapped in his arms.

The ache to be near him is immense, to the point where I'm just about to cave and go over to him—I'll make an excuse to my parents later—when the buxom blonde from earlier walks up to him. His eyes pull from mine to drop down to hers, and it's like a bucket of ice has been poured over me. I feel cold, and really, I only have myself to blame.

I thought I knew what I was getting into when I decided to be fuck buddies with a player like Matt, but in the past couple of weeks it's become clear he's not the guy he always pretends to be.

I don't know if that makes his sudden switch back to that guy better or worse.

Okay, it's worse. It's so much worse.

His eyes snap back to mine, something in them I'm afraid to name. The blonde is still clearly talking to him, but he doesn't look away from me, silently pleading to me with his eyes.

Pleading for what, I have no idea.

He's not supposed to mean anything, so why does this whole situation make me feel like someone's pouring salt on a fresh wound?

I look away, feeling my willpower to stay away from him waning and not willing to compete with buxom Barbie.

My dad turns to me. "How are you doing, honey?"

I look at him, trying to gauge if he's caught on to how my thoughts—and eyes—keep going to Matt. "What do you mean?"

"He means about the wedding," my mom says. "We were worried this would be hard for you after everything with Anthony." Her voice is kind and sympathetic, but it still grates on my nerves. We've hardly talked about Anthony since I told them why we broke up. I finally confessed to them about his infidelity to get them to stop asking if I was sure we couldn't work it out.

Yeah, I was sure.

"I'm fine," I say, adjusting my napkin in my lap and playing with my silverware to keep myself from having to look at them. "Honestly, it was probably for the best." I look up at Jack and

Paige who are laughing with a group of older couples. "We never loved each other like that."

My dad's hand settles softly on top of mine. "You'll have that someday, honey."

I offer him a small smile, and once again my eyes have a mind of their own and slide to the man behind him and across the room. Why can't I stop thinking about Matt when people say this stuff to me?

I'm relieved to see blonde Barbie is nowhere near him. Instead, he's talking to Luke Carter. My mom pulls my attention away from them and starts talking to me about work and how proud of me she is, especially since there's talk I might get promoted soon.

My gut churns at the idea. I'm exceptionally good at my job, but at the end of every day I feel drained and tired.

With all the other changes happening in my life, I guess it shouldn't come as a surprise to me that now I'm second-guessing my job. I got into marketing because—you guessed it—my parents thought I'd be good at it. And they were right. My dad was able to get me an interview with the Wolves straight out of college and I've worked there ever since.

But I don't love it. Most days lately, I don't even like it. Three months ago, if someone had offered me the promotion, I would've taken it in a heartbeat. But a lot has changed in three months. I'm no longer entirely content with just being the docile robot I've grown into.

And yet, you're here ignoring Matt because you know it would make your parents unhappy if you were seen together.

My shoulders sag at the thought. Maybe I haven't come as far as I hoped.

The catered dinner gets served and tastes like cardboard in my mouth, although I'm sure to everyone else it's delicious. Conversation flows but feels stilted. Speeches are given, laughs are had, but I feel like I'm watching it all happen to someone else, my thoughts so distracted and the war inside me raging on unbeknownst to those around me. On the outside, I'm composed, controlled, and poised. On the inside, I'm a mess.

The only person who's ever been able to calm the storm inside me is across the room, laughing with his friends. Although his smile never quite reaches his eyes, so maybe he's struggling as much as I am.

After the cake is cut, my dad turns to me. "Your mom and I are going to duck out. You ready to go?"

"Actually, I think I'll stay."

He frowns at me. "You sure?"

I nod. "Yeah, I'm going to hang out with Cassie and Max."

His brow is still furrowed in uncertainty, but he offers a small nod and kisses me on the forehead. My mom gives me a quick hug and then they head out of the room.

The moment they turn the corner and are out of sight, I feel his presence behind me.

Heat consumes my body, sending goose bumps up and down my arms.

"Do you have any idea how fucking gorgeous you look?" he asks, his voice husky and filled with the same want currently setting my body aflame.

I turn around, my shoulders grazing his chest in the process because he's standing so close.

His bright blue eyes are darker than normal, the longing in them so intense it steals the breath from my chest. If I thought he looked good from far away, he looks damn near edible up close. Why does he have to be so impossibly handsome? How is a woman supposed to resist him?

"I want to kiss you so badly," he whispers so only I can hear. His words slide through me, and the weight that's been bearing down on me since I got to this wedding finally lifts.

"Ditto," I say quietly. Our eyes are locked on each other, and I'm certain everyone in the room can tell there's something going on between us. Funny enough, now that my parents aren't here, I don't particularly care. I'm dying to touch him, to kiss him, to mark him as mine.

Even if he's only mine temporarily.

He holds his hand up. "Dance with me?" he asks softly.

I don't hesitate. I place my hand in his, and a bright smile lights up his whole face—his real smile—his eyes crinkling in the corners.

"I'd love to," I say.

He pulls me toward the dance floor and grins at the DJ who transitions it to a slow song.

I give him a *did you plan this* look?

He smiles and offers a carefree shrug before pulling me close, our bodies touching everywhere between our knees and our necks.

As our bodies sway to the mellow rhythm, I soak in the warmth and comfort of finally being wrapped in his strong arms.

"I've missed you all day," I whisper, letting my vulnerability show because I can't hide myself from him.

He leans back slightly as his eyes search mine, his expression serious and open before he leans down, his lips grazing my ear and sending a bolt of lust straight to my core as he whispers, "Ditto."

A soft smile fills my face, and he pulls back just enough for our gazes to lock, a silent conversation flowing between us.

No one else exists.

It's just the two of us and this song. My heart is full and content for the first time since he walked out of my office. I want to bask in this moment for as long as possible.

In the back of my mind, a little voice whispers that we're being reckless. It's blatantly obvious there's something more going on between us now. We used to think the worst of each other, and now we couldn't be any closer unless he was actually inside me.

But I ignore the voice because Matt makes me feel seen and heard. He knows more about me than any man ever has.

I'm not ready to move away from him.

I'm not ready to let him go.

But all good things come to an end—I should know that better than anyone.

You can't always get what you want.

TWENTY-SIX

Matt

Nikki's bright blue eyes feel like they're burrowing into my soul and taking up permanent residence there.

She makes me feel something I've never felt before. All day long, I've ached to hold her like this, and even though I know it's reckless to be this close to each other in front of everyone, I couldn't care any less than I do right now.

Because with Nikki in my arms, everything else fades. She's all that exists. She's all that matters.

It's terrifying, and yet, also freeing.

She makes me feel a level of contentment I don't think I've ever experienced, and hell if I'm going to stop it.

Her eyes are saying things I know her mouth never will, but I'll take it all the same, because in this moment it's clearer than ever that we're feeling the same thing. Today's been hard on both of us—pretending there's nothing between us when we've wanted nothing more than to be locked in each other's arms like we are now.

Every time that damn blonde hunted me down, I wished I could pull Nikki to my side and show the blonde I was taken.

Because I am.

I belong to Nikki now. Whether she is ready to admit it or not, it's where we are. We belong to each other.

I'm hers and she's mine.

I'm elated at the realization and feel like I just broke free from the emotional chains that have weighed me down for the last seventeen years. Chains I swore I didn't want to break free from, but now that they're gone, I never want to go back.

I don't want to go back to my life before Nikki.

I slide my thumb across the apple of her cheek, watching her eyes close and hearing her soft hum. Her eyes open slowly and the heat there has me wishing we were truly alone.

I'm just about to suggest we get out of here when Luke dances close to us, his roommate, Emma, in his arms—not as scandalously as Nikki in mine, but I'm still not convinced there's nothing going on with those two—and interrupts our moment.

"Matt," he hisses at me.

It takes a second for the note of panic to register, but I pull my gaze away from Nikki and look over at Luke. His eyes are wide with worry and he gestures his head behind me at the same time that I feel Nikki go stiff in my arms and let out a soft gasp.

I look down at her and see her gaze locked on something behind me. When I turn around, I understand the panic. Her dad—my coach—is standing at their table, her mother's shawl held loosely in his hands.

His gaze is glued to us, the rage in his eyes undeniable.

Fuck me.

Nikki pulls out of my arms, and I reluctantly let her, knowing if I let her go now, it's possible I'm going to lose her for good, but not sure what else to do.

"Dad," she whispers, taking a tentative step in his direction. He shakes his head once and she stops.

"Go get in the car, Nikki. I'm taking you home." His voice is cold and lifeless, sending chills down my spine. In all my time with the Wolves, I've never heard this tone.

"Now, Nikki."

Her body doesn't move. I can practically see the war she's having internally, and I'd give anything to make this easier for her, but I'm struggling to process everything myself.

Finally, she walks slowly back to the table, grabbing her purse and moving to stand in front of him.

"It was just a dance," she says softly, trying to control the situation.

Oh, my sweet, little control freak. She's not going to be able to talk her way out of this one. Even I can see that.

Her dad's eyes are still blazing into mine.

"Car, Nikki. Now."

She turns back to me, and seeing the pain in her eyes makes me feel like I've just been stabbed repeatedly in the heart.

I want to tell her everything will be fine, but I can't help thinking it would be a lie.

Dread slowly seeps over me, starting at my feet and moving swiftly up my body.

I have a feeling nothing is going to be fine after this.

I watch the gentle sway of her hips as she walks out of the room, away from me. Disappointment now joins the dread, swirling viciously inside me.

Once again, she's chosen her usual path.

My heart sinks in my chest. Did I honestly think she'd choose me over her family?

I'm nothing to her.

I walk toward Denton, noticing several people have stopped

and are watching, mostly players who know about Denton's rule against dating his daughter. Fortunately, our little scene hasn't disturbed the rest of the reception.

While it's felt life altering to me, only a handful of people have even noticed the hostility vibrating from my coach.

I don't speak, because I know I can't say anything to defend my actions here, and I refuse to regret my time with Nikki.

I'll never regret a second with her.

All I can do is prepare myself to be lambasted by a man I have admired and worked my ass off for.

"Fischer, I'm going to make your life a living hell if you ever come near my daughter again," he says, his voice so low and filled with rage I have to lean forward to catch it all.

"I still have another month on the campaign."

"Luther can take over."

I clear my throat. "No offense, sir, but that's Nikki's campaign. I don't think she'd appreciate you dictating her job for her."

He seethes as he speaks through clenched teeth, "You know nothing about my daughter! Stay the fuck away from her, Fischer. I mean it. She's not some plaything for you to toy with."

I see red and sneer at him, keeping my voice low, "You think I don't know that?" I lean into him. "Nikki isn't a plaything at all. It's not like that."

He gets in my face, our noses practically touching. "I'll tell you what it is—nothing! Whatever you were doing with Nikki is done. Stay away from her. If I hear you've seen her outside of a professional capacity, then your time with the Wolves will be done. Do you understand me?"

He doesn't wait for my response, simply turns around and storms out of the room. I watch his retreating figure until he rounds the corner and disappears.

Luke pats me on the shoulder. "You okay?"

I shake my head. "Not even close."

I think I just lost the best thing I ever had. Nikki will end things after this. I know it as sure as I know every play in our playbook.

Nikki will never choose me over her family.

TWENTY-SEVEN

Nikki

The text emblazoned on my phone taunts me and causes my stomach to twist.

Me: I can't do this with you anymore.

Matt: Yeah, I figured.

That's it. He didn't fight me on it at all.

I should be happy. We're ending this with no drama. It's a clean break.

Except it doesn't feel that way.

It feels like someone is beating a hammer on my heart even though it's already bloody, bruised, and broken. It hurts so much worse than when Anthony cheated on me.

Which should tell me something. But like the good daughter I've trained myself to be, I still go forward with my parents' wishes.

I'll never forget the look my dad shot me through the rearview mirror when he got in the car on Saturday after Jack and Paige's wedding.

He made it clear, in no uncertain terms, I was not to see Matt anymore. He even tried to put his foot down on my continued work on the campaign, suggesting Luther could take over, but I used what little backbone I was able to muster and told him the campaign was my job and there was only a month left. I could handle working professionally with Matt for a month.

Now I sit here on Cassie's couch, staring at my phone screen, holding back tears, and wishing he'd fight me on this. That he wouldn't let me end it so abruptly.

When an hour passes and still no more texts from him come, I finally let my tears fall free, embracing my heartache and knowing I'll only be able to allow myself this time to feel the pain of this. Once I go back to work on Monday, I'll have to be the Nikki everyone expects—cool, composed, and in control.

But tonight, I get to be me, the me no one but Matt and Cassie have ever really seen—confused, broken, and impossibly lonely.

For the first time in my life, I truly question if my plan to constantly please my parents is really worth it. All the sacrifices I've made throughout my life—giving up art after that fateful art show even though I still loved it, staying in LA instead of going to school in Boston like I wanted to, getting engaged to Anthony, going for marketing instead of graphic design. Every choice I've made has been based on what my parents wanted, all to make up for the guilt I felt over my sister's death. Where has that ever gotten me?

Here.

It's gotten me here, twenty-eight years old, sitting alone in someone's else's house because I don't have one of my own, wanting a man I can never really have unless I'm willing to epically piss off my parents, and feeling lonelier than I have in my entire life.

My shoulders slouch as I slump back in my office chair, looking out the window and taking in the overcast LA weather. LA is already a naturally smoggy city, but at least when it's sunny, it doesn't seem quite so dreary.

This overcast weather, though, matches how I'm feeling, so I guess I can't be upset by it. I rub my temples, hoping to ease the headache that's been brewing underneath the surface for the last hour. My tight bun isn't helping matters. I could wear my hair down, but I never do, and the thought of wearing it down now just makes me think about how much Matt loves when I let my hair flow loosely around my shoulders.

The tension in my shoulders strengthens, further encouraging the pounding in my head. There's a burning behind my already bloodshot and swollen eyes, but I refuse to cry at work. I have a reputation to maintain. I can fall apart later, when I'm in the safety of my bedroom and not at risk of someone walking in to see me having a breakdown.

Monday slogs on, slower than usual. My meetings feel endless, and the fluorescent lights that illuminate every room only continue to add to my aching head and tender eyes.

I work through lunch, since my appetite is nonexistent anyway. Sometime in the afternoon, Luther comes in to drop off the proofs from Matt's latest shoot on my desk.

He sits in the chair across from my desk, instead of leaving like I expect him to.

"Okay, spill," he says.

Confused, I ask, "Spill what?"

"You look like someone ran over your dog, and you've been less"—he gestures with his hand to encompass my whole body—"less, *you*."

I frown. "What does that mean?"

"Hun, you know I love you, but normally you have a very stone-cold exterior. You don't take shit from anyone and you're always in control. Your hair is always perfectly in place, your makeup on point, and your outfits professional without a wrinkle in sight.

"Today, however, you have a million flyaways, your eye makeup is a mess, and your suit jacket doesn't match your pants. If you're trying to be a trendsetter, it's not working. But I suspect it's because your head was somewhere else this morning. If this is delayed mourning over Anthony, that man is *so* not worth it, sweetie. He's a cockroach and not worth any tears."

My already tender heart lodges in my throat. God, do I really look that bad? I thought I was hiding it so well. Shit, did other people notice? Thinking back on the various meetings I've attended today, I can't recall anyone giving me weird looks, but then again, my head's not been in it all day.

My cheeks heat with embarrassment, which of course Luther catches immediately. I want to be mad that he's so observant, but I'm more focused on trying to hold back my tears. Everything feels so fragile right now, like I'm juggling delicate ceramic plates in the air and watching one by one as they come crashing down around me.

Luther reaches out and places his hand on mine, which is frozen to my desk. "Nikki, what's going on with you?" he asks delicately.

Oh God, and now he's not even being snarky or sassy. I've broken Luther!

That snaps me out of my frozen state, and I bury my face in my hands, feeling the heat of mortification on my cheeks and the wetness of my tears on my fingers.

Warm arms envelop me and pull me from my chair. With my hands still covering my face, I let go. I let out all the emotional turmoil I've been feeling since Saturday night.

Despite covering my face, when I pull back from Luther, I see a very noticeable wet spot on his shoulder from my tears. Placing my hand over it, I whisper, "I'm sorry about your shirt."

He shrugs. "It's just a shirt. It can be replaced. Now talk to me." The worry is clear in his tone, but I don't even know where to start. I haven't even talked to Cassie about any of this. Unable to find the words, I just shake my head.

I should've known better. Luther is relentless. Tipping my face back with his well-manicured hands, he says, "Nikki, I've never seen you like this. You need to talk about it. Trust me. Do I need to call Cassie in here?"

Pulling out of his embrace, I sit defeated back in my chair. "I...I don't know what to do anymore."

Luther sits on the edge of my desk. "About what?"

Shrugging, I whisper, "Everything."

"I'm going to need you to be a little more specific."

My head falls back against my chair, my eyes closing as I try to figure out where to begin.

"I was seeing someone. It wasn't supposed to be anything serious."

He nods knowingly, his look telling me he knows exactly who I'm talking about. "But it was?"

I nod. "He's so different than I thought he was. He's kind, caring, compassionate. He makes me laugh, challenges me to try new things, and pushes me out of my comfort zone, way out of my comfort zone, but it felt so freeing."

"Felt? What happened?"

"I had to end it. He's not someone my parents would approve of."

Luther rolls his eyes. "Well, they don't have to date him. You do."

I shake my head, wishing I could explain everything to him, but I can't. "I can't disappoint them," I whisper.

Instead of disappointing my parents, I'm now faced with Luther's disappointment. I can see it clearly on his face.

"Don't, okay?" I beg him. "Don't tell me I need to put myself first. I hear it enough from Cassie. I finally listened to her, and look where it got me? I've never been so miserable. So whether or not you agree with my reasons, I need you to support them and just help me get over this. I *cannot* fall apart at work."

He bites his lip, fighting the words I can practically see in his eyes. Finally, he nods and recommends an ice pack for my eyes plus chocolate for my heartache. We agree to have a "girls'" night with Cassie so they can help me wallow properly, something I've never done over a guy before. After we make our plans, Luther goes to leave so he can get his own work done.

He stops at the threshold of my office. "Did it ever occur to you that you might be miserable because it was actually real?"

His parting words slam into me, and instead of waiting for a response, he walks out of my office, leaving me to process them on my own.

I turn back to the window and the overcast sky outside, Luther's words on an endless loop in my head, until the only words I'm hearing are *it was real*.

TWENTY-EIGHT

Matt

I take another sip of my beer and look around the crowded bar where Luke and I are hanging out tonight. He's avoiding his roommate, Emma, and I'm avoiding the thoughts that keep bombarding me whenever I have a minute to myself.

While a part of me wishes I could drown my sorrows, I refuse to become my dad. Besides, I have a Wolves event tomorrow I have to go to as part of the campaign, and I'm going to need a clear head if I'm going to manage staying away from Nikki.

And not let her see how much not being with her is killing me.

"Matt, did you hear a word I just said?"

I glance over at my friend, who's staring at me, one brown brow arched. "Sorry, what'd you say?"

He shakes his head. "What's going on with you? I haven't seen you like this, like, ever. Hell, if I didn't know any better, I'd say you were hung up on a woman."

I just stare at him, not refuting his suggestion because it would be a lie, and I don't lie to my friends.

His eyes go wide, and his carefree grin drops. "Oh shit," he says in a hushed whisper. "You are, aren't you? Holy shit, someone finally got under your skin. Who is she?"

"It doesn't matter now," I mutter, taking another swig of my beer.

He studies me. "Based on the look on your face, I'd say it does." His face pales. "Wait a minute, this isn't about Nikki Denton, is it?"

Again, I don't respond.

Luke runs his fingers through his already disheveled hair. "Fuck, dude, you *cannot* be hung up on Denton's daughter. She's a big no-go. I figured you guys might have a thing based on what happened at the wedding, but I thought it was just a quick, easy lay for you."

I shake my head. "She's different."

"Uh, yeah, she's off-limits. Like, never-should've-touched-her-in-the-first-place off-limits. What the hell were you thinking?"

I shrug. Fuck if I know what I was thinking when I agreed to that stupid fuck buddies plan. I was thinking with my dick like I usually do when it comes to women. I never in a million years thought my heart would get involved.

It never has before.

But what I told Luke is true. She's different. She's so much more than anyone gives her credit for.

She's smart as a whip, funny, kind, and more passionate than that tight hair bun of hers suggests.

I just wish she were brave enough to finally stand up to her parents.

Brave enough to be with me.

Answering Luke's question, I respond, "It doesn't matter anymore. It's over now."

He watches me carefully. "Was it because Denton saw you

dancing with his daughter? Cause if looks could kill, you'd definitely be dead already."

"Yeah. She's a good little princess, so she decided not to fuck the team playboy anymore."

My stomach churns at the words before they even leave my mouth, but I can't take them back now. They aren't true. Not really. I know Nikki is probably letting this eat at her, maybe more than even I am. But there is still an element of truth to it. She'll never stop being the good daughter who does what her parents want and expect, even when it means sacrificing her own happiness.

I take another sip of my beer, starting to understand my dad a little better. There's a certain appeal to getting wasted and not having to think about how much this fucking hurts. But I refuse to be that guy.

I just need to find someone else. There are hundreds—hell, thousands—of women who I could have in this city. Fuck, I bet I could find at least half a dozen who would suck me off in the bar bathroom with just a glance from me.

Somehow the idea doesn't appeal like it used to. Instead, it sends a sharp pain to my chest and another twist in my stomach. The idea of hooking up with someone else feels like cheating.

Which is stupid since Nikki and I weren't even really together. We were just fucking.

Yeah, okay, keep telling yourself that.

I finish the last of my beer and then stand, patting Luke on the back. "I'm gonna head home. I'll see you tomorrow."

He squints at me, clearly trying to assess if I'm okay.

I'm not, but it doesn't matter. I have a job to do, and I'm not going to let my team down.

He must see enough that suggests I'll be fine, because he offers me a pat on the back and then goes back to his own drink.

When I get home, I go straight to my gym room and work

out for two hours until my body and mind are so exhausted I can hardly keep my eyes open.

Just what I was going for.

I fall like a brick onto my bed, asleep as soon as my head hits the pillow.

The stadium is busy with kids and families. We have a game tonight, but there's a family event beforehand for a group of kids from a local hospital who have all recovered from cancer. A bunch of players came together to start a foundation to help support the pediatric cancer ward, and now every year we invite them for a free game, with a meet and greet before and all the Wolves' swag their little hearts desire.

These kids have overcome so much, it feels like the least we could do. I got involved in the early stages but remained a silent partner. It didn't exactly fit my playboy image, and I wasn't sure parents would be happy having me involved, with how notorious I am for fooling around.

Well, *was*.

A bald boy who looks about five walks up to me, his smile big and showing off his two missing teeth.

"You're Matt Fischer," he says with a hint of awe and wonder that still feels surreal, no matter how long I play professionally.

It's also a humbling reminder that kids look up to me. Maybe it wouldn't be such a bad idea to change my image. Maybe something good can come out of my heartache.

Like she's been called by my thoughts, Nikki appears on the sidelines, her pantsuit looking sharp.

On closer inspection, I notice her hair is pulled back in a low bun at the nape of her neck, instead of her usual tight knot high on her head. She offers a smile to the family clearly talking to her, but her eyes have lost their shine and her smile never reaches them.

I take two steps forward before I register what my body's doing and stop myself. I can't go to her.

My chest tightens and my stomach clenches, seeing her so close and yet knowing she's so far away from me. Farther than just this field.

She must sense me watching her because her eyes look up and land on mine. What little smile there was drops completely from her face. Her usually bright blue eyes look pained. Her gaze searches mine like she's trying to tell me something or get me to understand something.

All I understand is that she chose her parents' happiness, and clearly that choice is costing both of us.

I'm sure she can see the pain on my face. I'm not hiding it from her. I don't want to hide anything from her anymore.

Standing here, I'm torn between wanting this damn campaign to be over so I don't have to see her all the time and wanting it to never end because it's my only opportunity to be close to her now.

I turn around and start walking over to another group of players, overthinking the Nikki situation like a teenage girl crushing on a dude who's way out of her league.

Feelings suck.

How do guys like Jack and Will handle this?

I've seen them with their women, and they make it look so easy. I know it's not, but still, they make it look like the best thing in the whole world.

Like loving their women finally brought them to life.

All it's brought me is pain and suffering.

I stop dead in my tracks. Wait a minute. Am I...am I *in love?*

Is that what this god-awful pain in my chest is? Is this why things feel so different with Nikki? Because I love her?

Fuck me.

The event drags on after that—my revelation making me feel like I'm in a fog. I can feel Nikki wherever I go on the field. At one point the photographer asks us both to come over so we can give our opinions on a couple of shots that'll be used for my campaign.

The air thickens the closer we get, the invisible string that seems to tether us to each other tightening like a noose around my heart.

I can't tease her like I could before. I can't call her princess because all it'll make me think of now are all the times I used it while I was buried deep inside her.

It feels awkward and uncomfortable. If the photographer can sense it, he doesn't let on.

I come up beside Nikki, her sweet citrus scent hitting my nose and flooding my veins with so much want it nearly topples me over. I press my chest against her shoulder, looking over her at the photographer's display screen. Her breath hitches at the contact.

My pants get tight, and I know I shouldn't but I can't help myself as I graze my fingers against hers, never looking away from the screen.

Her body leans against mine infinitesimally, but it's enough that I notice. I ache to hold her, to grab her hand and storm off this field so I can take her somewhere private and bury myself inside her so deep she can't deny what's between us.

"How do these look to you, Matt?" the photographer asks.

I couldn't care less about the pictures. "They look great."

"Awesome. Nikki, what do you think?"

She makes a noise in her throat causing the photographer to look at her.

"Nikki?"

She audibly swallows and lifts her chin, attempting to be more composed than she really is. "They look good. Are we done here, then?"

The photographer looks back at his screen, nodding. While he yammers on and on about the next steps, I continue to graze my fingers ever so gently against hers. Her breathing gets noticeably shallower and her chest heaves slightly.

The photographer must finish whatever he was saying—I stopped listening a while ago—because he starts walking away. Nikki moves away from me, but I grab her hand to stop her.

"Nikki," I whisper, knowing I sound like a lovesick sap and not giving two shits.

Fuck, I miss her, and it's only been a couple of days.

Her head turns to the side, her eyes downcast, not looking at me but acknowledging my whispered word and the plea behind it.

"I can't," she whispers back, her voice breaking.

A single tear slides down her cheek, confirming she's as broken up about this as I am.

But she still won't choose me.

And it's becoming increasingly clear to me that I'm desperate for her to do just that.

Reluctantly, I pull my fingers back, and she immediate steps forward. Each step away from me takes a piece of my heart with her.

Fuck love.

TWENTY-NINE

Nikki

"You ready for this?"

I don't look over at Cassie sitting in the passenger seat of my car. Instead, I stare out the window at the ostentatious house I used to share with Anthony. This house isn't me at all. The sharp lines of the modern architecture make it look like someone stacked a bunch of metal boxes together, and the garden is hideous with no flowers, just the same green shrubbery roping around the house. A shudder slides through me.

What the hell was I thinking ever agreeing to live here?

On that note, how the hell did I think I would *ever* be happy with Anthony?

A laugh escapes as I realize how much my life has changed in just a few short months. Calm courses through me at the knowledge that I'm not the same woman as the one who walked out of this monstrosity of a house.

I may still have a long way to go to become the woman I want to be, but it's a relief to discover how far I've already come.

"I'm ready." I share a look with Cassie, one that tells her this is still what I want, and a relieved smile crosses her face.

The walk to the front door goes by in a blink. When I enter,

I stop in the foyer and let my gaze wander around, seeing things with a whole new perspective.

I never noticed how beige everything was. Literally. All the colors around the house are different shades of cream, beige, and white, with the only splash of color coming from those ridiculous paintings that look like kindergartners made them rather than artists charging upwards of fifteen thousand dollars.

What the fuck was I thinking becomes a mantra in my head as I walk through each room. Cassie walks quietly behind me, here as moral support for my inevitable encounter with Anthony.

As if he knows I'm thinking about him, Anthony appears around the corner coming from the kitchen.

He looks up from his phone, a cup of coffee suspended on its way to his mouth, his face morphing into one of surprise. "You're here."

"I told you I was coming today." My spine is stiff straight, my body braced for whatever he might throw at me.

He glances down at his phone. "It's barely eight in the morning. I expected you'd come tonight after work."

"I took the day off."

His brow furrows. "You didn't need to do that. You could've come by tonight. I had dinner planned out and everything." He looks behind me and frowns at Cassie. When I peek back at her, she's glaring at him.

It takes everything in me not to laugh.

I turn back to Anthony, my face composed, mostly. By the disapproving frown he now directs toward me, I can tell I'm not hiding my humor as well as I hoped.

Oh well.

He leans forward and lowers his voice. "I was really hoping we could talk about things."

I stare at him curiously, his voice grating on my nerves. Has he always sounded so nasally and pompous?

We were together for over a year. How did I not notice that before? I look at him more carefully, taking in his pointed nose, weak chin, and muddy-brown eyes that seem dull in comparison to the brilliant blue eyes I've stared into so recently.

My heart squeezes painfully in my chest, and I brush the thought aside quickly.

I can't think about Matt right now.

I need to focus on one disaster at a time. And this is one chapter of my life I'm ready to slam closed.

"Anthony, you cheated on me. There's nothing to talk about."

"Babe, it was just that one time. It—"

I cut him off. "Did you think I wouldn't find out about Nadine?"

His jaw goes slack, and his eyes go back and forth between mine, like he's searching to see if my gaze will give away how much I know.

His eyes harden, before he collects his composure and speaks to me in his typical condescending tone, "Babe, that was a long time ago and you'd been so busy and then couldn't go on that romantic trip I'd spent so much time planning."

Is he fucking serious right now?

"I was sick, you fucking douchebag!"

His eyes go wide in surprise and he gapes at me. I hear Cassie snicker behind me. His reaction is pretty humorous, until I realize the reason he's shocked is because this is only the second time I've stood up to him, and that's only if you count leaving him as the first time.

Of course he's shocked. This is completely out of character for the Nikki he knew.

But I'm not that woman anymore. I stand tall, confidence

oozing from my pores as I stare at this pathetic excuse for a man. He can try to gaslight me all he wants, but I'm not going to just sit back and take it.

"We're done, Anthony. There's nothing to discuss. You own the house, and I'm glad for that because"—I look around, disgust covering my features—"this house is fucking hideous. I'm just here for my stuff and then I'll be out of your hair for good."

He stands there frozen in place while I turn around and head up the stairs toward the bedroom I shared with him. I go immediately to my closet, grab all my travel suitcases, and lay them on the bed. We have boxes in the car, but as I look around the room, I realize there's nothing here I want apart from my clothes and some pictures on my dresser, all of which will fit in my suitcases. Nothing else in this house is mine. They're all things Anthony chose.

God, I really didn't have a backbone at all, did I?

To accept this life without a second thought for as long as I did.

I sit heavily on the bed, and my gaze slides across the room, landing on a picture of Nora and me laughing in our bathing suits, our mouths and chins red from the cherry popsicles we'd just eaten. It was taken the summer before she died. While my eyes pore over the picture, my fingers brush across my silver ring.

I did this all wrong.

Nora wouldn't have wanted me to live my life like I have. Instead of being subservient to my parents, she would've wanted me to do anything and everything I ever dreamed of.

To live a big life.

An exceptional life.

While I've never lacked for anything, my life has only ever been mediocre. It's been as bland and boring as these beige walls that are quickly giving me a headache.

A streak of familiar blue infiltrates my thoughts again—Matt's eyes, so vivid it takes my breath away.

My heart sinks into my stomach.

No, I really haven't done any of this right at all.

A knock pulls my attention to the door. Cassie pops her head in. "Need any help?"

I offer her a small smile and a nod. We make quick work of packing up everything from my closet, drawers, and bathroom.

"Is that all?" She sounds surprised I don't want more.

I look around again, already knowing this is the only room that held anything of value. "Yeah, I guess it is."

"Alright then. Are you ready to blow this popsicle stand?" She does a silly happy dance.

I laugh and shake my head at her antics. "Yeah, I'm ready."

And I am.

I'm ready for whatever my future holds.

But even more than that, I'm ready to finally make it *mine*.

I'm so ready.

I've spent the last two weeks not only trying to move on from Matt—from what was only supposed to be sex, yet so obviously became something more—but also trying to get my life together. In some ways, I've excelled.

I finally confronted Anthony and got the rest of my things. I still wish I'd taken a picture of the look on his face when I stood up to him. It was priceless.

I finally moved out of Cassie and Max's place into my own two-bedroom condo in Santa Monica.

But there are still areas of my life where I'm struggling.

Every morning I wake up expecting to feel more like my old self, like Matt hasn't fundamentally shifted my core being.

Every morning I end up missing him more, not less. My heart pleads with me to reunite with him, but I hold steadfast in my decision—no matter how much my heart aches when I think about him, or my lungs burn while I try to breathe, or tears sting my now regularly sleep-deprived eyes.

Although, the more of my life that I take control over, the more I question if I made the right decision in the first place.

I roll out of bed, my bare feet touching the cold hard laminate wood floors in my light and airy bedroom. I slide my feet into my purple slippers nearby and walk over to the oversized chair I put in the corner of the room near the window. I grab the light pink throw blanket resting on the arm of the plush chair and wrap it around my shoulders, hoping it'll warm me up, and knowing even a heater couldn't warm up the cold chill that seems to have permanently seeped into my bones since I ended things with Matt.

Instead of going to the kitchen and starting my day with a cup of coffee, I curl up in the chair and watch the birds flit over the ocean. The view was the main reason I chose this condo. I'm still several blocks from the beach, but every morning, I get to look out and watch the waves crash on the sand.

There's something soothing about watching the waves creep over the sand and then slide back out to sea. The ocean is so vast, it makes my problems seem small, inconsequential in the grand scheme of things.

Even if I feel like I'm constantly drowning from how much I miss him.

It wasn't supposed to be like this.

I wasn't actually supposed to fall for the biggest manwhore in the league. All the women I've seen him with in the past float through my brain, and my stomach lurches at the thought that he's probably already had sex with someone else since I broke things off.

Oh God.

But what did I even expect from him? For him to remain celibate? Please! He could have any woman he wants—and often has. I probably wasn't even the best lay he's ever had.

Ugh, that thought is especially depressing.

On that delightful note, I push myself up from my cozy chair knowing if I don't get moving, I'll never make it to work on time.

The drive to work goes by in a blur, my mind in a haze like it has been for weeks. As I walk down the hall toward my office, I see Luther up ahead pacing in front of my door.

"Luther? Everything okay?"

He looks up quickly. "Where the fuck have you been? You're never late."

I look at the time on my phone and then back at him. "And I'm still not. In fact, I'm ten minutes early."

He shakes his head, his eyes wide, his voice urgent. "Did you forget about the campaign meeting with Matt, his agent, and the GM?"

All the blood drains from my face. "Oh shit," I whisper.

Luther nods his head aggressively. "Oh shit is right. You're twenty minutes late."

I shove him aside and open the door to my office, throwing down my purse and coat and shuffling through the papers on my desk looking for the documents I need.

I slide my fingers through my hair hanging loose around my shoulders, as I try to figure out how I forgot about this meeting.

Because you've been trying to forget about everything Matt related.

Shit. Shit. Shit.

"Nikki, are you feeling okay?"

I don't glance up. "I'm fine. Why?"

Where the hell is that damn document for the last photoshoot of the campaign?

"You're wearing your hair down," I vaguely hear Luther say. "You never wear your hair down."

His words finally register, and I slide my fingers through my hair again, realizing he's right.

Shit, did I even brush my hair when I got ready? I can't remember.

I look up at him, and my eyes must convey my panic because he walks over to me like he's approaching a cornered dog. "Okay, this is fine. Honestly, it has that just-fucked mussed-up look about it, which is very in right now." He pauses, his eyes scanning my body so critically I feel naked. He waves his hand at my body. "Actually, this whole thing you've got going on right now is really working for you. You look hot, girl."

"What?" I choke out.

He nods. "You do. I mean, it doesn't seem like you. Not the composed Nikki I've come to know and love, but I like it."

He looks down at his watch. "Shit, okay, come on, hustle up. We gotta get back in there."

I give up on the document, knowing it's here somewhere, but I'm so flustered it could be right in front of my face and I'd probably miss it.

"Okay, okay, let's go."

Luther and I rush down to the conference room. I stop at the threshold of the room, the sight of Matt's tall frame causing my heart to stutter in my chest. His sandy-brown hair looks disheveled like it did when I would run my fingers through it. I can still practically feel the soft strands against my skin. Luther clears his throat behind me and puts his hand against the small of my back to move me forward.

Matt turns just as Luther's hand rests on my back, and his gaze locks on Luther's hand. Instantly, Matt's brow furrows, his jaw clenches, and his mouth sets in a hard line. His blue eyes shoot to mine, and all the breath leaves my lungs at the accusation in his gaze, and even more so at the hurt lying just underneath.

I look up at Luther and then back at Matt. He couldn't possibly think there's something going on between me and Luther.

Could he?

I subtly offer a shake of my head, hoping he understands what I'm trying to tell him. He looks away, not giving me any signs he got my silent message, and my heart sinks.

I hate this. I hate this with every fiber of my being. I want to scream at him and tell him he's ridiculous if he thinks I could possibly get over him that quickly, while I want to ask in the same breath if his jealousy means he's not hooking up with anyone else yet.

I drag a breath into my deprived lungs, but it's shallow, and the weight of my unrelenting guilt, pain, and uncertainty about everything is crushing.

My gaze works its way around the room, watching everyone else act like everything is business as usual while I sit here silently crumbling into nothing. How did so much change in such a short amount of time?

My eyes slide to the man sitting across the oak table from me, and I know exactly how.

Matt.

Matt changed everything for me. As if he can feel my eyes on him, his own meet mine. I can see so much in those light blues, and I have to actively fight my body from climbing over this table to get to him and wrap him in my arms and never let go.

He breaks away from our silent stare-off, and I feel like someone just turned off all the lights. The darkness isn't new, but when you've seen everything in the light, it feels more brutal.

I try to refocus on the meeting, but my heart's not in it. I don't love this job, even if I'm damn good at it.

Right now, there's not much I love about my life. I love my new apartment, and I love my friends.

That's it.

I think back to the realization I had when I packed up all my things from Anthony's.

Nora wouldn't have wanted this for you.

God, she'd be so furious with me for how I've lived my life. But it's too late to change things now.

Right?

I look over to Matt and find his penetrating gaze already settled on me. I feel the pressure of other eyes and look over to Luther, but my eyes scan the room in the process, and I realize *everyone* is staring at me. My cheeks heat, my blush fortunately hidden beneath my makeup so it's not so noticeable to anyone else.

Luther leans over, whispering quietly, "Are you sure you're okay?"

I clear my throat and nod. Speaking to the room, I say, "Sorry, I missed that last bit."

Our general manager, Richard Mitchell, squints at me. "Are you feeling well, Nikki? I've never known you to be so distracted at work."

I keep my face composed, even though I physically want to crumple in my seat at the hint of censure in his tone.

I put on my business smile, the one that's faker than Rich's wife's boobs. "I'm fine. Thank you for your concern. Now, can someone please summarize what we were just talking about?"

Matt's smooth voice washes over me. "They want to add a

photoshoot with the cheerleaders. They'd like to appeal to the male fans and thought they'd capitalize on my playboy status."

His tone doesn't reveal how he feels about this, and I wish it did. Does he want to be seen as a playboy still? Even though that's not what he is, or at least that's not *all* he is.

I cave and ask, "How do you feel about that?"

He shrugs, but I know him well enough now to see his shrug isn't as carefree as it appears. "I'm here for whatever the team wants me to do." His ice-blue eyes pierce mine. "How do you feel about it?"

"I hate it."

The words are out of my mouth before I even have a chance to think about them. Matt's eyes go wide at the same time I'm sure mine do. I can't believe I just said that out loud.

Luther tries to cover for me while Matt and I continue our stare-off, his gaze full of questions and tinged with hope.

The truth I've been trying to deny for weeks barrels into me. I want him.

I want him for myself, and I'm miserable without him.

Without really thinking about how unprofessional it is, I stand abruptly from my chair, my gaze never leaving Matt's.

"Matt, can I talk to you in my office, please?"

He doesn't look at his agent for permission. He just continues looking at me. My heart lodges in my throat, worried he's going to say no.

Without a word, he stands up and walks to the door. He holds it open and then gestures for me to go through. We walk silently to my office, the air between us vibrating with more longing than I've ever encountered in my entire life.

I open my office door and allow him to walk in ahead of me. The second the door shuts behind me, he spins around and presses me against the door.

Our lips meet before I have a chance to even blink, speak, or think. Our mouths move in that practiced way between lovers, fitting perfectly and moving in just the way we know the other likes. Our tongues join quickly, both of us moaning at finally being connected again.

Instinctively, my hands slide through Matt's hair, and now I'm good and truly consumed by him. I can feel his silky strands on my fingers, smell his manly scent, and taste him on my tongue.

I never want to stop. I don't even know if I can. Being apart was torture, but this contact is pure heaven.

He gently pulls his lips away but leans his forehead against mine, his breath washing over my face with each heavy pant. We're almost panting in sync.

"Fuck, Nikki, what are you doing to me?" he whispers.

"Whatever it is, you're doing it to me too," I whisper back.

He pulls away completely, pacing around my office, while his hands slide through his hair.

"Are you just fucking with me right now? What is this to you?" He gestures between us, his tone angry, but the hurt in his eyes clear as day.

I wonder if he's as scared of this as I am.

Here goes nothing.

"I want you, Matt," I say softly. I feel the sting of tears behind my eyes, but I know he deserves the whole truth. "I'm not ready for my dad to know, but I want you. I want you to be mine because as much as I've tried to fight it, I'm yours."

THIRTY

Matt

Her words are the sweetest thing I've ever heard in my entire life. In the blink of an eye, I have her back in my arms and my lips are molded to hers. She tastes just as sweet as she always has.

Fuck, I've missed her.

She melts into my embrace, her hands wrapping around my neck and her lips moving hungrily against mine. She lets out a soft moan that vibrates through my whole body and sends blood straight to my needy cock.

She pulls back, and I reluctantly let her. Her sky-blue eyes are vulnerable and scared, causing my heart to stall in my chest.

"Are you really okay with keeping this a secret until I'm ready to tell my family?"

"Are you really mine?"

"Yes." She doesn't even hesitate. The word comes out strong and sure.

"Then we can keep it a secret for as long as you need. I just don't want to be apart from you anymore."

"Me either," she says, her gaze locked on my lips. I watch in fascination as her pupils dilate, and her tongue darts out to slide across her lips. She looks hungry—hungry for me—and I can't deny her anything anymore.

I pull her close to me, her soft breasts pressing against my hard chest, and cup her porcelain cheek in my large palm. I lean down and bite her bottom lip playfully, causing a soft smile to pull her lips up at the corners.

Her eyes gleam as she cups my cheek with one of her soft, small hands, her thumb delicately gliding across my cheek. The motion sends another ripple of want pulsing through me, but more than anything I just want to bask in this moment with her.

This is so much more than sex.

It both terrifies me and makes me feel more alive than I've ever been. The words claw at my throat, begging to be let free, but fear holds them back. I've never been so vulnerable with a woman before. With our gazes entwined the same way I know our hearts are, I give her all of me.

"I'm yours," I whisper.

My breath catches in my throat while her eyes search mine. I know she can see the truth there because I'm stripped bare and letting her see it all. I really am hers. She owns me. These past few weeks have made that fact abundantly clear.

I will never belong to anyone other than Nikki Denton.

Her eyes shine with tears, but they're lit up like a damn Christmas tree with happiness. She gets up on her tiptoes and pulls my lips the rest of the way until they meet hers. Our kiss is long and slow, filled with forgiveness for the pain we've caused each other and sweet relief at being together again.

A knock at her door pulls us from our reverie.

"Yeah," she calls out.

"Are you two ever planning to come back? Rich is about to lose his shit," Luther says from the other side.

She looks at me. "You ready to go back?"

"After you," I reply.

She smiles, drops one more quick kiss on my lips, and then walks over to the door, opening it with a flourish and a smile.

Luther looks at her curiously and then up at me standing behind her. His eyes light up with amusement, and he purses his lips knowingly.

"Glad to see you two worked everything out."

Nikki smiles playfully at him. "Let it go, Luther."

"Girls' night?"

She shrugs and hedges, "Maybe."

"It better be a whole lot more than maybe or I'll text Cassie right now."

I watch them banter back and forth wondering what the hell they're talking about. I *think* I know, but it's almost like they're speaking in code. Luther finally lets out a huff and then flounces in front of us—and yes, flounces is exactly how he walks away.

Looking down at Nikki, I ask, "What was all that about?"

"He wants the dirt on you, which is something we usually do during our girls' nights."

Thinking back on how he touched her earlier and the ugly green monster that nearly consumed me in that moment, I confirm, "Luther's gay, right?"

She huffs out a laugh. "Definitely gay." She pats me on the back with a knowing look on her face. "You have nothing to worry about."

"I know," I reply nonchalantly, but I can't deny the relief flowing through my veins knowing I don't have to worry about competition from someone who sees her nearly every day.

She laughs at me, and it's clear she's not buying my chill exterior.

We reach the room and I see my agent, Steven, talking

closely with Rich. They both look up when we enter, Steven's eyes looking a lot more friendly than Rich's.

"About damn time," Rich mutters under his breath, but loud enough for everyone to hear.

Nikki's body stiffens next to me, her mouth opening and closing like she wants to respond but can't find the words.

"Apparently, Miss Denton has worked with me enough she can read me like a book and knew I wasn't happy about the suggestion."

My agent looks at me curiously but doesn't dispute my claim.

"And what weren't you happy with?" Rich asks.

"I used to be a playboy, yes. No one here in this room will deny it, least of all me, but that's not what I want to be known for. I want my legacy to be about how I play football, not how I am in bed."

The words are more truthful than I meant for them to be. I didn't used to care—sleeping around went hand in hand with being a star player for the Wolves.

Things are different now.

I'm different.

Nikki makes me want to be more. Ultimately, I want to be a man she's not ashamed to introduce to her parents.

Rich looks at me with disbelief written all over his face. "Matt, do you know how many men would kill to be in your position? You get more action than most guys get from their own damn hand."

I flush at his description of me and glance at Nikki, worried of how this picture looks to her. I'm surprised by the glower on her face.

"Matt is more than his good looks or history with women. He's one of our star players, not to mention his work with the children's cancer foundation and the Fresh Start program."

My eyebrows practically reach the ceiling. "How'd you know about that?" I ask her.

Nikki looks at me and opens her mouth, but Rich interrupts before she gets a chance to respond. "I didn't know you were part of Fresh Start. How'd you get involved with them?"

I look between him and Nikki before facing him. "I was looking up area programs to assist with so I might qualify for an NFL community outreach award."

It's a lie. When I look back at Nikki, I can tell she knows it too.

Fresh Start is a program for recovering alcoholics and drug addicts who need just that, a fresh start. I got involved when I felt like I hit a dead end with my dad. I wanted to know recovery was possible, and if my dad wouldn't let me help him, at least the Fresh Start folks would.

I never told Nikki about Fresh Start, so I have no idea how she found out.

"Well, Fresh Start doesn't have the same sex appeal as our original idea, but if you're really opposed to being surrounded by sexy half-naked women for a photoshoot, then we could focus on your support for an important community program. It would certainly make the Wolves look good," Rich says.

If people find out I'm involved in Fresh Start, they might start digging around about my dad. I've done a good job keeping him out of the spotlight, and I don't need him dragged in now when he's spiraling even more than normal.

My gaze catches Nikki's. Her eyes are bright with excitement and her gorgeous smile is wide on her face. I can tell she likes the Fresh Start angle, but she has to understand why that's also a no-go for me. Her smile falls when she catches my hesitation.

Her brows furrow in determination and she turns back to Rich. "We need a third option. I was actually thinking we could pull Jack, Will, and Luke in for a foursome shoot. The men who run our offense. Matt doesn't work by himself, and this would give us the perfect opportunity to show what a powerhouse the Wolves are."

Rich looks at her, a frown on his face, and then glances at me. "You wouldn't get all the spotlight with that option."

"I'm okay with that."

He purses his lips, but then shakes his head. "Fine, fine. But only if we make them look really good. Strong for the men who want to be them, and sexy for the women who want to be with them. Got it?" He gives his instructions to Luther and Nikki while collecting his phone and papers off the table.

He pats me on the back and then walks out without another word.

"So, we need to convince Jack Fuller, Will Edmonson, and Luke Carter to do a sexy photoshoot with Matt?" Luther asks, summarizing the final idea that Nikki offered up.

She nods at him.

"Easy peasy," he says sarcastically. Nikki winces, clearly hearing it too. He continues, "Especially seeing as how Jack was very clear he didn't want to be involved in any campaigns this year, Will is focused on planning his wedding, and Luke's game has been slipping lately, so being in a photoshoot should be the last of his concerns."

Nikki bites her bottom lip. "I'll talk to them."

Luther affirms, "Damn right you will. I'm not dealing with that one."

"It's one photoshoot. They'll do it. It'll be fine."

He tosses her a look that tells me it won't be as fine as she thinks.

I interject before Luther can say more. "I've never known any of those guys to be prima donnas. Hell, I'll talk to them.

They're doing me a huge favor if they're on board with it. The other two options sound about as appealing as eating dog shit."

Nikki grimaces and mumbles, "Thanks for the visual."

I grin at her and respond, "Anytime, Princess."

She smiles and shakes her head.

We're back.

THIRTY-ONE

Nikki

I fumble with my apartment door, Matt at my back sucking at my neck and sending goosebumps all down my body and heat straight to my core.

If I could just get the damn key in the lock—oh God, that feels good.

I'm so distracted I can't even think straight.

"If you don't open that door in the next thirty seconds, I'm gonna fuck you right here," Matt mumbles into my neck as he continues sucking and licking in such a way that I feel I might combust.

"I can't concentrate with you doing that."

"Well, I'm not going to stop, so I guess we're doing it right here."

He spins me around and takes my lips with his, owning me completely with his kiss. My moan vibrates between us, needy and demanding that he never stop. He can take me right here. I don't even care anymore. I just need him inside me, like yesterday.

He groans and pulls away from me, panting heavily. "Give

me the keys. I can't stand the idea of some other fucker seeing what's mine."

His voice is gravelly and deep, but it doesn't take away from the significance of his words. Of what we've already admitted to each other.

I'm his. He's mine.

We belong to each other.

Warmth and belonging seep through my bones, contentment close on its heels. I've never felt this way with anyone else, which should terrify me, especially since I have no idea how I'll ever tell my dad I'm dating one of his players. But right now I can't seem to find the will to care.

I just want Matt. In any way I can have him.

He manages to get the door open while I'm lost in my thoughts. He grabs my hand, pulling me into my apartment and then slamming the door behind me. In an instant, my back is pushed against the closed door, and his lips are back on mine.

Our hands are everywhere, trying to reclaim each other with every touch. It's been so long since we were last together, we're both hungry for the connection, desperate for it.

A niggle of doubt works its way to the surface—maybe it hasn't been that long for him.

I pull away from his lips. "Matt," I pant his name, trying to restore breath to my lungs.

"Huh?" His mouth is already working back down my neck, his large hands cupping my breasts. My head falls back on the door and I look at the ceiling, trying to get my thoughts in order. I place both hands on his head and gently pull him up enough until his eyes meet mine. He must see the seriousness in my expression because he stops attempting to kiss me and just stares at me.

His eyebrows draw together when I still don't speak—

mainly because I'm trying to find the words to ask what I'm afraid to ask.

"What's wrong?"

I shake my head and then give up. Closing my eyes—because I don't want to see the guilt in his expression when he confirms my fears—I blurt out, "I know it probably hasn't been that long since you've had sex, but I haven't been with anyone since we were last together. I just needed you to know." The last sentence is barely a whisper. My body is locked, tight and tense with nervous energy surging through every inch of me.

Silence.

He doesn't say anything. I can't even hear him breathing anymore, but I still don't open my eyes. I can't look at him right now. His eyes always give him away, and I already know the words will cut me enough.

"Nikki, look at me." His voice is soft, quiet. I can't tell if he's about to break my heart or not. Although, what right do I even have to be upset about him hooking up with other women? I let him go! What did I expect?

"Nikki."

Slowly, my eyelids rise, revealing the world an inch at a time until my eyes meet his. There's so much warmth and softness in his gaze.

"You really think I could hook up with anyone else?"

"I know I don't have a right to be mad at you. I let you go. I know—"

"Stop," he interrupts my ramble, which is probably for the best because who knows what was about to pop out of my mouth.

He brings one hand up to cup my cheek. The rough texture of his palm is oddly soothing against my soft cheek, grounding me in this moment, in him.

"I wasn't with anyone else. There's been no one since you."

I feel like Miley Cyrus just took a wrecking ball to my sternum for the impact his words have on me.

"What?" Even I can hear how breathy and disbelieving I sound.

"There's been no one. Only you, Nikki." He drops his forehead to mine, the warmth of his breath washing over me with his next words. "Only ever you."

The truth is clear in his eyes, and there's a hint of something else there—something I'm not sure I'm ready to see, something I might be feeling too.

I smash my lips on his, showing him with my mouth how much his words mean to me, how much *he* means to me.

If I thought we were frantic for each other before, we've taken it to a whole new level now. We rip at each other's clothes desperately, our lips only ever disconnecting long enough for our shirts to come off.

My hallway feels miles long as we work our way toward my bedroom. We crash through my bedroom door—fucking finally —naked as the day we were born and alternating between laughter and moans as we explore each other with our hands and mouths on our way to the bed.

As soon as he slides inside me, everything slows down, our frantic energy zeroing in on where we're joined. His eyes pierce mine, and I'm no longer able to deny what I see buried in those sexy blues.

Neither of us are ready to say it, but our bodies are speaking clearly enough for both of us to feel the unspoken declaration. When every ounce of pleasure gets wrung from us, we collapse on my bed, sweat-slickened bodies drained and chests heaving.

Matt pulls me close to him and then proceeds to pull the covers over us.

"You're not leaving?"

"I'm not leaving." His voice is strong and sure, his words meaning so much more than just him staying the night.

My lips curve up in a soft smile and I cuddle closer to him, soaking in the feeling of his strong arms wrapped around me.

That night, for the first time, we fall asleep together outside of the hotel, holding each other tight, our hearts open, not just our bodies.

It might just be the best night of sleep I've ever had.

The only noise in the room is the clinking of the silverware against the blue ceramic plates my mother loves. I take another bite of food, not tasting a single bite of the usually succulent pot roast. My dad sits stoically to my right, refusing to look at me, a scowl permanently etched on his face. My mom has been yammering on about the weather.

The *weather*.

You know things are bad when the only safe topic is the damn weather. I can't help but feel angry and frustrated with my dad and how he's behaving. Unfortunately, that feeling is conflicting with my need to constantly please my parents and make them proud of me.

I'm letting them down. What's really sad is they don't even know how much I'm letting them down because this is just their reaction at thinking Matt and I *were* a thing—past tense. If they only knew that he slept in my bed all night last night and I woke up with his mouth between my legs bringing me insane amounts of pleasure, their disappointment probably wouldn't even fit in this too big house of theirs.

I pick up my water glass and take a long sip, the cool water doing nothing to ease the tension in my shoulders brought on by my guilt and frustration.

I look at my mom, whose eyes keep darting up to look over at my dad. She glances at me and offers me a small apologetic smile before darting her gaze back to my dad and then looking down at her plate. Okay. This is ridiculous. I can't take this anymore.

I turn to my right. "Dad, are you really not going to talk to me at all tonight? You've hardly spoken to me in the last two weeks, and if this is the way things are going to continue, maybe I shouldn't even come over for our weekly dinners anymore."

He continues to chew his roast, not even offering me a glance. My body tenses and my eyes burn with the start of tears I refuse to let fall. I feel sick to my stomach that I just spoke to him like that, but I know it's well past time I stand my ground.

He has no idea what I've sacrificed for him in the past. Why can't he give me this one thing without me feeling like the worst child he could have?

"Dad." My voice cracks a little at the end, and I know he caught it because his fork freezes on its way to his mouth. His eyes finally dart to mine before he drops his fork, allowing it to clang loudly against his plate. He grabs his napkin from his lap and wipes his mouth before dropping it on the table at the same time that he pushes out of his chair.

"I've had enough. I'm going to my office."

His words are spoken to my mom, who nods mutely. I stare at my dad's back as he walks out of the room, unable to hide the hurt overwhelming me. I bite my lip to keep my emotions in check. I'm about to get up and leave when my mom places her hand delicately on top of mine on the table.

"I'm sorry, Nikki. I tried talking to him, but you know how stubborn your dad is."

"That doesn't excuse his behavior." I shake my head, wishing I could tell her everything I'm feeling. Wishing she could see how good I've been my whole life *for* them, and yet the one time I do something for me, they act like the sky is falling. I look at my mom and realize she actually seems understanding and open, so maybe it's just my dad who's the real problem.

My mom takes a deep breath, her body sagging in her chair. "I know it doesn't. Maybe it would help if you talked to him one on one."

The idea sounds less than appealing, but I know better than anyone to always say goodbye like it might be the last time. I can't leave things like this with him.

Excusing myself from the table, I make my way through the hallway displaying family pictures from my life. Nora's face is nowhere to be found. We didn't live in this house back then, and when we moved my parents decided to keep her pictures private. I'm pretty sure my mom has a stash somewhere in her room, like it's some sordid secret.

My gut twists. I wish Nora were here. God, how different things might be if she was.

I knock on my dad's office door. Instead of waiting for him to let me in—which I know he probably won't due to his attitude right now—I just walk in.

He's sitting at his desk, looking over playbooks with a video playing in the background of a recent game.

"I can't leave. Not until you talk to me."

"I have nothing to say," he says, his voice harder and gruffer than normal.

"Then you can listen."

He doesn't look up, but his papers remain still on his desk, so I assume he's listening.

"It's not fair for you to be mad at me about Matt."

His head shoots up, and the anger in his eyes stuns me speechless.

"I have one rule for my players—ONE! They are to stay the

fuck away from my daughter. I have every right to be *furious* at Matt for coming anywhere near you. Hell, even you knew better. I've always made it clear you were never to get personally involved with any of my players."

"Dad, you haven't even given him a chance."

His gaze turns glacial and his voice lowers. "Are you still seeing him?"

I take a deep breath, my heart beating furiously in my chest. "Yes."

He stares at me, the silence beating down on me until I feel like I can't breathe. Finally he shakes his head. "No. Matt is a playboy, Nikki. If you think you mean anything to him, you're fooling yourself. Matt isn't good enough for you. And knowing that you're choosing to be with him..."—he stops himself and then sighs—"I've never been so disappointed in you, Nikki."

All the breath leaves my lungs, and I feel like I've just been slapped across the face, the sting of his words burning into me. Before I even have a chance to hold them back, tears fall from my eyes in large drops and slide down my cheeks.

I stare at my dad, his words shattering me. It goes against every instinct I've built over the last twenty years to disappoint my parents, especially my dad after what he went through losing Nora and being the one who was in the car with her.

I wish he could understand I just wanted this *one* thing. This one person for myself. I didn't choose Matt because of my dad or the team, but because of who Matt is underneath it all. He's such a good man, but I can tell any argument I try will be lost on my dad. The anger is still fierce in his eyes, even as he watches his only daughter break under the weight of his derision.

The only daughter he has left.

I spin around and rush from the room, through the house that now feels like it belongs to a stranger, and out into the cool

Los Angeles night, grabbing my purse by the door on my way out. I suck air into my lungs, my chest heaving as tears fall down my face.

My car feels like a safe haven, cocooning me away from the disappointment lingering heavily from his brutal words. The drive home is a blur, my emotions at war inside me. Part of me is so angry at my dad—angry that he's willing to let this cause a rift between us and angry that he can't see what I've sacrificed for him. But the other part of me is dying inside as his words repeat on an endless loop in my head—the words an acknowledgement that all my hard work and sacrifice has been for naught because I've gone and disappointed him anyway.

I pull up to my condo, my mind distracted as I turn off my car and start walking up the stairs. It takes me a second to realize that somebody is sitting a few steps above me. When I look up at his face, I'm left breathless for the second time tonight, but for an entirely different reason.

Matt's blue eyes are filled with concern. "Nikki, what's wrong?" He stands up immediately and wraps his arms around me, encasing me in a hug that breaks down what little strength I had left. I grip his shirt, sobbing into his chest, allowing his warmth to wrap around me while he comforts me with soft words telling me he's here for me. He's got me.

He does have me.

That's what's so terrifying. If any other man from my past had caused the rift with my dad that Matt has, I would've walked away without a second thought. But I can't just walk away from Matt. He makes me feel so much, like I'm a whole person. Like my dreams, my opinions, my wants actually matter.

It's the first time I've felt this way since I was eight, and call me selfish, but I'm just not ready to let it go. To let *him* go.

Just once in my life, I wish my dad could see this. That I need this man. That he makes me feel strong. I already tried to give him up, and I was miserable the entire time we were apart. I don't want to go back to that person. I feel like I've been a shell of myself, and Matt has brought me back to life. He pushes me and challenges me. But most importantly, he makes me happy.

I lift my face from his chest and look into his perfect blue eyes that seem to see deep into my soul. Without a word, I get up on my tiptoes and gently place my lips on his. He returns the kiss softly but then pulls away. His thumb brushes a stray tear from my cheek.

"What's wrong?" he whispers.

I shake my head. "Nothing."

He gives me a disbelieving look. "Try again, Princess. The truth this time."

"I had dinner with my parents tonight and it did not go well." My body feels heavy from exhaustion, and I lean into Matt, letting his strength seep into me. I trust him and feel safe to let out all I'm feeling while his arms are wrapped around me.

"My dad said he was disappointed in me. I can't remember a single moment in my life where he's been disappointed in me. Not before my sister died, and certainly not after. I've always done exactly what they wanted." I pull back slightly, looking at his handsome face as it sets in a frown, concern still present in his gaze. My voice quiet and broken, I say, "I just...I just want to be with you, and I want my dad to accept us together. You..." The words stick in my throat. "You make me feel different. I like who I am with you. I don't want to give you up."

He runs his fingers through my hair and drops a kiss to my forehead, the gesture tender and endearing and exactly what I need right now. "I don't want you to give me up either." He pulls me closer to him, our bodies pressed together and his arms holding me tight. "We'll figure it out, okay?"

Without lifting my head, I nod into his chest. My breathing finally calms and the tension I've carried since that disastrous dinner is slowly fading from my shoulders. I let Matt lead me into my condo and take off my clothes until we're both just in our underwear. He pulls back the covers and gestures for me to get in bed. I do without hesitation. Besides, what woman in her right mind would argue about getting into bed with Matt?

He scoots in behind me and molds his front to my back. His arms wrap around me and I fall asleep being held by the man I am undoubtedly falling in love with.

THIRTY-TWO

Matt

Practice is grueling, and way more than usual. Coach Denton is ripping every guy on this team a new asshole, and I have a pretty good idea why. My sympathy for the guy, though, is nonexistent since I held Nikki while she cried after the way he treated her.

I can see all she's sacrificed for her family. Why the fuck can't he?

Luke wanders over to me and grouses, "What crawled up Denton's ass and died?"

"His own fucking ego."

I can feel Luke's gaze burning a hole in the side of my head. "You know something, don't you?"

I shrug.

"Dude, seriously, I'm your best friend. I deserve to get the inside scoop. What is it?"

I shake my head. This is one time I'm not going to be telling my best friend any details about my current romantic entanglements. For starters, Nikki's not like the other women I've hooked up with. But I'm also not going to say anything because it's not my story to tell. Nikki confided in me, and I have no intention of breaking her trust.

Luke stares at me in amazement. "When did you become so pussy whipped, Fischer?"

"Apparently when Nikki Denton stormed into my life."

That woman has had me twisted from the very beginning. Even when I still thought she was a stuck-up, spoiled, ice princess. I know better now, and I'll be the first to admit she's changed me permanently.

After another hour of getting bitched at by Denton, he finally cuts us loose. The locker room is filled with grumbling about what's gotten into Coach. When he walks through the locker room on his way to his office, I see his shoulders tight with tension and his face frozen in the same angry scowl he's been wearing all day.

I reach into my cubby and grab my cellphone, powering it on and instantly seeing a text from Nikki. Warmth fills my veins, and I can feel the pull of my ridiculous smile. This woman has turned me into the biggest lovesick sap.

Love.

Yeah, I said it. Not to her, obviously. I'm not ready. Love was always a foreign concept to me, but I'm starting to understand its appeal. I feel like every fucking superhero wrapped into one whenever I have Nikki in my arms, or when she smiles at me.

She's changed my perspective about a lot of things.

Nikki: Are we still on for tonight?

Oh yeah. We're definitely on. The thought of burying myself so far inside her no one knows where she ends and I begin is the only thing that's gotten me through this hellacious day.

Me: Definitely. Practice is just finishing up. I'll

swing by your place and pick you up in about an hour. Pack a bag.

Nikki: A bag, huh? A bit presumptuous, don't you think? ;)

Me: Keep it up, Princess, and see what that sass gets you.

Nikki: Promises, promises.

"Seriously, do you even have any balls left?"

I glance up to see Luke looking at me, amusement written all over his face. "What?"

"You have the goofiest fucking grin on your face. It's like you're some teenage girl whose crush finally noticed her."

"Shut the fuck up."

"Whatever, dude, it's true. Nikki must have one hell of a pussy."

Faster than he can blink, I shove him against his cubby.

"What the fuck, Matt?"

"Don't talk about her like that. It's not like that with her."

His eyes are wide, his mouth open in shock. After a beat, he raises his hands in surrender. "Okay, sorry. I didn't realize. I mean it, man. I never would've said that if I knew it was that serious."

"It is."

Silence hits my ears, and I gaze around the room to see all the guys looking at me. Several with knowing grins—mainly Jack and Will—but most looking dumbfounded by my totally-out-of-character actions. Movement to my left catches my attention, and I turn just in time to see Coach Denton walk back into his office.

How much did he see?

"It's cool, guys, go back to what you were doing," Luke shouts out, breaking up the tension hanging in the air.

I go back to my cubby and finish getting changed, more eager than ever to get out of here and get to Nikki.

An hour later, I'm pulling up to her condo. I've barely gotten out of the car when I look up to see her coming down the stairs, an overnight bag in her hand and a smile on her face that could bring a man to his knees.

Did I say could?

Cause I'm pretty sure—okay, positive—she's definitely brought me to mine. I still can't get over seeing Nikki dressed casually in skinny jeans and a teal top that brightens her eyes. Her blonde hair hangs in loose waves around her face and down her shoulders.

She's so fucking sexy—more than she realizes.

I look at her now and can't believe I ever thought she was cold. Nikki is the epitome of warmth and light.

"Hey, stud, you have a little something right...here." She gestures down her own chin as she squints at me. I don't miss her mocking tone, and she's probably not wrong. I think I am drooling a little.

Sue me—she's hot and I'm a fucking guy.

While she's putting her bag in the back seat of my car, I walk around to meet her by her door. She walks straight into my arms, no hesitation, her face bright and open, although her eyes are noticeably dimmer than they usually are, no doubt from the stress over this rift with her dad. I pull her as close as I can and lean down to take her lips with mine. God, I've been dying to kiss her since I left her condo this morning.

I've never craved a woman like this before, but I feel a little addicted. It doesn't matter how much we kiss, touch, or stroke. I want more.

I want her. Always.

Fuck, I'm turning into a softie.

I pull away, breaking the kiss but still holding her close. "I missed you today."

"You did?" she asks with happy surprise.

"Yeah."

She bites her lip and looks at me hesitantly, scrutinizing my face. I watch her in silence, dying to know what she's thinking.

"How was practice?" she asks softly.

Oh. I shrug.

"That's not really an answer, Matt."

Sliding my hands down her arms, I take her hands in mine and squeeze softly. "It sucked. Your dad was in a particularly pissy mood and decided to take it out on the team."

Worry creases her brow, and she goes back to biting her lip. I hate the turmoil I see written all over her face. I know she's trying to remain strong for me, but I hate that by choosing to be with me, she's causing a rift in her family, mainly because of the stress that rift is causing her. If she didn't care, I wouldn't care. But since she does, and since it's obvious this is killing her, it's killing me.

What scares me most is I'm getting dangerously close to doing whatever it takes to make her happy, even if that means letting her go.

I push the thought aside, knowing I'm not there yet. There's still a chance things could work out. I'm going to hold on to that for as long as I can.

I drop another kiss to her mouth and then gesture for her to get in the car.

I'm taking Nikki on a date.

A real date.

Our first date.

I hope she doesn't hate what I have planned.

We drive in companionable silence to the beach. I had to pay a pretty penny for special permits, but I've found if you have enough money you can do just about anything in LA. I pull up along a special access road tucked just out of view. It's mainly a place only locals know about, but I had a friend growing up who lived in this neighborhood and told me about it.

I park the car and look at her. Her eyes are wide with curiosity, and her gorgeous pink lips are slightly parted. She turns to me, and I soak in the trust I see in those brilliant blues.

"Where are we?"

"I've never been on a date before," I say tentatively.

Her smile drops from surprise. "What?"

I nod, my hand gripping my neck in a nervous gesture I wish wasn't quite so obvious. "I've always been..." *Ok, seriously bad idea to get her thinking about all the women you've fucked. Good job, asshole.* I scrub my hands over my face. "Fuck, I'm messing this up."

She places her hand on top of my leg and offers me the sweet smile I know she reserves just for me. "I promise you're not."

I take a deep breath. "I'm rich enough I could've taken you to some fancy restaurant, but I didn't really feel like that fits...*us.* I wanted something a little bit more intimate and special."

"Okay," she says softly, still not sure where I'm going.

"Come on, it's easier to show you."

I get out of the car, my nerves causing a riot in my body. I can't remember ever being nervous around a woman. I shouldn't even be this anxious around Nikki, but I want to please her, and not just with my body. I want this to make her happy.

I want to make her happy.

I walk around to my trunk and pop it open, exposing the

giant wicker picnic basket. Nikki gets out of the car and walks to the back until she's standing next to me. I peek at her from the corner of my eye and see a smile growing on her face.

She turns to me, her eyes glistening with tears that would make me fucking panic if it weren't for the smile accompanying them. "We're having a picnic."

"Yeah, on the beach, with a bonfire."

She looks around. "I thought you could only have bonfires at the pits at Huntington Beach?"

I shake my head. "When you have money, you can have bonfires wherever you want."

Her hand rests on my arm. "I love it, Matt. It's perfect," she says as she leans up, her lips ready for the taking.

And boy, do I take them. I grip the back of her head in my large hand, my fingers sliding through her silken blonde strands. We moan into each other's mouths, our tongues sliding across each other in an erotic form of foreplay I've never appreciated until Nikki.

Everything is better with her.

We break apart, breathing heavy, both of us reluctant to actually let each other go, but I'm determined to have a real date with her. To show her this is so much more than sex for me.

To show her what she means to me, even if I'm not ready to say it.

We walk hand in hand down the quiet, deserted beach toward where a bonfire has already been set up. It really does pay to know people.

Our date goes better than I hoped it would. Our conversation is easy like it always is. For the first time, I can talk with someone about anything and everything. She laughs at my jokes and teases me mercilessly, but I love every second of it, soaking in her vibrant warmth and attention.

When the weather starts to get too chilly, and we realize

several hours have gone by, I drive us back to my house. This was the other part of the night I was nervous about. I pull into my garage and shut off the engine before getting out of the car and grabbing her overnight bag from the back. We walk silently into my house and down the hallway that extends from the garage. The hallway opens up into my open concept living room, dining room, and kitchen.

"Do you want a tour?"

"Sure," she says softly, offering me a nod at the same time.

We walk quietly next to each other while I point out all the different rooms in my house—an entertainment room, gym, two guest bedrooms, and my room, which also has a balcony over-looking the pool.

We're both staring down at the bright blue water of my pool from my balcony when she turns to me and asks, "Is it weird having me here?"

My gaze slides from the blue of the pool to the blue of her eyes. "No," I reply honestly. "I thought it would be, but it's not."

She nibbles her bottom lip before asking, "Why were you worried?"

I shrug. "Because I've never brought a woman here before."

Her mouth drops open in shock, and I can't stop myself from teasing her. I chuck her chin with my knuckle. "Careful there, Princess, you're gonna catch flies."

She slaps my arm, but the teasing snaps her out of her shock. "You've really never had a woman here?"

I shake my head, suddenly uncomfortable, but also wanting to explain it to her, to help her see how different she is.

"I'd meet women at their places or hotels usually. Hotels were easiest. I made sure none of them knew where I lived, so I wouldn't have to see them again."

She looks at me sadly. "Weren't you ever lonely?"

I look back at the pool, letting my thoughts swirl through my mind and out of my mouth. "I didn't think so. For the longest time, it felt like the only option. I didn't think I was cut out for a relationship. I'd seen the downside of love and was dragged through it with my parents. I didn't want to go through that myself. Meaningless sex just seemed like a safe bet. I got my needs met, and women got to say they screwed a famous NFL player. It was win-win."

I turn to her. "I didn't realize how truly empty it felt until you. It was starting to feel...I don't know...unsatisfying before we started our arrangement. But then every time you and I were together, I just wanted more. I didn't want you to leave. Hell, I didn't want to leave you." I slide my thumb across the apple of her cheek, her gaze locked on mine.

"You changed everything for me, Nikki."

I love you.

The words claw at my throat, but I can't let them out. Not yet. Instead, I kiss her hard, pouring all of my feelings into the kiss and hoping she can feel the words I'm too afraid to say.

Yeah, afraid. I'm afraid. I'll admit it.

With this kiss—with my love—I'm giving her the power to destroy me, and I don't even care because if the alternative is to live an empty life of never having known this feeling, I wouldn't trade this for that in a million years.

With the light of a full moon streaming through my windows, I make love to Nikki Denton and give her everything I am.

I can only hope someday I'll be enough to earn her love in return.

The incessant ringing of my phone wakes me up from my deep sleep. Nikki mumbles my name, and I kiss the back of her head before I roll over and grab my phone from the nightstand. I don't recognize the number, but the area code is local. I decide to dismiss the call, figuring whoever it is can leave a message. Before I even get a chance to snuggle back against Nikki, my phone is ringing again, the same unknown number displayed on the screen.

Curious now, I answer. "Hello?"

"Is this Matt Fischer?"

"Yes," I say cautiously.

"Mr. Fischer, this is Officer Bennett with the LAPD. Is Mark Fischer your father?"

I sit up now, my body bracing for the hit I can already see coming. "Yes. Is he okay?"

I feel the bed shift as Nikki sits up, holding a sheet over her naked chest. I glance over at her, worry coating her features.

The officer clears his throat. "I'm sorry, Mr. Fischer, but your father was found unresponsive this morning outside Billy's Tavern. EMTs were called, but there was nothing they could do. Your father is dead."

The words echo around my head, my body frozen in shock. How many times did I prepare myself for this call? And yet I feel completely unprepared.

He can't be gone.

"There has to be some mistake." My voice is gravelly, both from sleep and from the grief I'm barely holding back.

"I'm very sorry for your loss. We'll need you to come down to the coroner's office today to confirm his identity."

"Right. Sure." I can hardly breathe as I hang up the phone.

"Matt?" Nikki's voice flows over me.

I turn to her and lose the fight with my emotions, tears now streaming silently down my face. Her arms immediately wrap around me, and she hugs me tight.

"What's wrong? Who was that?"

I pull her closer, trying to find comfort. In all the times I imagined getting this call, I always pictured myself alone. I'm glad that's not my reality.

I pull back enough to look at her. "My dad died."

Tears immediately fill her eyes and she pulls me closer, allowing me to bury my head in her neck as I feel the truth start to settle deep in my bones.

My dad's gone.

THIRTY-THREE

Nikki

The minister says one final prayer and then the casket gets lowered into the ground. I squeeze Matt's hand, sending him all the strength I can. I would give anything to be able to take his pain away. Players from the team stand around him, dressed in black suits with somber expressions. They pat him on the back before dispersing to their vehicles. As each player says their goodbye, Matt's hand never leaves mine, even when a few try to wrap him in a hug.

The crowd parts as more people leave, and my breath catches when my gaze clashes with my dad's. I watch his gaze drop to my hand in Matt's before his expression shutters and he turns around and walks away.

My heart sinks, and I let a tear fall before quickly wiping it away. Matt looks at me.

"You okay?" he asks.

I grip his hand tighter. "I should be asking you that."

He turns to me and slides his fingers through my hair, watching the movement before he looks back at me. "I'm glad you're here."

"There's nowhere else I'd be," I say softly, getting up on my toes to place a tender kiss on his lips.

I slide my thumb across his cheek before falling back on my heels. Luke walks up and gives Matt a hug.

"I'm so sorry, man. Is there anything I can do?"

"No, everything's been taken care of, but I appreciate the offer."

"Anytime. If you think of anything, or just need to get out of the house, give me a call." Luke looks at me. "Take care of him, okay?"

Matt wraps his arm around me and pulls me close to his side. "She's already gone above and beyond."

He says it with a smile, but it never reaches his eyes. Apart from the moment after he got the call about his dad, Matt hasn't cried, at least not around me. He's been stoic and focused on taking care of the funeral arrangements and getting his dad's house cleared out.

He's been reserved, but I can't help feeling like there's a torrent of emotion brewing under the surface.

I wish he'd talk to me about how he's feeling, but instead he just wants to hold me or make love to me.

I watch carefully as Matt says goodbye to some of the other players on the team. His shoulders sag when the last car drives away.

He pulls me into his arms and holds me close, burying his face in my hair. I hold him tighter, loving this man with everything I have and knowing I'll do anything I can to help him through this.

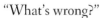

"What's wrong?"

I look up from my phone to see Cassie looking at me, a frown on her face and concern in her eyes. As soon as I feel the tear slip down my cheek, I know there's no sense in hiding the truth from her, even though I haven't had time to process it myself.

"My mom just called me. My dad is canceling our weekly family dinner. He can't even look at me."

Tears overwhelm me, and I bury my head in my shaky hands. On top of helping Matt deal with his grief over losing his dad, this is just one last thing I wasn't prepared for. I feel ridiculous and childish for crying like this over a fight with my dad, but our relationship has *never* been like this. Even after Nora died, when I blamed myself so completely for her loss and expected everyone else to, my dad always welcomed me with open arms.

The thought that he's so disappointed in me he can't even look at me shatters my heart into a million pieces.

Matt's such an amazing man, more than anyone gives him credit for. I'm so angry at my dad for not only judging me so harshly, but making unfair judgements about Matt, especially now that Matt is dealing with the loss of his dad.

Cassie pulls a chair up next to me and rubs my back while I try to compose myself. On top of everything else, my work has been slipping. Probably because my heart's not in it anymore, especially since I started looking into freelancing as a graphic designer. I reached out to one of my graphic design professors from college and am now seriously considering switching careers.

Who knows how my parents will take that news. At this rate, they'll probably think I need a lobotomy or that an alien has invaded their daughter.

At least that's how they're acting.

My dad acts like he's two seconds away from cutting me out of the family altogether.

My heart clenches at the idea. After what happened to Nora, how could he treat me this way without talking to me about things? He hasn't even given me a chance to explain or for me to show him how wonderful Matt is to me. Shouldn't that be the only thing that matters? Shouldn't my happiness be more important than his stupid pride?

Like it has for days, my heartache morphs to anger. It's been going back and forth between those two emotions for the last three weeks.

I throw my phone on my desk and run my fingers through my loose hair. "Gah, I'm so damn annoyed with him." I turn to Cassie. "He won't even talk to me about Matt. I've tried several times since our last family dinner together when he told me what a giant disappointment I am to him, and he refuses to even answer my calls or texts now. Who the hell does that to their only daughter?"

Cassie stares at me sympathetically, her hand continuing to rub soothing circles on my back.

I'm about to continue my rant when a tap on the door causes Cassie and I to both look up. Matt and Luther stand there looking at us—Luther with worry, Matt with concern and a trace of anger.

"What happened, honey?" Luther asks.

Before I can respond, Matt spits out, "Was it your dad?"

My gaze locks on his and I nod.

He shakes his head and runs his fingers through his hair. "What did he do now?"

"He's not talking to me anymore, and my mom just called to cancel dinner."

Luther walks over to me and asks as he sits down on the edge of my desk, "Why would he stop talking to you?"

I look behind Luther to Matt, whose gaze is locked on me. His eyes are sad, the blues dulled from their usual bright hue.

His mouth is set in a hard line, and his body is fraught with tension.

The fact he feels so strongly in my defense only makes me love him even more. How did I ever think he was a shallow playboy?

I turn back to Luther, who's looking between Matt and me.

"Because Matt and I are dating."

"So, your dad's mad you're dating one of his players?"

The smile falls slowly off my face. "Yes and no. It's a little more complicated."

"It's because of the player she's dating specifically," Matt says quietly, but his words land like a bomb.

I glance over at Matt and see him looking at me, torment clear in his gaze, along with something else that puts me on edge. The feeling of dread on the horizon settles deep in my belly. I can't tell what he's thinking, but I don't think I'm going to like it. His lack of communication since his dad died doesn't ease my concern any.

My mouth opens to ask him, to get reassurance that he's okay—that we're okay—but he speaks first.

"I need to head out so I'm not late to practice." He looks at Luther and Cassie. "Can you two make sure she gets home okay?"

They both nod while I stare at him, begging him silently to look at me, but he doesn't. His eyes look everywhere *but* at me, which only strengthens the unease growing in my gut.

Finally, as though he can't stop himself, his gaze meets mine, and the pain there nearly sucks all the air from my lungs.

"I'll call you after practice."

I nod, unable to speak, fear holding my tongue hostage at the look in his eyes.

I can't lose you too. Please don't pull away.

I plead with my eyes, begging him silently with everything

inside me. He walks toward me, around Luther and Cassie, and lifts me from my chair.

His hands slide into my hair, and his lips descend on mine in a kiss that shatters me completely.

I've never experienced one before, but I'm almost certain this is what a goodbye kiss feels like.

He pulls away, his eyes haunted and sad, before dropping a kiss to my forehead and turning toward the door.

"Matt..." The word is a whisper, but I know he hears it because he pauses. Without turning around, he shakes his head and then walks out the door, taking my heart with him.

THIRTY-FOUR

Matt

I didn't want it to come to this, but I know what I have to do.

I call my agent on the way to practice, running my idea by him. He says it would be nearly impossible to break my contract with the Wolves unless I get Coach Denton on board, especially given the fact they've just put a bunch of promotional dollars behind me this season.

"Coach Denton won't be a problem," I tell him.

I can hear the hesitation in Steven's tone, but he says he'll work up a proposal on his end. I'm about to hang up when I hear him say something.

"What was that?" I ask.

"What happened? I thought you loved the Wolves. Why are you trying to leave?"

Because I fell in love with the one woman I was never supposed to, and being with me is slowly tearing her apart.

Because if I have to give her up, there's no way I can stay with the Wolves and still be near her without wanting to be with her.

Because if I go through with this, I'll never be able to look her dad in the eye without wanting to beat him to a pulp for forcing me to give up the only woman I've ever loved.

Because now that my dad's gone, Nikki is the only person tying me to this city, and losing my dad has made me realize all she is risking by being with me.

Even I know I'm not worth it.

"It's personal."

Understatement.

"Will you tell me the full story if I make this happen?"

"Maybe."

"Fair enough. I'll call you when I've got something worked out."

"Thanks." I hang up the phone, dread settling deep in my bones. My whole body feels heavy and tired. My heart pumps furiously in my chest, knowing what's coming and begging me not to rip it out.

Unfortunately, what my heart wants no longer matters. I can't stand to see Nikki so broken up like this. Every day, her dad has done something small that has hurt her in ways I doubt he's fully aware of. I won't be the reason she loses her family, and that seems to be the direction things are going since her dad is being a stubborn jackass.

My recent loss only strengthens my resolve to do what needs to be done.

But that doesn't make it easy.

I can't help being a little mad at Nikki. For always being the good daughter, which has put her in this position to begin with. For always putting her parents first, so they never saw who she really was, who she could be. For making me fall in love with her.

I know it's not really rational, but who said love was rational?

I pull up outside the training facility and take a deep breath, prepping my body and mind for what I'm about to do.

I'm early, so none of the other players should be here yet, but Coach Denton will be.

The blue walls taunt me while I walk down the long hallway to the locker room, feeling like I'm a dead man walking.

Which, I mean, I am. Because after this, I'll be walking around without a heart anyway.

So, there's that.

My gaze catches on the Wolves logo, and my heart stalls in my chest. I never in a million years thought I'd voluntarily leave this team. I've given everything I have to this team. I love this team.

But I love Nikki more.

I'm about to give it all up for her, and I can't be sorry about that, not if it means she gets her family back. I know how much they mean to her, and I won't be the one who takes them away.

I push through the wooden door into the locker room and halt in my tracks as soon as I see the lone figure standing at his cubby. He turns to me, his blue eyes looking at me curiously and his brow pinched.

"Hey Matt, what are you doing here so early?" Jack inquires.

I swallow hard and force out, "I didn't think anyone else would be here. I need to talk to Denton."

Jack's gaze gets hawklike as he stares at me. "I always get here this early. I like getting a little extra time in."

I nod.

Jack turns to look behind him where Denton's office is. He looks back at me. "He's in his office. He's not in the best mood, but that seems to be the new normal."

My gaze scans over to Denton's office door. "Yeah," I say softly.

Jack crosses his arms and leans his shoulder against the edge of his cubby. "You wouldn't know anything about that, would you?"

"I might."

He lets his arms fall to his sides and takes a step toward me. "You're not planning to do something stupid, are you?"

"Why do you ask?"

"Because you have the look of a man who would do anything—and I mean *anything*, even something monumentally stupid—for the woman he loves."

I ignore his comment and start walking toward Denton's office, each step feeling heavier than the last, like my feet are in blocks of cement.

Jack's hand shoots out and grabs my bicep. "Matt, I mean it. Don't do something you'll regret."

My gaze never leaves Denton's closed door. "I'm not."

Jack lets me go, and I move forward, determination the only thing driving me.

I don't knock on Denton's door. Instead, I open the thick, heavy wooden door and push my body through. He looks up from the game tape he's watching, his scowl deepening.

His voice is gruff and angry. "What the fuck do you want, Fischer?"

"I want you to talk to Nikki again."

His eyes flare and his face reddens with rage. He stands up, his knuckles white from the grip he has on the edge of his desk. "Don't you fucking talk to me about my daughter."

"You have no idea what you're putting her through, what she's done for you, and you continue to treat her like garbage because of me."

"You don't know anything about my relationship with my daughter."

"Actually, I think I know more than you do."

His mouth opens to dispute my claim, but I don't give him the chance.

"Did you know she wanted to be a graphic designer?" I can practically see the words he was about to spit out get stuck in his throat. I continue, "Did you know she switched to marketing because your wife said she'd be great at it and you said you'd love to have her working with the Wolves, so she'd be close by?"

His eyes get that faraway look people have when they're searching their brain for a memory. I keep going, on a roll now, and desperate for him to see Nikki for who she really is.

"Since she was eight years old, she's done everything for *you*. Trying to be the perfect daughter to make up for the one you lost."

His face scrunches up in pain, and I don't miss the glisten in his eyes from tears, but I refuse to stop now. "She has blamed herself for what happened to Nora every day for the last twenty years, and she's tried to be the perfect daughter for you, sacrificing so much more than you can even imagine. She's sacrificed her happiness for *yours*. And now you punish her because of me? Fuck you, Denton. I may not deserve your daughter, but you sure as fuck don't either with how you've treated her. You don't deserve all she's given up to make you and your wife happy."

I take a breath, my heart stopping in my chest and begging me not to speak the words about to tumble out of my mouth.

"I won't be the reason she loses her family. I love her too fucking much to hurt her that way," I say, my voice hoarse and choked. His eyes shoot up to mine, but I keep going, my voice gaining strength from my conviction that I'm doing the right thing, even if it's killing me—each word out of my mouth a dagger to my heart. "If you really can't stand to see us together, then I'll end it. I'll give her up if it means she can keep you guys. Your silent treatment is tearing her apart, and I can't stand to see her heartbroken like this. But if I do this, I can't stay here. You need to convince Rich to trade me to another team."

His brow furrows in confusion, the fire and rage previously there now only simmering.

"You would leave the Wolves for Nikki?"

I nod reluctantly. "She doesn't love me." The quiet words I'm saying feel like glass scraping my throat, but they're the truth. "She loves you both and this is killing her."

He stares at me a moment, and I don't miss how his voice is softer when he speaks. "What makes you think she doesn't love you? She's been fighting with me for weeks, so obviously you mean something to her."

"She cares for me, and I'm sure she'll be upset when I end it, but in the long run she'll be happier having her family back than trading you guys for me, which is what you're forcing her to do. I won't make her choose."

Denton watches me carefully. "Because you're taking yourself out of the picture."

I'm unable to speak because the idea of not being with her is finally setting in, and I think it would feel better if someone just ripped all my insides out.

Denton and I stare at each other, some kind of understanding passing through his features, while I stand there numb and slowly shattering from within.

But I can't back down now. Nikki's happiness is on the line. I've just lost the last of my family. I refuse to be the reason Nikki loses hers.

"Does Nikki know you're here right now? That you're doing this?"

I shake my head.

Denton slowly sits back in his seat, his gaze still locked on me. He rests his chin in his hand on the arm of his chair, staring at me, processing what I've confessed, what I'm willing to lose for his daughter.

Finally, he nods. "Okay."

Without another word, I walk out of his office. The second the door closes behind me, I lean against the wall on the side, hidden from his view. I bend over, resting my hands on my bent knees and fighting back the vomit threatening to come up.

The weight of what I've just agreed to sits heavily on my shoulders. I should be concerned I'm essentially throwing my career away, that I'll have to move soon, but that's not what's making my body feel like it's heavy with lead.

Fuck, I have to give up Nikki.

I slide down the wall, holding my head in my hands as reality beats me down, my heart finally disintegrating in my chest.

I'm not ready.

I'm not ready to lose her.

I try to hold on to the fact that in the long run, this will make her happiest. That she'd never be happy with me if it caused a permanent rift with her family.

Nikki's happiness is all that matters.

Who needs a heart anyway?

THIRTY-FIVE

Nikki

My finger shakes slightly as I extend my hand out and press heavily on the silver doorbell outside Matt's front door. Restlessness has been tormenting me all day since Matt left my office. I don't want this shit with my dad to interfere with what we've got going. Not when I finally feel like I found someone I can be myself with.

The door swings open, and my breath catches in my throat at the sight of Matt in a towel. God, he's so delicious. Instinctively, I lick my bottom lip before catching it between my teeth. Matt's eyes lock on the movement, and there's no denying the heat there. His gaze slides up to mine, and I'm left breathless by the desire in his eyes.

But there's something else there too. He quickly looks away and gestures for me to come in.

"Make yourself at home. I'm gonna run upstairs and throw some sweats on." He drops a quick kiss on my head before rushing up the stairs. I look around his place and make my way over to the couch. Matt's phone buzzes repeatedly on the end table on the other side of the couch, making me curious. Just when I'm about to go over and check it out, he comes back down the stairs wearing black sweats and a Wolves T-shirt.

Instead of sitting on the couch with me, he sits on a chair across from me. He rests his elbows on his knees and grips his hands.

"I'm glad you came over tonight."

"Things felt kind of weird when you left my office earlier."

He glances down at his hands, before looking back up at me. The look in his eyes steals my breath. "I'm working on a trade deal. It should be finalized this week."

"What?" I ask, my voice breathy and weak as devastation slams through my body.

He drops his gaze, looking at the grey carpet underneath his feet.

What. The. Actual. Fuck?

"Are you fucking kidding me right now, Matt?"

He looks up at me then, clearly hearing the anger in my tone. You'd have to be deaf not to. I'm hoping he can't hear the hurt that's there too, because I'm fucking devastated and it's taking everything in me not to break down.

This has to be a terrible joke. Or displaced grief. He loves this team. There's no way he'd choose to leave voluntarily.

His face is stoic, his eyes the only piece of him revealing any hint to how he's really feeling.

"I've decided to look at different teams. I don't think I should stay with the Wolves."

I try to calm my frantically beating heart. "Where does that leave us, then?"

"There would be no us."

He says it so easily, like he's reciting the weather. My mouth drops open in shock, and my eyes sting from the tears I'm just barely holding back.

"I don't understand," I choke out quietly.

He sits there staring at me before quietly responding, "We should've never gotten back together. I'm not the right guy for you."

"Isn't that my decision to make? Don't I get to decide if you're right for me or not?"

"Nikki, don't make this harder than it already is."

"Why are you doing this?" I don't understand. We were fine yesterday. Fucking yesterday! What could possibly change in twenty-four hours when we'd finally found our groove?

"Now that my dad's gone, there's really nothing keeping me here."

I fight against the tears slowly filling my eyes as reality crashes down on me. Nothing keeping him here? Am I really nothing to him? After all we've been through together?

He shakes his head, running his hands through his hair and finally losing the stoicism. "Fuck. This was just supposed to be sex. It wasn't supposed to cause you family grief. I just think it'd be better if we broke things off now, before we get any deeper."

Any deeper? Is he fucking serious right now?

I'm in love with him. I'm already in as deep as it gets.

I stare at him, shock and hurt reverberating through my body like he's just ripped my heart right out of my chest and cut it up in front of me.

I can't believe this is happening.

Something in me shuts down—the part of me Matt was bringing back to life.

I stand from the couch, my movements choppy and robotic while I grab my purse.

"Nikki?" I can hear the apprehension in his tone, but I can't give him anything.

I have nothing left to give.

I turn to him, my face a mask hiding my emotions from him.

My words are quiet, but miraculously composed. "Fine. If that's what you want." I don't even recognize my own voice.

Matt frowns, doubt crossing his features, before he grips the back of his neck with his hand.

Without another word, I walk through his house and out the door. I don't stop moving until I get inside my car. I put the keys in the ignition on autopilot and start the car. But instead of driving away, I sit there, my eyes glassy and unseeing, my hands white-knuckling the steering wheel. My emotions are a river of white rapids, and I'm convinced this steering wheel is the only thing keeping me grounded and above water.

I fight the tears, knowing the second I let one out, the rest will follow quickly.

Stupidly, I look back at Matt's house only to see him standing in the doorway, anguish on his face. I want to go to him, to soothe that look in his eyes, to kiss him and love him.

But I can't.

Because he doesn't want me.

Because the woman he'd brought back to life has completely disappeared.

In her place is the shell of a woman I was before.

I shift my gear into drive and speed away from Matt, my heart still a bloody mess on his living room floor.

It doesn't matter. It'll never belong to anyone else.

I never should've tried to be someone I'm not. I should've just stayed the good daughter. Then none of this would've happened.

The drive to my condo is a blur. I'm two seconds away from breaking and can't think about anything but getting inside my house so I can fall apart in private.

The second the door closes behind me, the first tear falls. I don't stop it. I can't anymore, even if I wanted to. Instead, I let myself feel all the pain coursing through me, allowing myself this one night to be completely brokenhearted before I suck it up and go back to being the good daughter.

If this is what fighting for what I want gets me, then it's not worth the pain.

The polished silverware clinks against the plate as I move my peas around.

"Nikki, I just found out Mrs. Peterson's grandson, who used to work in Silicon Valley, just moved to LA. He's single and quite the eligible bachelor, I hear. He's twenty-nine and just started his own start-up. It's apparently taking off. He's into tech or something along those lines."

I look up at my mom, fake interest on my face. I'm a pro at this expression. "Oh, really?"

After Matt shattered my heart, I called my mom and told her we needed to have family dinner, whether my dad wanted to be there or not. Seeing as how he's sitting to my right, I'm guessing he didn't see a problem with it. He even said hello to me when I got here, which I suppose is improvement.

I should be grateful something is getting back to normal, but I feel so empty, I'm worried my carefully composed expression is slipping.

My mom continues, "Yeah, I was thinking maybe we could invite him to the next family dinner. It might be good for you to move on from Anthony."

"From Anthony?" The words are out of my mouth before I can reel them back. I look over at my dad who's already looking at me. He gives me a subtle shake of his head, but the message is clear.

My mom didn't know Matt and I were still together.

I sit back in my chair, reeling from the realization that I have to pretend like Matt meant nothing to me. Emotion clogs my throat—I'm out of practice in regards to my poker face, and I'm already feeling raw and tender from my breakup with Matt. I swallow the emotion down, using all the strength I possess to hold myself together and get through this dinner.

I need things to go back to normal.

I thought constantly sacrificing my happiness for my parents was getting painful and tedious.

Turns out losing the love of your life is so much worse.

Going back to the old me feels like sunshine and roses compared to that.

Okay, maybe sunshine and roses isn't quite accurate.

I glance up and see my dad scrutinizing me. I glance away and take a drink of my water.

"Nikki?"

I turn to my mom. "Hmm?"

"What do you think? About being set up with Mrs. Peterson's grandson. I saw a picture. He's a real catch."

How fabulous for him. I observe my mom's obvious excitement at the idea of setting me up, and even though the thought makes me want to vomit, I swallow it down and nod.

"Sure."

I pick up my fork, which now feels like I'm lifting fifty pounds in my hands, and continue to shovel food around my plate.

"Great," my mom responds with less enthusiasm than she had before, but I don't look at her.

The table shakes as my dad uses it to push his chair out and stand up.

"Nikki, can I have a word with you in my office?"

He doesn't wait for my answer but simply walks away expecting me to follow. Which I do, because that's what a good daughter does.

When I get to his office, he's already sitting at his desk. "What's up, Dad?"

He frowns at me. "That's what I was about to ask you."

"I'm not sure what you mean."

"You just agreed to be set up on a date."

I shrug. "That shouldn't surprise you. Mom was also the one who introduced me to Anthony."

"I don't think Matt would appreciate you going on a date with another man."

My heart stops. "What?"

Confusion fills my dad's features. "Matt. Your boyfriend."

I shake my head, digging down deep for strength and knowing I'm going to be depleted for days after this damn dinner.

"We're not together anymore," I say, my voice sounding hollow to my ears.

My dad's face goes slack, his jaw opening in slight shock and his eyes wide. "What?"

I don't think I can repeat myself. The words feel like broken glass every time I say them.

My insides feel cut up enough. Instead, I just shrug my shoulders.

Then realization dawns on me and I find my voice enough to ask, "Did you know about the trade?"

"He's not getting traded." His voice is strong, the coach in him coming out.

I stare dumbfounded at him because I know Matt's doing everything in his power to get traded. At least that's what he implied when he broke up with me.

My dad takes pity on me. "Let me rephrase—there's no way I'm letting him get traded."

Now I'm the one who's confused. "What do you mean?"

His eyes are sad. "Do you really think I'd trade my daughter's boyfriend, knowing how that would hurt her?"

A tear slides down my cheek, and I whisper, "He's not my boyfriend anymore."

"Did you break up with him?"

I shake my head.

My dad rubs his hand over his hair, staring at the wall, lost in thought. "That stupid idiot," he mutters. He looks back at me. "This is my fault."

I shake my head again, even though I'm sure it partially is. Isn't that one of the excuses Matt gave me when he broke my heart?

Either way, it doesn't matter. Pointing fingers doesn't change anything.

My dad watches me carefully before asking softly, "Do you love him?"

My gaze, which had been drawn to my hands while I fidgeted with my silver ring, shoots up to meet his. I bite my lip and nod, another tear letting loose down my face.

He nods. "Yeah, that's what I figured after his little speech in my office."

"What speech?"

My dad continues to shake his head, almost like he can't believe the situation he's found himself in.

"He told me if I didn't want him around you anymore, then I needed to support a trade deal." Dad's gaze pierces mine. "He was willing to give up the Wolves for you. I may not have approved of you two together, but I know what the team means to him. I know what kind of sacrifice it would be for him to leave." My dad's brows pinch together. "He said you didn't love him, so it was better this way."

My jaw opens on a sharp inhale as my eyes go wide.

"What?" The word is a breathy whisper, but my dad still hears it.

"He was convinced you didn't love him, so this was the best thing." His expression turns sad. "Matt said our fight was tearing you apart, and he couldn't stand to see you hurting."

It all clicks. His distance at my office. The anguish on his face when he watched me drive away. "So he removed himself."

My dad nods. "Like I said, he's a stupid idiot."

My knees weaken as everything comes into sharp clarity.

Matt hated seeing me hurting to the point he was willing to give up the team he loves so my dad wouldn't be mad at me anymore.

But most importantly, Matt loves me.

He loves me.

But he thinks I don't love him. How could he ever think that when I was willing to sacrifice my relationship with my parents to be with him? When I stood by his side as he grieved the loss of his dad?

Because you never told him.

Oh. My. God.

I sit heavily in the chair in front of my dad's desk, my tears drying up as I absorb the information that's just been placed in front of me.

My dad's voice pulls me from my thoughts. "I wouldn't have approved the trade."

My gaze slides up and lands on his. "Why not? I thought you didn't want us together."

He sits down in his chair, sighing heavily. "I didn't. Not until he came to my office and laid his cards on the table and showed he was willing to give it all up for you." He leans forward. "Do you know what it would do to his career to leave this team right now? He's at the top of his game, but part of that is because the offensive line has found their groove and are strongest together. That's a dynamic you don't always get on a team. It takes years to develop. Matt's strongest on this team with Jack, Will, and Luke. When they're on the field, they can't be stopped. Knowing he's willing to give that all up for you was more than enough to show he's serious. It was different when I thought he was just playing you like I'd seen him do with other women." He twists his head from side to side. "Okay, maybe not like other women. It did seem different with you from the beginning, but I was too stubborn to see it at the time."

He leans forward, reaching out for my hand, which I place in his. "I'm so sorry, Nikki. This is my fault. If I hadn't shut you out, I would've seen this earlier. I thought...well, I thought he didn't deserve you."

"He's not that guy, you know—the player. That might've been the way he was with women, or at least the persona he put forth, but he's so much more. He's caring, generous, funny. He pushes me and challenges me in the best possible way. He forces me out of my comfort zone, which is honestly what I've been craving for a long time."

I take a deep breath and admit, "Dad, I shut down after Nora died."

He cuts me off. "Nikki, we don't need to—"

"Yes, we do. This is stuff I should've said a long time ago." Emotion clogs my throat but I push through the words I've needed to say for years. "I blamed myself for Nora's death." I ignore my dad's horrified expression and continue, "I thought if I hadn't been so selfish and demanded you both be at my stupid art show, then the accident would've never happened, and Nora would still be here. You and Mom were both so lost in grief and I felt so responsible that I decided to be the perfect daughter—to do whatever you both wanted—to make up for it. And I did. I went into marketing because you both wanted me to. I got engaged to Anthony because you both liked him. I stayed in LA for college instead of going to Boston like I wanted because you both hated the idea of me being so far away. Everything I've done for the last twenty years, I did because I thought that's what *you* wanted, not because it's what *I* wanted."

My dad's eyes are watery with tears, his voice choked when he says, "Not until Matt."

I nod in confirmation.

"And then I acted like a fucking child about it."

I nod slowly, the emotion I held back to confess how I feel now sliding down my cheeks in wet streaks. But my body also feels lighter, as if by finally being open with him, I've let go of the heavy burden I've carried for years.

"I'm so sorry, Nikki," he says as he pushes out of his chair and rounds his desk to me. I stand and wrap my arms around his middle, letting him pull me into a tight hug, while both of us grieve together. He continues to mumble apologies into my hair while we stand there, holding each other tight.

Finally, I pull away. "I can't go back to being the woman I was before, Dad. I don't want to. I was so miserable," I confess.

His heartbreak is transparent on his face. "I don't want that either, Nikki. I might not always like or agree with your choices, but I promise never to shut down on you again."

We hug again, and a calmness comes over me. We're going to be okay, no matter what I do.

Now I just need to find a way to show Matt that I love him.

Because if tonight has taught me anything, it's that I do need to fight for what I want if I'm ever going to be happy with my life.

And there's nothing I want more than Matt.

THIRTY-SIX

Matt

"What do you mean he won't agree?"

"Uh, I don't know how to make it any clearer to you, Matt. Denton is refusing to agree to the trade deal unless you meet with him first."

"I already fucking met with him," I mumble. I'm not ready to relive that experience so soon—it was painful enough the first time.

I haven't talked to Nikki in two days, and it already feels like a lifetime. I have to go in to see how the final shoot for the campaign came together, and I feel like a meth addict waiting for his next hit, only instead of meth, I'm addicted to Nikki fucking Denton.

"Matt, if you really want this deal to go through, then you need to talk to Denton."

The problem is I don't want the deal to go through. I don't want to leave Nikki.

But what I want stopped mattering the second I fell for her.

Isn't that how it works when you love someone—their happiness is more important to you than your own?

If I have to feel this miserable for the rest of my life, it'll be worth it if I know she's happy. That she's got her family, even if I don't think they deserve her.

Not that I do either.

"And in case I haven't said it enough, I'm not a fan of this deal. Not to mention, I don't think Rich is really on board either. If the Patriots weren't offering an obscene amount of money for you, I doubt he'd even go for it."

"This deal has to go through."

"As your agent, I'm advising you against it, but if this is how you want to crash your career, then by all means, go ahead. But you'll have to talk to Denton before it happens. I'd recommend sooner than later."

"I'll head over to the stadium right after I stop by the business office. Luther wanted me to sign off on the final proofs. I'm on my way there now."

"Okay. Give me a call when it's done."

"Will do."

I hang up with my none-too-pleased-with-me agent. I don't blame him. It's not exactly like he's getting a raise with this trade deal, but it's the best we could finagle if I want to get off the team as soon as possible.

Which I have to do, because if I stay any longer, I'm afraid my resolve to stay away from Nikki will crumble. Being this close to her—in the same city, working for the same team—is like having the perfectly hanging fruit just out of my reach. If I stay much longer, I'm going to grab a ladder and haul ass up the tree just to get to her.

It's another perfect sunny California day, but the air is crisp and chilly alluding to the time of year. The bright sunny sky does nothing to lighten my tempestuous mood, though. My fingers twitch against the steering wheel as I pull into a parking space in the underground garage. Sitting back in my seat, I lean my head back and close my eyes, trying to turn off all the emotions Nikki brings out in me. She's so close. Knowing she's in the building right above me makes my body light up like a damn Christmas tree, itching to go to her.

I just need to stay strong for this one last meeting.

Pressing the elevator button sends a sinking sensation to my stomach, nerves swirling around and my fight or flight responses firing.

Run away or fight for the woman I've fallen in love with.

There's no choice really, even though I wish there was.

Her happiness is what matters. And her family is what makes her happy.

I need to keep reminding myself and fight against the instinct telling me to fight for her.

I enter the elevator and press the button for the marketing floor. Tension tightens my muscles, my body bracing for an impact like I would on the field. The familiar feeling eases some of my stress. Maybe I should've been treating this whole thing like I was on the field from the beginning—always braced for the hit that's inevitable. I knew from the beginning not to get attached to Nikki. I'd never gotten attached to any woman before, so I didn't prepare myself for what it would feel like when I finally did.

Lesson fucking learned.

With my game face firmly in place, my shoulders fraught with tension, and my stomach clenched like a lineman will be hitting me at any moment, I walk through the halls of the marketing department toward the familiar conference room where we've held all our business meetings.

"Matt."

Her voice sweeps over me like warm water after a tough day, easing the muscle tension in my body, until I remember she's the reason I'm supposed to have my guard up to begin with.

I turn around, my breath catching in my lungs at the sight of her in front of me after so many days apart. Fuck, she's gorgeous.

Inside and out.

Her blue eyes scan my body from head to toe and back again before locking on mine. There's something in them that stops me from completely putting my guard up with her. Almost like they're pleading with me for something—for what, I have no idea. I've already given her everything I have.

"Can we talk for a minute in private?" Her voice is soft and unsure, like she thinks I'll reject her. Doesn't she know, I don't have it in me to ever tell her no? Even when I know it would be better for my heart if I did.

"Sure."

She gestures to her open door a couple of feet behind her and I walk past her into her office. Her scent assaults my nose and causes my heart to ache in my chest. I will never be able to smell citrus and vanilla and *not* think about Nikki.

The click of the door latching closed hits my ears like a bullet just went off next to me. The second click of the lock engaging forces me to turn around, my heart pumping so rapidly in my chest, I'm convinced she can see it.

Nikki leans back against the door, her hands behind her and her eyes filled with hesitation. She closes them briefly and then opens them up, all hesitation gone, and determination fierce in her gaze.

"I love you."

My jaw drops and my eyes search hers, while it feels like my heart has stalled completely in my chest at her words. I must've heard her wrong.

"What?" I choke out.

Her brow gets that little pucker it does when she's worried, and she chews the inside of her lip before standing tall and opening her gorgeous, luscious mouth to repeat the three most beautiful words I've ever heard in my life.

"I love you."

In two long strides, I reach her, my hands going straight to her pink cheeks and my lips crashing against hers in a kiss that consumes me completely. Her hands grip my hips as she pulls me flush to her body, moaning into my mouth, and setting my blood on fire. Wetness on my hand causes me to pull away and look at her face. Tears are streaming from her eyes as they go back and forth between mine, searching.

"You love me?" I whisper, still disbelieving.

She nods. Another tear escapes her beautiful eyes.

"I love you more," I say softly.

A relieved laugh escapes her. "I highly doubt that. I was willing to fight with my dad for you."

"I was willing to give you up, so you wouldn't have to choose."

She shakes her head, her eyes never leaving mine. "I don't want you to give me up. I don't want you to go to another team, but if you still want to, then I'm coming with you."

I pull back completely. "What?"

"If you really want to leave the Wolves, then I'm going with you."

I stare at this incredible woman in awe. "You'd move for me? Away from your family?"

"Where you go, Fischer, I go. That's what you do when you love someone."

I intend to drop a quick kiss on her lips in recognition of what she's willing to sacrifice, but the second they connect, I get greedy and take her lips in a searing kiss meant to permanently tie us together. She belongs to me the same way I belong to her.

But I guess that's always been the case, whether I was fully aware of it or not. I was down the minute we made contact.

Nikki

EPILOGUE

6 months later

I squeal as Matt tosses me on the bed and then pounces on top of me, his body caging me in and sending excitement through me. His lips come down on mine, hungry after several days apart. My fingers slide through his thick hair, holding him to me as much as I can.

I'll never get tired of these moments with him.

"Fuck, I want you," he mumbles as he kisses my neck, moving down toward my collarbone, "but we have to get ready to go."

I nibble at his ear before whispering, "Can't we stay in tonight and go out tomorrow?"

He pulls back and looks at me, his gaze determined. "No, but we can definitely finish this later tonight."

He sits up and gets off the bed, while I let out a groan in frustration. He's been gone for days for sponsorship promos, and I'm desperate to feel him buried inside me.

"Come on, Princess. Trust me, I'll make it worth your while."

"You better," I huff as I reluctantly get up and head to my closet.

My closet in our house.

Three months ago, Matt asked me to move in with him. Of course I said yes. At that point, we spent every moment we could together, so it only made sense.

I still get moments where it hits me how far we've come.

How far *I've* come.

I can say with complete certainty I've never been happier in my entire life. Shortly after Matt and I got back together, I quit my job with the Wolves and now work as a freelance graphic designer. Matt stayed with the team and is now prepping for next season, under my dad's watchful eye.

In the six months we've been back together, Matt and I have become each other's rocks, our relationship set on a strong unbreakable foundation we both plan to build a future on.

Together.

I quickly get dressed in a red short-sleeved lace sheath dress I never would've dared to wear before Matt and I got together.

I slide on my favorite pair of black stilettos and grab my black clutch before meeting Matt in the living room where he insisted on waiting because he was afraid he'd see me and not be able to keep his hands off of me.

Based on the desire in his eyes when I walk in the room, he was probably right.

His mouth opens and closes before he rubs his hand over his jaw and finds his words. "Fuck, Nikki...How the hell did I get so lucky? What did I ever do to deserve you?"

I smile up at him and run my hands over the lapel of his dark gray suit jacket. "Funny, I ask myself all the time what I did to deserve *you*."

He shakes his head like he doesn't quite believe me. He still thinks he's the one who lucked out here, but he's wrong.

I'm the lucky one.

No one has ever loved me so completely. And I mean *me*. Not the me I present to the world, but the me who has bouts of insecurity and still deals with the occasional misplaced guilt. He loves me always, and for that I will always be convinced I'm the lucky one.

He takes my hand, pulling it up to his mouth so he can kiss it before wrapping his arm around me and pulling me out to his car.

"If we stay in this house for another minute, I'm going to forget our plans."

I wouldn't be opposed, but I can tell this is important to him —whatever it is.

We make small talk during our drive, telling each other about how our week was, sharing details we didn't share over the phone or updates that happened after our nightly phone calls. When he makes a turn down a familiar side street, a smile breaks out on my face.

I know exactly where we're going—the secluded beach where we had our first date. I glance over at him just as he glances at me and our eyes meet.

"It's been a while since we've been back here."

"I know, but it's special, so I thought..."

He doesn't finish his thought, but he's said enough that my heart lodges in my throat. *He thought...what?*

My brain is going a mile a minute thinking about the different ways he could finish that sentence, but the one causing hope to bloom in my chest is the idea he wanted this night to be special.

I'm afraid to hope, because we really have only officially been a couple for six months, but I'm also so madly in love with him I can only wish this night is leading where I hope it is.

We walk down to the beach, hand in hand, Matt carrying a

picnic basket in his other hand while I carry my heels. The sound of the waves crashing on the beach soothes my nerves, leaving only hope and excitement in their place.

Matt sets up our picnic and we eat, continuing our earlier light conversations from the car. By the time we're both done eating, I've almost forgotten about where I thought this night was heading.

Almost.

But then Matt clears his throat, his expression turning serious, and my breath stutters in my lungs as I wait for the words I'm dying to hear.

"Nikki...I...,"—he lets out a breath and runs his fingers nervously through his hair. "I planned a whole speech, but I can't remember it now, so I guess this is going to be off the cuff. I brought you here tonight because I wanted to tell you how much you mean to me."

He reaches over, capturing my hand in his and holding it tight. "I never thought I'd fall in love. All I'd ever seen was how love made people weak. I had no idea it had the ability to make me feel so *strong*. These past six months—hell, and the three months before that—have been the happiest in my entire life. *You* make me the happiest I've been in my entire life. I want to spend the rest of my life making you happy, too, Nikki. I want a family with you and a life with you. I want it all."

My eyes are beginning to blur with tears, but I can't stop staring at this gorgeous man as he bares his heart to me, his words matching my own feelings. He rolls to his knees, bending one in front of him, and pulls a small blue box out of the picnic basket.

His eyes capture mine, and I swear no one else in the world exists except for us.

"Nikki, will you marry me?" Movement catches my attention, and I look down to see he's opened the box to display the most beautiful oval cut diamond engagement ring with a halo of ruby stones surrounding it. The diamond in the middle has to be at least two carats.

It's the most beautiful piece of jewelry I've ever seen, and I can no longer hold the tears back as I realize I'm about to have everything I've ever wanted.

A man who loves me unconditionally and is committed fully to me.

Without another moment's hesitation, I whisper the only answer I could ever give him.

"Yes!"

THE END

Thank you so much for reading Down by Contact. If you loved this book, I would be forever grateful if you'd leave a review.

Luke and Emma's story is up next. Buy Taking the Handoff today! Keep reading for a sneak peek at chapter 1.

Curious about Max and Cassie's story? Subscribe to my newsletter to read their novella.

TAKING THE HANDOFF PREVIEW

Chapter 1 – Emma

"No."

"Drew..."

"No, absolutely not."

I stare at my brother while he looks around my brand-new apartment in MacArthur Park. I look around the apartment which only a month ago was an exciting new prospect. Unfortunately, I can understand my overprotective older brother's dismay.

This place doesn't look anything like the pictures, and I'm pretty sure we witnessed a drug deal outside before we walked in.

I'm actually surprised Drew made it this far. I thought he was going to turn around right there and demand I move back home to Seattle.

But I've come this far. I'm not giving up on my dream now.

"It's not that bad..."

Drew throws me a *get real* look and I turn back to the room before us.

Ok, it is that bad.

The pictures made it look like such a cute little place. Maybe I should've done a little more research on the neighborhood.

You know what, it's fine. This is just a small hiccup. It doesn't change my plans and hopefully I won't have to live here long, but I *do* have to live here because it's all I can afford. My parents refused to help because they think I'm chasing after a silly dream that will never make me a living. Drew offered to help, but he's got his own bills to pay. He can't afford to pay for me, too.

And frankly, I don't want him to.

This is my first real adventure into adulthood and I'm ready for it. I was desperate to get out of Seattle and away from my overbearing and judgmental parents. They might not be so judgy if I was a lawyer like my brother, but I'm not. I'm a singer. It's the only thing I've ever really loved to do. I went to college and got a degree in business, but I felt like I was dying the entire time.

Maybe that's dramatic, but it's the truth.

I have no idea where my creative gene came from because my parents, Mark and Patricia Delaney, don't have a creative bone in their bodies. They're clinical, methodical, and disciplined. It's what makes them such great doctors. They were thrilled to have a son who thought similarly to them. Unfortunately, four years after Drew was born, they were gifted with me, their constant disappointment. I was the weird kid who put on a "circus" performance on the playground jungle gym pretending I was some Cirque de Soleil prodigy when really I was just sliding down the sloped parallel bars with my hands out and thinking I looked cool because I switched sides while doing it. I had very few friends and probably would've been plagued by constant bullies if it weren't for Drew and his best friend, Luke Carter.

The thought of Luke awakens butterflies in my stomach that I immediately push aside.

I look around my small apartment, beginning to feel the spark of creativity that zings through my veins as I see all the possibilities of this space come to life in my mind. The steady beats of a new song start in the back of my mind, and I dig in my purse for the notebook I keep for moments just like this. I jot down the few lines that started repeating in my head moments ago before tucking it back in my purse.

I look up to see Drew staring at me, a small smile on his face.

"Did this hell hole inspire you?"

I roll my eyes at his exaggeration. It's not a hell hole. It's not nice, or as posh as he's used to, but it's mine and I'll make it look nice. I don't see any signs of rodents, so that's a plus.

"You can't honestly believe I'm going to let you live here, Emma."

I stare at him, "Of course, you are, because it's not up to you. I'm the one paying the rent. Don't stress about it, D. It'll be fine. I'll spruce it up and it'll look cute in no time."

He shakes his head, "You're so determined to make this work that you're willing to live in this shit stain of an apartment?"

"Can you please stop talking about my apartment like that. It's got potential. And it's in my budget. It'll be fine."

It has to be fine. I don't have a backup plan, and singing is the only thing that's ever given me true joy and happiness. I moved to Los Angeles to pursue a career and I'm not going to let my overprotective brother stand in my way, even if a small part of me worries he might be right about this apartment.

Drew squints at me and then shakes his head in disbelief, "I'll be back. I've got to make a call."

"Who are you calling?"

"Don't worry about it."

"You're not calling mom and dad, are you?"

He must hear the hint of worry in my tone because his expression softens, and he shakes his head before coming over and placing both hands on my shoulders. "I'm not calling mom and dad. I promise. Don't worry about them. They'll come around. Keep following your dreams, Squish. You know I've always got your back when it comes to them, right?"

I nod and fight back the tears I feel burning behind my eyes. I will not cry, even if my brother's words soothe the ever-present worry that I will forever be a disappointment to my parents. At least I'll always have Drew.

Pre-order Now!
Releasing September 2, 2021

AFTERWORD

I honestly can't believe this is my third full-length novel. Some days it still feels surreal that I'm actually a published author. I feel so grateful every day to be a part of the amazing writing community I've found and to have people like you read my books. Thank you so much from the bottom of my heart.

I couldn't have done any of this without the help of some really incredible people.

To my romance newbies, I love you so much. Thank you for being my sounding board, for loving my characters as much as I do, and for sharing my TikTok love language :) You ladies keep me sane and I'd be lost without you.

To my incredible cover designer, Kate Farlow. Thank you so so much for continually blowing me away with these covers.

To my editors, Happily Editing Anns for putting up with all my overused words and pointing them out to me so I can put out the best book possible.

To Christian Hogue, who has no idea who I am. Thank you for being the ultimate muse for Matt. I thoroughly enjoyed looking at your Instagram and watching your stories on a daily basis while I was writing this book. Not gonna lie, as handsome as you are, it's your dog that really did it for me. I'm a sucker for cute dogs.

To my best friend and soul sister, Rikki. We've been watching 10 Things I Hate About You every time we see each other for 10 years and it's just recently that I realized I turned into a real life Ms. Perky. Thanks for putting up with my crazy antics. Love you!

To my husband, for loving me unconditionally and for picking up the slack in our household so I could write. Thank you for always believing in my dreams and pushing me to pursue them. I love you more than words could ever describe.

And last, but never least, to my baby boy, thank you for being the miracle you are and always pushing me to be the best mom and example I can be. I live for your smiles and laughter.

ABOUT THE AUTHOR

Cadence Keys writes steamy contemporary romance novels full of heart, heat, and HEAs. She loves football (especially seeing all those tight ends), coffee (it sustains her), and watching Gilmore Girl marathons (witty banter for the win). She has been writing for almost a decade, but only recently got the gumption to really do something with her work. She looks forward to publishing many more novels.

You can also find more information about all future releases at www.cadencekeysauthor.com/

facebook.com/cadencekeysauthor

twitter.com/cadencewrites

instagram.com/cadencekeysauthor

bookbub.com/profile/cadence-keys

goodreads.com/cadencekeysauthor

ALSO BY CADENCE KEYS

LA Wolves Series

In the Grasp

Across the Middle

Down by Contact

Taking the Handoff

Defending the Backfield

Rapturous Intent Rockstar Series

Noble Intent

Forbidden Intent

Devoted Intent

Promised Intent

Printed in Great Britain
by Amazon

22055245R00158